W9-AEO-552

STRANGERS NO MORE

Tales of Alien Life by
Science Fiction Masters
Isaac Asimov, Philip José Farmer,
Marion Zimmer Bradley and More

DOVER PUBLICATIONS, INC.
Mineola, New York

SF

Bibliographical Note

Strangers No More: Tales of Alien Life by Science Fiction Masters Isaac Asimov, Philip José Farmer, Marion Zimmer Bradley and More!, first published by Dover Publications, Inc., in 2017, is a new anthology of stories reprinted from standard editions.

Library of Congress Cataloging-in-Publication Data

Title: Strangers no more : tales of alien life by science fiction masters Isaac Asimov,
  Philip José Farmer, Marion Zimmer Bradley and more!.
Description: Mineola, New York: Dover Publications, Inc., 2017.
Identifiers: LCCN 2016047852 | ISBN 9780486795072 | ISBN 0486795071
Subjects: LCSH: Science fiction, American. | Extraterrestrial beings—Fiction.
Classification: LCC PS648.S3 S79 2017 | DDC 813/.0876208—dc23
  LC record available at https://lccn.loc.gov/2016047852

Manufactured in the United States by LSC Communications
79507101   2017
www.doverpublications.com

CONTENTS

Stanley G. Weinbaum
  A Martian Odyssey (1949)   1

Isaac Asimov
  Youth (1952)   30

Robert Sheckley
  Warrior Race (1952)   63

Marion Zimmer Bradley
  Year of the Big Thaw (1954)   76

Philip José Farmer
  Rastignac the Devil (1954)   84

Clifford D. Simak
  The World That Couldn't Be (1958)   139

Al Sevcik
  Alien Offer (1959)   182

Fredric Brown
  Earthmen Bearing Gifts (1964)   198

STRANGERS
NO MORE

A MARTIAN ODYSSEY

STANLEY G. WEINBAUM

Jarvis stretched himself as luxuriously as he could in the cramped general quarters of the *Ares*.

"Air you can breathe!" he exulted. "It feels as thick as soup after the thin stuff out there!" He nodded at the Martian landscape stretching flat and desolate in the light of the nearer moon, beyond the glass of the port.

The other three stared at him sympathetically—Putz, the engineer, Leroy, the biologist, and Harrison, the astronomer and captain of the expedition. Dick Jarvis was chemist of the famous crew, the *Ares* expedition, first human beings to set foot on the mysterious neighbor of the earth, the planet Mars. This, of course, was in the old days, less than twenty years after the mad American Doheny perfected the atomic blast at the cost of his life, and only a decade after the equally mad Cardoza rode on it to the moon. They were true pioneers, these four of the *Ares*. Except for a half-dozen moon expeditions and the ill-fated de Lancey flight aimed at the seductive orb of Venus, they were the first men to feel other gravity than earth's, and certainly the first successful crew to leave the earth-moon system. And they deserved that success when one considers the difficulties and discomforts—the months spent in acclimatization chambers back on earth, learning to breathe the air as tenuous as that of Mars, the challenging of the void in the tiny rocket driven by the cranky reaction motors of the twenty-first century, and mostly the facing of an absolutely unknown world.

1

Jarvis stretched and fingered the raw and peeling tip of his frost-bitten nose. He sighed again contentedly.

"Well," exploded Harrison abruptly, "are we going to hear what happened? You set out all shipshape in an auxiliary rocket, we don't get a peep for ten days, and finally Putz here picks you out of a lunatic ant-heap with a freak ostrich as your pal! Spill it, man!"

"Speel?" queried Leroy perplexedly. "Speel what?"

"He means 'spiel'," explained Putz soberly. "It iss to tell."

Jarvis met Harrison's amused glance without the shadow of a smile. "That's right, Karl," he said in grave agreement with Putz. "*Ich spiel es!*" He grunted comfortably and began.

"According to orders," he said, "I watched Karl here take off toward the North, and then I got into my flying sweat-box and headed South. You'll remember, Cap—we had orders not to land, but just scout about for points of interest. I set the two cameras clicking and buzzed along, riding pretty high—about two thousand feet—for a couple of reasons. First, it gave the cameras a greater field, and second, the under-jets travel so far in this half-vacuum they call air here that they stir up dust if you move low."

"We know all that from Putz," grunted Harrison. "I wish you'd saved the films, though. They'd have paid the cost of this junket; remember how the public mobbed the first moon pictures?"

"The films are safe," retorted Jarvis. "Well," he resumed, "as I said, I buzzed along at a pretty good clip; just as we figured, the wings haven't much lift in this air at less than a hundred miles per hour, and even then I had to use the under-jets.

"So, with the speed and the altitude and the blurring caused by the under-jets, the seeing wasn't any too good. I could see enough, though, to distinguish that what I sailed over was just more of this grey plain that we'd been examining the whole week since our landing—same blobby growths and the same eternal carpet of crawling little plant-animals, or biopods, as Leroy calls them. So I sailed along, calling back my position every hour as instructed, and not knowing whether you heard me."

"I did!" snapped Harrison.

"A hundred and fifty miles south," continued Jarvis imperturbably, "the surface changed to a sort of low plateau, nothing but desert and orange-tinted sand. I figured that we were right in our guess, then, and this grey plain we dropped on was really the Mare Cimmerium which would make my orange desert the region called Xanthus. If I were right, I ought to hit another grey plain, the Mare Chronium in another couple of hundred miles, and then another orange desert, Thyle I or II. And so I did."

"Putz verified our position a week and a half ago!" grumbled the captain. "Let's get to the point."

"Coming!" remarked Jarvis. "Twenty miles into Thyle—believe it or not—I crossed a canal!"

"Putz photographed a hundred! Let's hear something new!"

"And did he also see a city?"

"Twenty of 'em, if you call those heaps of mud cities!"

"Well," observed Jarvis, "from here on I'll be telling a few things Putz didn't see!" He rubbed his tingling nose, and continued. "I knew that I had sixteen hours of daylight at this season, so eight hours—eight hundred miles—from here, I decided to turn back. I was still over Thyle, whether I or II I'm not sure, not more than twenty-five miles into it. And right there, Putz's pet motor quit!"

"Quit? How?" Putz was solicitous.

"The atomic blast got weak. I started losing altitude right away, and suddenly there I was with a thump right in the middle of Thyle! Smashed my nose on the window, too!" He rubbed the injured member ruefully.

"Did you maybe try vashing der combustion chamber mit acid sulphuric?" inquired Putz. "Sometimes der lead giffs a secondary radiation—"

"Naw!" said Jarvis disgustedly. "I wouldn't try that, of course—not more than ten times! Besides, the bump flattened the landing gear and busted off the under-jets. Suppose I got the thing working—what then? Ten miles with the blast coming right out of the bottom and I'd have melted the floor from under me!" He rubbed his nose again. "Lucky for me a pound only weighs seven ounces here, or I'd have been mashed flat!"

"I could have fixed!" ejaculated the engineer. "I bet it vas not serious."

"Probably not," agreed Jarvis sarcastically. "Only it wouldn't fly. Nothing serious, but I had my choice of waiting to be picked up or trying to walk back—eight hundred miles, and perhaps twenty days before we had to leave! Forty miles a day! Well," he concluded, "I chose to walk. Just as much chance of being picked up, and it kept me busy."

"We'd have found you," said Harrison.

"No doubt. Anyway, I rigged up a harness from some seat straps, and put the water tank on my back, took a cartridge belt and revolver, and some iron rations, and started out."

"Water tank!" exclaimed the little biologist, Leroy. "She weigh one-quarter ton!"

"Wasn't full. Weighed about two hundred and fifty pounds earth-weight, which is eighty-five here. Then, besides, my own personal two hundred and ten pounds is only seventy on Mars, so, tank and all, I grossed a hundred and fifty-five, or fifty-five pounds less than my everyday earth-weight. I figured on that when I undertook the forty-mile daily stroll. Oh—of course I took a thermoskin sleeping bag for these wintry Martian nights.

"Off I went, bouncing along pretty quickly. Eight hours of daylight meant twenty miles or more. It got tiresome, of course—plugging along over a soft sand desert with nothing to see, not even Leroy's crawling biopods. But an hour or so brought me to the canal—just a dry ditch about four hundred feet wide, and straight as a railroad on its own company map.

"There'd been water in it sometime, though. The ditch was covered with what looked like a nice green lawn. Only, as I approached, the lawn moved out of my way!"

"Eh?" said Leroy.

"Yeah, it was a relative of your biopods. I caught one—a little grass-like blade about as long as my finger, with two thin, stemmy legs."

"He is where?" Leroy was eager.

"He is let go! I had to move, so I plowed along with the walking grass opening in front and closing behind. And then I was out on the orange desert of Thyle again.

"I plugged steadily along, cussing the sand that made going so tiresome, and, incidentally, cussing that cranky motor of yours, Karl. It was just before twilight that I reached the edge of Thyle, and looked down over the grey Mare Chronium. And I knew there was seventy-five miles of *that* to be walked over, and then a couple of hundred miles of that Xanthus desert, and about as much more Mare Cimmerium. Was I pleased? I started cussing you fellows for not picking me up!"

"We were trying, you sap!" said Harrison.

"That didn't help. Well, I figured I might as well use what was left of daylight in getting down the cliff that bounded Thyle. I found an easy place, and down I went. Mare Chronium was just the same sort of place as this—crazy leafless plants and a bunch of crawlers; I gave it a glance and hauled out my sleeping bag. Up to that time, you know, I hadn't seen anything worth worrying about on this half-dead world—nothing dangerous, that is."

"Did you?" queried Harrison.

"*Did I!* You'll hear about it when I come to it. Well, I was just about to turn in when suddenly I heard the wildest sort of shenanigans!"

"Vot iss shenanigans?" inquired Putz.

"He says, 'Je ne sais quoi,'" explained Leroy. "It is to say, 'I don't know what.'"

"That's right," agreed Jarvis. "I didn't know what, so I sneaked over to find out. There was a racket like a flock of crows eating a bunch of canaries—whistles, cackles, caws, trills, and what have you. I rounded a clump of stumps, and there was Tweel!"

"Tweel?" said Harrison, and "Tveel?" said Leroy and Putz.

"That freak ostrich," explained the narrator. "At least, Tweel is as near as I can pronounce it without sputtering. He called it something like 'Trrrweerrlll.'"

"What was he doing?" asked the Captain.

"He was being eaten! And squealing, of course, as anyone would."

"Eaten! By what?"

"I found out later. All I could see then was a bunch of black ropy arms tangled around what looked like, as Putz described it to you, an ostrich. I wasn't going to interfere, naturally; if both creatures were dangerous, I'd have one less to worry about.

"But the bird-like thing was putting up a good battle, dealing vicious blows with an eighteen-inch beak, between screeches. And besides, I caught a glimpse or two of what was on the end of those arms!" Jarvis shuddered. "But the clincher was when I noticed a little black bag or case hung about the neck of the bird-thing! It was intelligent! That or tame, I assumed. Anyway, it clinched my decision. I pulled out my automatic and fired into what I could see of its antagonist.

"There was a flurry of tentacles and a spurt of black corruption, and then the thing, with a disgusting sucking noise, pulled itself and its arms into a hole in the ground. The other let out a series of clacks, staggered around on legs about as thick as golf sticks, and turned suddenly to face me. I held my weapon ready, and the two of us stared at each other.

"The Martian wasn't a bird, really. It wasn't even birdlike, except just at first glance. It had a beak all right, and a few feathery appendages, but the beak wasn't really a beak. It was somewhat flexible; I could see the tip bend slowly from side to side; it was almost like a cross between a beak and a trunk. It had four-toed feet, and four fingered things—hands, you'd have to call them, and a little roundish body, and a long neck ending in a tiny head—and that beak. It stood an inch or so taller than I, and—well, Putz saw it!"

The engineer nodded. "*Ja!* I saw!"

Jarvis continued. "So—we stared at each other. Finally the creature went into a series of clackings and twitterings and held out its hands toward me, empty. I took that as a gesture of friendship."

"Perhaps," suggested Harrison, "it looked at that nose of yours and thought you were its brother!"

"Huh! You can be funny without talking! Anyway, I put up my gun and said 'Aw, don't mention it,' or something of the sort, and the thing came over and we were pals.

"By that time, the sun was pretty low and I knew that I'd better build a fire or get into my thermo-skin. I decided on the fire. I picked a spot at the base of the Thyle cliff, where the rock could reflect a little heat on my back. I started breaking off chunks of this desiccated Martian vegetation, and my companion caught the idea and brought in an armful. I reached for a match, but the Martian fished into his pouch and brought out something that looked like a glowing coal; one touch of it, and the fire was blazing—and you all know what a job we have starting a fire in this atmosphere!

"And that bag of his!" continued the narrator. "That was a manufactured article, my friends; press an end and she popped open—press the middle and she sealed so perfectly you couldn't see the line. Better than zippers.

"Well, we stared at the fire a while and I decided to attempt some sort of communication with the Martian. I pointed at myself and said 'Dick'; he caught the drift immediately, stretched a bony claw at me and repeated 'Tick.' Then I pointed at him, and he gave that whistle I called Tweel; I can't imitate his accent. Things were going smoothly; to emphasize the names, I repeated 'Dick,' and then, pointing at him, 'Tweel.'

"There we stuck! He gave some clacks that sounded negative, and said something like 'P-p-p-proot.' And that was just the beginning; I was always 'Tick,' but as for him—part of the time he was 'Tweel,' and part of the time he was 'P-p-p-proot,' and part of the time he was sixteen other noises!

"We just couldn't connect. I tried 'rock,' and I tried 'star,' and 'tree,' and 'fire,' and Lord knows what else, and try as I would, I couldn't get a single word! Nothing was the same for two successive minutes, and if that's a language, I'm an alchemist! Finally I gave it up and called him Tweel, and that seemed to do.

"But Tweel hung on to some of my words. He remembered a couple of them, which I suppose is a great achievement if you're used to a language you have to make up as you go along. But I couldn't get the hang of his talk; either I missed some subtle point or we just didn't *think* alike—and I rather believe the latter view.

"I've other reasons for believing that. After a while I gave up the language business, and tried mathematics. I scratched two plus two equals four on the ground, and demonstrated it with pebbles. Again Tweel caught the idea, and informed me that three plus three equals six. Once more we seemed to be getting somewhere.

"So, knowing that Tweel had at least a grammar school education, I drew a circle for the sun, pointing first at it, and then at the last glow of the sun. Then I sketched in Mercury, and Venus, and Mother Earth, and Mars, and finally, pointing to Mars, I swept my hand around in a sort of inclusive gesture to indicate that Mars was our current environment. I was working up to putting over the idea that my home was on the earth.

"Tweel understood my diagram all right. He poked his beak at it, and with a great deal of trilling and clucking, he added Deimos and Phobos to Mars, and then sketched in the earth's moon!

"Do you see what that proves? It proves that Tweel's race uses telescopes—that they're civilized!"

"Does not!" snapped Harrison. "The moon is visible from here as a fifth magnitude star. They could see its revolution with the naked eye."

"The moon, yes!" said Jarvis. "You've missed my point. Mercury isn't visible! And Tweel knew of Mercury because he placed the Moon at the *third* planet, not the second. If he didn't know Mercury, he'd put the earth second, and Mars third, instead of fourth! See?"

"Humph!" said Harrison.

"Anyway," proceeded Jarvis, "I went on with my lesson. Things were going smoothly, and it looked as if I could put the idea over. I pointed at the earth on my diagram, and then at myself, and then, to clinch it, I pointed to myself and then to the earth itself shining bright green almost at the zenith.

"Tweel set up such an excited clacking that I was certain he understood. He jumped up and down, and suddenly he pointed at himself and then at the sky, and then at himself and at the sky again. He pointed at his middle and then at Arcturus, at his head and then at Spica, at his feet and then at half a dozen stars, while I just gaped at him. Then, all of a sudden, he gave a tremendous leap. Man, what a hop! He shot straight up into the starlight, seventy-five feet if an inch! I saw him silhouetted against the sky, saw him turn and come down at me head first, and land smack on his beak like a javelin! There he stuck square in the center of my sun-circle in the sand—a bull's eye!"

"Nuts!" observed the captain. "Plain nuts!"

"That's what I thought, too! I just stared at him open-mouthed while he pulled his head out of the sand and stood up. Then I figured he'd missed my point, and I went through the whole blamed rigamarole again, and it ended the same way, with Tweel on his nose in the middle of my picture!"

"Maybe it's a religious rite," suggested Harrison.

"Maybe," said Jarvis dubiously. "Well, there we were. We could exchange ideas up to a certain point, and then—blooey! Something in us was different, unrelated; I don't doubt that Tweel thought me just as screwy as I thought him. Our minds simply looked at the world from different viewpoints, and perhaps his viewpoint is as true as ours. But—we couldn't get together, that's all. Yet, in spite of all difficulties, I *liked* Tweel, and I have a queer certainty that he liked me."

"Nuts!" repeated the captain. "Just daffy!"

"Yeah? Wait and see. A couple of times I've thought that perhaps we—" He paused, and then resumed his narrative. "Anyway,

I finally gave it up, and got into my thermo-skin to sleep. The fire hadn't kept me any too warm, but that damned sleeping bag did. Got stuffy five minutes after I closed myself in. I opened it a little and bingo! Some eighty-below-zero air hit my nose, and that's when I got this pleasant little frostbite to add to the bump I acquired during the crash of my rocket.

"I don't know what Tweel made of my sleeping. He sat around, but when I woke up, he was gone. I'd just crawled out of my bag, though, when I heard some twittering, and there he came, sailing down from that three-story Thyle cliff to alight on his beak beside me. I pointed to myself and toward the north, and he pointed at himself and toward the south, but when I loaded up and started away, he came along.

"Man, how he traveled! A hundred and fifty feet at a jump, sailing through the air stretched out like a spear, and landing on his beak. He seemed surprised at my plodding, but after a few moments he fell in beside me, only every few minutes he'd go into one of his leaps, and stick his nose into the sand a block ahead of me. Then he'd come shooting back at me; it made me nervous at first to see that beak of his coming at me like a spear, but he always ended in the sand at my side.

"So the two of us plugged along across the Mare Chronium. Same sort of place as this—same crazy plants and same little green biopods growing in the sand, or crawling out of your way. We talked—not that we understood each other, you know, but just for company. I sang songs, and I suspect Tweel did too; at least, some of his trillings and twitterings had a subtle sort of rhythm.

"Then, for variety, Tweel would display his smattering of English words. He'd point to an outcropping and say 'rock,' and point to a pebble and say it again; or he'd touch my arm and say 'Tick,' and then repeat it. He seemed terrifically amused that the same word meant the same thing twice in succession, or that the same word could apply to two different objects. It set me wondering if perhaps his language wasn't like the primitive speech of some earth people—you know, Captain, like the Negritoes, for instance, who haven't any generic words. No word for food or water or man—words for good food and bad food, or rain water and sea water, or strong man and weak man—but no names for general classes. They're too primitive to understand that rain water and sea water are just different aspects of the same thing. But that wasn't the case with Tweel; it was just that we were somehow mysteriously different—our minds were alien to each other. And yet—we *liked* each other!"

"Looney, that's all," remarked Harrison. "That's why you two were so fond of each other."

"Well, I like *you!*" countered Jarvis wickedly. "Anyway," he resumed, "don't get the idea that there was anything screwy about Tweel. In fact, I'm not so sure but that he couldn't teach our highly praised human intelligence a trick or two. Oh, he wasn't an intellectual superman, I guess; but don't overlook the point that he managed to understand a little of my mental workings, and I never even got a glimmering of his."

"Because he didn't have any!" suggested the captain, while Putz and Leroy blinked attentively.

"You can judge of that when I'm through," said Jarvis. "Well, we plugged along across the Mare Chronium all that day, and all the next. Mare Chronium—Sea of Time! Say, I was willing to agree with Schiaparelli's name by the end of that march! Just that grey, endless plain of weird plants, and never a sign of any other life. It was so monotonous that I was even glad to see the desert of Xanthus toward the evening of the second day.

"I was fair worn out, but Tweel seemed as fresh as ever, for all I never saw him drink or eat. I think he could have crossed the Mare Chronium in a couple of hours with those block-long nose dives of his, but he stuck along with me. I offered him some water once or twice; he took the cup from me and sucked the liquid into his beak, and then carefully squirted it all back into the cup and gravely returned it.

"Just as we sighted Xanthus, or the cliffs that bounded it, one of those nasty sand clouds blew along, not as bad as the one we had here, but mean to travel against. I pulled the transparent flap of my thermo-skin bag across my face and managed pretty well, and I noticed that Tweel used some feathery appendages growing like a mustache at the base of his beak to cover his nostrils, and some similar fuzz to shield his eyes."

"He is a desert creature!" ejaculated the little biologist, Leroy.

"Huh? Why?"

"He drink no water—he is adapt' for sand storm—"

"Proves nothing! There's not enough water to waste anywhere on this desiccated pill called Mars. We'd call all of it desert on earth, you know." He paused. "Anyway, after the sand storm blew over, a little wind kept blowing in our faces, not strong enough to stir the sand. But suddenly things came drifting along from the Xanthus cliffs—small, transparent spheres, for all the world like glass tennis balls! But light—they were almost light enough to float even in this thin air—empty, too; at least, I cracked open a couple and nothing came out but a bad smell. I asked Tweel about them, but all he said was 'No, no, no,' which I took to mean that he knew nothing about them. So they went bouncing by like tumbleweeds, or like soap bubbles, and we plugged on toward Xanthus. Tweel pointed at one of the crystal balls once and said 'rock,' but I was too tired to argue with him. Later I discovered what he meant.

"We came to the bottom of the Xanthus cliffs finally, when there wasn't much daylight left. I decided to sleep on the plateau if possible; anything dangerous, I reasoned, would be more likely to prowl through the vegetation of the Mare Chronium than the sand of Xanthus. Not that I'd seen a single sign of menace, except the rope-armed black thing that had trapped Tweel, and apparently that didn't prowl at all, but lured its victims within reach. It couldn't lure me while I slept, especially as Tweel didn't seem to sleep at all, but simply sat patiently around all night. I wondered how the creature had managed to trap Tweel, but there wasn't any way of asking him. I found that out too, later; it's devilish!

"However, we were ambling around the base of the Xanthus barrier looking for an easy spot to climb. At least, I was. Tweel could have leaped it easily, for the cliffs were lower than Thyle—perhaps sixty feet. I found a place and started up, swearing at the water tank strapped to my back—it didn't bother me except when climbing—and suddenly I heard a sound that I thought I recognized!

"You know how deceptive sounds are in this thin air. A shot sounds like the pop of a cork. But this sound was the drone of a rocket, and sure enough, there went our second auxiliary about ten miles to westward, between me and the sunset!"

"Vas me!" said Putz. "I hunt for you."

"Yeah; I knew that, but what good did it do me? I hung on to the cliff and yelled and waved with one hand. Tweel saw it too, and set up a trilling and twittering, leaping to the top of the barrier and then high into the air. And while I watched, the machine droned on into the shadows to the south.

"I scrambled to the top of the cliff. Tweel was still pointing and trilling excitedly, shooting up toward the sky and coming down head-on to stick upside down on his beak in the sand. I pointed toward the south and at myself, and he said, 'Yes—Yes—Yes'; but somehow I gathered that he thought the flying thing was a relative of mine, probably a parent. Perhaps I did his intellect an injustice; I think now that I did.

"I was bitterly disappointed by the failure to attract attention. I pulled out my thermo-skin bag and crawled into it, as the night chill was already apparent. Tweel stuck his beak into the sand and drew up his legs and arms and looked for all the world like one of those leafless shrubs out there. I think he stayed that way all night."

"Protective mimicry!" ejaculated Leroy. "See? He is desert creature!"

"In the morning," resumed Jarvis, "we started off again. We hadn't gone a hundred yards into Xanthus when I saw something queer! This is one thing Putz didn't photograph, I'll wager!

"There was a line of little pyramids—tiny ones, not more than six inches high, stretching across Xanthus as far as I could see! Little buildings made of pygmy bricks, they were, hollow inside and truncated, or at least broken at the top and empty. I pointed at them and said 'What?' to Tweel, but he gave some negative twitters to indicate, I suppose, that he didn't know. So off we went, following the row of pyramids because they ran north, and I was going north.

"Man, we trailed that line for hours! After a while, I noticed another queer thing: they were getting larger. Same number of bricks in each one, but the bricks were larger.

"By noon they were shoulder high. I looked into a couple—all just the same, broken at the top and empty. I examined a brick or two as well; they were silica, and old as creation itself!"

"How you know?" asked Leroy.

"They were weathered—edges rounded. Silica doesn't weather easily even on earth, and in this climate—!"

"How old you think?"

"Fifty thousand—a hundred thousand years. How can I tell? The little ones we saw in the morning were older—perhaps ten times as old. Crumbling. How old would that make *them*? Half a million years? Who knows?" Jarvis paused a moment. "Well," he resumed, "we followed the line. Tweel pointed at them and said 'rock' once or twice, but he'd done that many times before. Besides, he was more or less right about these.

"I tried questioning him. I pointed at a pyramid and asked 'People?' and indicated the two of us. He set up a negative sort of clucking and said, 'No, no, no. No one-one-two. No two-two-four,' meanwhile rubbing his stomach. I just stared at him and he went through the business again. 'No one-one-two. No two-two-four.' I just gaped at him."

"That proves it!" exclaimed Harrison. "Nuts!"

"You think so?" queried Jarvis sardonically. "Well, I figured it out different! 'No one-one-two!' You don't get it, of course, do you?"

"Nope—nor do you!"

"I think I do! Tweel was using the few English words he knew to put over a very complex idea. What, let me ask, does mathematics make you think of?"

"Why—of astronomy. Or—or logic!"

"That's it! 'No one-one-two!' Tweel was telling me that the build-ers of the pyramids weren't people—or that they weren't intelligent, that they weren't reasoning creatures! Get it?"

"Huh! I'll be damned!"

"You probably will."

"Why," put in Leroy, "he rub his belly?"

"Why? Because, my dear biologist, that's where his brains are! Not in his tiny head—in his middle!"

"*C'est* impossible!"

"Not on Mars, it isn't! This flora and fauna aren't earthly; your bio-pods prove that!" Jarvis grinned and took up his narrative. "Anyway, we plugged along across Xanthus and in about the middle of the afternoon, something else queer happened. The pyramids ended."

"Ended!"

"Yeah; the queer part was that the last one—and now they were ten-footers—was capped! See? Whatever built it was still inside; we'd trailed 'em from their half-million-year-old origin to the present.

"Tweel and I noticed it about the same time. I yanked out my auto-matic (I had a clip of Boland explosive bullets in it) and Tweel, quick as a sleight-of-hand trick, snapped a queer little glass revolver out of his bag. It was much like our weapons, except that the grip was larger to accommodate his four-taloned hand. And we held our weapons ready while we sneaked up along the lines of empty pyramids.

"Tweel saw the movement first. The top tiers of bricks were heav-ing, shaking, and suddenly slid down the sides with a thin crash. And then—something—something was coming out!

"A long, silvery-grey arm appeared, dragging after it an armored body. Armored, I mean, with scales, silver-grey and dull-shining. The arm heaved the body out of the hole; the beast crashed to the sand.

"It was a nondescript creature—body like a big grey cask, arm and a sort of mouth-hole at one end; stiff, pointed tail at the other—and that's all. No other limbs, no eyes, ears, nose—nothing! The thing dragged itself a few yards, inserted its pointed tail in the sand, pushed itself upright, and just sat.

"Tweel and I watched it for ten minutes before it moved. Then, with a creaking and rustling like—oh, like crumpling stiff paper—its arm moved to the mouth-hole and out came a brick! The arm placed the brick carefully on the ground, and the thing was still again.

"Another ten minutes—another brick. Just one of Nature's bricklayers. I was about to slip away and move on when Tweel pointed at the thing and said 'rock'! I went 'huh?' and he said it again. Then, to the accompaniment of some of his trilling, he said, 'No—no—,' and gave two or three whistling breaths.

"Well, I got his meaning, for a wonder! I said, 'No breath?' and demonstrated the word. Tweel was ecstatic; he said, 'Yes, yes, yes! No, no, no breet!' Then he gave a leap and sailed out to land on his nose about one pace from the monster!

"I was startled, you can imagine! The arm was going up for a brick, and I expected to see Tweel caught and mangled, but—nothing happened! Tweel pounded on the creature, and the arm took the brick and placed it neatly beside the first. Tweel rapped on its body again, and said 'rock,' and I got up nerve enough to take a look myself.

"Tweel was right again. The creature *was* rock, and it didn't breathe!"

"How you know?" snapped Leroy, his black eyes blazing interest.

"Because I'm a chemist. The beast was made of silica! There must have been pure silicon in the sand, and it lived on that. Get it? We, and Tweel, and those plants out there, and even the biopods are *carbon* life; this thing lived by a different set of chemical reactions. It was silicon life!"

"*La vie silicieuse!*" shouted Leroy. "I have suspect, and now it is proof! I must go see! *Il faut que je—*"

"All right! All right!" said Jarvis. "You can go see. Anyhow, there the thing was, alive and yet not alive, moving every ten minutes, and then only to remove a brick. Those bricks were its waste matter. See, Frenchy? We're carbon, and our waste is carbon dioxide, and this thing is silicon, and *its* waste is silicon dioxide—silica. But silica is a solid, hence the bricks. And it builds itself in, and when it is covered, it moves over to a fresh place to start over. No wonder it creaked! A living creature half a million years old!"

"How you know how old?" Leroy was frantic.

"We trailed its pyramids from the beginning, didn't we? If this weren't the original pyramid builder, the series would have ended somewhere before we found him, wouldn't it?—ended and started over with the small ones. That's simple enough, isn't it?

"But he reproduces, or tries to. Before the third brick came out, there was a little rustle and out popped a whole stream of those little crystal balls. They're his spores, or eggs, or seeds—call 'em what you want. They went bouncing by across Xanthus just as they'd bounced by us back in the Mare Chronium. I've a hunch how they work, too—this is for your information, Leroy. I think the crystal shell of silica is no more than a protective covering, like an eggshell, and that the active principle is the smell inside. It's some sort of gas that attacks silicon, and if the shell is broken near a supply of that element, some reaction starts that ultimately develops into a beast like that one."

"You should try!" exclaimed the little Frenchman. "We must break one to see!"

"Yeah? Well, I did. I smashed a couple against the sand. Would you like to come back in about ten thousand years to see if I planted some pyramid monsters? You'd most likely be able to tell by that time!" Jarvis paused and drew a deep breath. "Lord! That queer creature! Do you picture it? Blind, deaf, nerveless, brainless—just a mechanism, and yet—immortal! Bound to go on making bricks, building pyramids, as long as silicon and oxygen exist, and even afterwards it'll just stop. It won't be dead. If the accidents of a million years bring it its food again, there it'll be, ready to run again, while brains and civilizations are part of the past. A queer beast—yet I met a stranger one!"

"If you did, it must have been in your dreams!" growled Harrison.

"You're right!" said Jarvis soberly. "In a way, you're right. The dream-beast! That's the best name for it—and it's the most fiendish, terrifying creation one could imagine! More dangerous than a lion, more insidious than a snake!"

"Tell me!" begged Leroy. "I must go see!"

"Not *this* devil!" He paused again. "Well," he resumed, "Tweel and I left the pyramid creature and plowed along through Xanthus. I was tired and a little disheartened by Putz's failure to pick me up, and Tweel's trilling got on my nerves, as did his flying nosedives. So I just strode along without a word, hour after hour across that monotonous desert.

"Toward mid-afternoon we came in sight of a low dark line on the horizon. I knew what it was. It was a canal; I'd crossed it in the rocket and it meant that we were just one-third of the way across Xanthus. Pleasant thought, wasn't it? And still, I was keeping up to schedule.

"We approached the canal slowly; I remembered that this one was bordered by a wide fringe of vegetation and that Mudheap City was on it.

"I was tired, as I said. I kept thinking of a good hot meal, and then from that I jumped to reflections of how nice and home-like even Borneo would seem after this crazy planet, and from that, to thoughts of little old New York, and then to thinking about a girl I know there—Fancy Long. Know her?"

"Vision entertainer," said Harrison. "I've tuned her in. Nice blonde—dances and sings on the *Yerba Mate* hour."

"That's her," said Jarvis ungrammatically. "I know her pretty well—just friends, get me?—though she came down to see us off in the *Ares*. Well, I was thinking about her, feeling pretty lonesome, and all the time we were approaching that line of rubbery plants.

"And then—I said, 'What 'n Hell!' and stared. And there she was—Fancy Long, standing plain as day under one of those crackbrained trees, and smiling and waving just the way I remembered her when we left!"

"Now you're nuts, too!" observed the captain.

"Boy, I almost agreed with you! I stared and pinched myself and closed my eyes and then stared again—and every time, there was

Fancy Long smiling and waving! Tweel saw something, too; he was trilling and clucking away, but I scarcely heard him. I was bounding toward her over the sand, too amazed even to ask myself questions.

"I wasn't twenty feet from her when Tweel caught me with one of his flying leaps. He grabbed my arm, yelling, 'No—no—no!' in his squeaky voice. I tried to shake him off—he was as light as if he were built of bamboo—but he dug his claws in and yelled. And finally some sort of sanity returned to me and I stopped less than ten feet from her. There she stood, looking as solid as Putz's head!"

"Vot?" said the engineer.

"She smiled and waved, and waved and smiled, and I stood there dumb as Leroy, while Tweel squeaked and chattered. I *knew* it couldn't be real, yet—there she was!

"Finally I said, 'Fancy! Fancy Long!' She just kept on smiling and waving, but looking as real as if I hadn't left her thirty-seven million miles away.

"Tweel had his glass pistol out, pointing it at her. I grabbed his arm, but he tried to push me away. He pointed at her and said, 'No breet! No breet!' and I understood that he meant that the Fancy Long thing wasn't alive. Man, my head was whirling!

"Still, it gave me the jitters to see him pointing his weapon at her. I don't know why I stood there watching him take careful aim, but I did. Then he squeezed the handle of his weapon; there was a little puff of steam, and Fancy Long was gone! And in her place was one of those writhing, black, rope-armed horrors like the one I'd saved Tweel from!

"The dream-beast! I stood there dizzy, watching it die while Tweel trilled and whistled. Finally he touched my arm, pointed at the twisting thing, and said, 'You one-one-two, he one-one-two.' After he'd repeated it eight or ten times, I got it. Do any of you?"

"*Oui!*" shrilled Leroy. "*Moi—je le comprends!* He mean you think of something, the beast he know, and you see it! *Un chien*—a hungry dog, he would see the big bone with meat! Or smell it—not?"

"Right!" said Jarvis. "The dream-beast uses its victim's longings and desires to trap its prey. The bird at nesting season would see its mate, the fox, prowling for its own prey, would see a helpless rabbit!"

"How he do?" queried Leroy.

"How do I know? How does a snake back on earth charm a bird into its very jaws? And aren't there deep-sea fish that lure their victims into their mouths? Lord!" Jarvis shuddered. "Do you see how insidious the monster is? We're warned now—but henceforth we can't trust even our eyes. You might see me—I might see one of you—and back of it may be nothing but another of those black horrors!"

"How'd your friend know?" asked the captain abruptly.

"Tweel? I wonder! Perhaps he was thinking of something that couldn't possibly have interested me, and when I started to run, he realized that I saw something different and was warned. Or perhaps the dream-beast can only project a single vision, and Tweel saw what I saw—or nothing. I couldn't ask him. But it's just another proof that his intelligence is equal to ours or greater."

"He's daffy, I tell you!" said Harrison. "What makes you think his intellect ranks with the human?"

"Plenty of things! First, the pyramid-beast. He hadn't seen one before; he said as much. Yet he recognized it as a dead-alive automaton of silicon."

"He could have heard of it," objected Harrison. "He lives around here, you know."

"Well how about the language? I couldn't pick up a single idea of his and he learned six or seven words of mine. And do you realize what complex ideas he put over with no more than those six or seven words? The pyramid-monster—the dream-beast! In a single phrase he told me that one was a harmless automaton and the other a deadly hypnotist. What about that?"

"Huh!" said the captain.

"*Huh* if you wish! Could you have done it knowing only six words of English? Could you go even further, as Tweel did, and tell me that another creature was of a sort of intelligence so different from ours that understanding was impossible—even more impossible than that between Tweel and me?"

"Eh? What was that?"

"Later. The point I'm making is that Tweel and his race are worthy of our friendship. Somewhere on Mars—and you'll find I'm right—is a civilization and culture equal to ours, and maybe more than equal. And communication is possible between them and us; Tweel proves that. It may take years of patient trial, for their minds are alien, but less alien than the next minds we encountered—if they *are* minds."

"The next ones? What next ones?"

"The people of the mud cities along the canals." Jarvis frowned, then resumed his narrative. "I thought the dream-beast and the silicon-monster were the strangest beings conceivable, but I was wrong. These creatures are still more alien, less understandable than either and far less comprehensible than Tweel, with whom friendship is possible, and even, by patience and concentration, the exchange of ideas.

"Well," he continued, "we left the dream-beast dying, dragging itself back into its hole, and we moved toward the canal. There was a carpet of that queer walking-grass scampering out of our way, and when we reached the bank, there was a yellow trickle of water flowing. The mound city I'd noticed from the rocket was a mile or so to the right and I was curious enough to want to take a look at it.

"It had seemed deserted from my previous glimpse of it, and if any creatures were lurking in it—well, Tweel and I were both armed. And by the way, that crystal weapon of Tweel's was an interesting device; I took a look at it after the dream-beast episode. It fired a little glass splinter, poisoned, I suppose, and I guess it held at least a hundred of 'em to a load. The propellent was steam—just plain steam!"

"Shteam!" echoed Putz. "From vot come, shteam?"

"From water, of course! You could see the water through the transparent handle and about a gill of another liquid, thick and yellowish. When Tweel squeezed the handle—there was no trigger—a drop of water and a drop of the yellow stuff squirted into the firing chamber, and the water vaporized—pop!—like that. It's not so difficult; I think we could develop the same principle. Concentrated sulphuric acid will heat water almost to boiling, and so will quicklime, and there's potassium and sodium—

"Of course, his weapon hadn't the range of mine, but it wasn't so bad in this thin air, and it *did* hold as many shots as a cowboy's gun in a Western movie. It was effective, too, at least against Martian life; I tried it out, aiming at one of the crazy plants, and darned if the plant didn't wither up and fall apart! That's why I think the glass splinters were poisoned.

"Anyway, we trudged along toward the mud-heap city and I began to wonder whether the city builders dug the canals. I pointed to the city and then at the canal, and Tweel said 'No—no—no!' and gestured toward the south. I took it to mean that some other race had created the canal system, perhaps Tweel's people. I don't know; maybe there's still another intelligent race on the planet, or a dozen others. Mars is a queer little world.

"A hundred yards from the city we crossed a sort of road—just a hard-packed mud trail, and then, all of a sudden, along came one of the mound builders!

"Man, talk about fantastic beings! It looked rather like a barrel trotting along on four legs with four other arms or tentacles. It had no head, just body and members and a row of eyes completely around it. The top end of the barrel-body was a diaphragm stretched as tight as a drum head, and that was all. It was pushing a little coppery cart and tore right past us like the proverbial bat out of Hell. It didn't even notice us, although I thought the eyes on my side shifted a little as it passed.

"A moment later another came along, pushing another empty cart. Same thing—it just scooted past us. Well, I wasn't going to be ignored by a bunch of barrels playing train, so when the third one approached, I planted myself in the way—ready to jump, of course, if the thing didn't stop.

"But it did. It stopped and set up a sort of drumming from the diaphragm on top. And I held out both hands and said, 'We are friends!' And what do you suppose the thing did?"

"Said, 'Pleased to meet you,' I'll bet!" suggested Harrison.

"I couldn't have been more surprised if it had! It drummed on its diaphragm, and then suddenly boomed out, 'We are v-r-r-riends!' and gave its pushcart a vicious poke at me! I jumped aside, and away it went while I stared dumbly after it.

"A minute later another one came hurrying along. This one didn't pause, but simply drummed out, 'We are v-r-r-riends!' and scurried by. How did it learn the phrase? Were all of the creatures in some sort of communication with each other? Were they all parts of some central organism? I don't know, though I think Tweel does.

"Anyway, the creatures went sailing past us, every one greeting us with the same statement. It got to be funny; I never thought to find so many friends on this God-forsaken ball! Finally I made a puzzled gesture to Tweel; I guess he understood, for he said, 'One-one-two—yes!—two-two-four—no!' Get it?"

"Sure," said Harrison. "It's a Martian nursery rhyme."

"Yeah! Well, I was getting used to Tweel's symbolism, and I figured it out this way. 'One-one-two—yes!' The creatures were intelligent. 'Two-two-four—no!' Their intelligence was not of our order, but something different and beyond the logic of two and two is four. Maybe I missed his meaning. Perhaps he meant that their minds were of low degree, able to figure out the simple things—'One-one-two—yes!'—but not more difficult things—'Two-two-four—no!' But I think from what we saw later that he meant the other.

"After a few moments, the creatures came rushing back—first one, then another. Their pushcarts were full of stones, sand, chunks of rubbery plants, and such rubbish as that. They droned out their friendly greeting, which didn't really sound so friendly, and dashed on. The third one I assumed to be my first acquaintance and I decided to have another chat with him. I stepped into his path again and waited.

"Up he came, booming out his 'We are v-r-r-riends' and stopped. I looked at him; four or five of his eyes looked at me. He tried his password again and gave a shove on his cart, but I stood firm. And then the—the dashed creature reached out one of his arms, and two finger-like nippers tweaked my nose!"

"Haw!" roared Harrison. "Maybe the things have a sense of beauty!"

"Laugh!" grumbled Jarvis. "I'd already had a nasty bump and a mean frostbite on that nose. Anyway, I yelled 'Ouch!' and jumped aside and the creature dashed away; but from then on, their greeting was 'We are v-r-r-riends! Ouch!' Queer beasts!

"Tweel and I followed the road squarely up to the nearest mound. The creatures were coming and going, paying us not the slightest attention, fetching their loads of rubbish. The road simply dived into an opening, and slanted down like an old mine, and in and out darted the barrel-people, greeting us with their eternal phrase.

"I looked in; there was a light somewhere below, and I was curious to see it. It didn't look like a flame or torch, you understand, but more like a civilized light, and I thought that I might get some clue as to the creatures' development. So in I went and Tweel tagged along, not without a few trills and twitters, however.

"The light was curious; it sputtered and flared like an old arc light, but came from a single black rod set in the wall of the corridor. It was electric, beyond doubt. The creatures were fairly civilized, apparently.

"Then I saw another light shining on something that glittered and I went on to look at that, but it was only a heap of shiny sand. I turned toward the entrance to leave, and the Devil take me if it wasn't gone!

"I suppose the corridor had curved, or I'd stepped into a side passage. Anyway, I walked back in that direction I thought we'd come, and all I saw was more dimlit corridor. The place was a labyrinth! There was nothing but twisting passages running every way, lit by occasional lights, and now and then a creature running by, sometimes with a pushcart, sometimes without.

"Well, I wasn't much worried at first. Tweel and I had only come a few steps from the entrance. But every move we made after that seemed to get us in deeper. Finally I tried following one of the creatures with an empty cart, thinking that he'd be going out for his rubbish, but he ran around aimlessly, into one passage and out another. When he started dashing around a pillar like one of these Japanese waltzing mice, I gave up, dumped my water tank on the floor, and sat down.

"Tweel was as lost as I. I pointed up and he said 'No—no—no!' in a sort of helpless trill. And we couldn't get any help from the natives. They paid no attention at all, except to assure us they were friends—ouch!

"Lord! I don't know how many hours or days we wandered around there! I slept twice from sheer exhaustion; Tweel never seemed to need sleep. We tried following only the upward corridors, but they'd run uphill a ways and then curve downwards. The temperature in that damned ant hill was constant; you couldn't tell night from day and after my first sleep I didn't know whether I'd slept one hour or thirteen, so I couldn't tell from my watch whether it was midnight or noon.

"We saw plenty of strange things. There were machines running in some of the corridors, but they didn't seem to be doing anything— just wheels turning. And several times I saw two barrel-beasts with a little one growing between them, joined to both."

"Parthenogenesis!" exulted Leroy. "Parthenogenesis by budding like *les tulipes!*"

"If you say so, Frenchy," agreed Jarvis. "The things never noticed us at all, except, as I say, to greet us with 'We are v-r-r-riends! Ouch!' They seemed to have no home-life of any sort, but just scurried around with their pushcarts, bringing in rubbish. And finally I discovered what they did with it.

"We'd had a little luck with a corridor, one that slanted upwards for a great distance. I was feeling that we ought to be close to the surface when suddenly the passage debouched into a domed chamber, the only one we'd seen. And man!—I felt like dancing when I saw what looked like daylight through a crevice in the roof.

"There was a—a sort of machine in the chamber, just an enormous wheel that turned slowly, and one of the creatures was in the act of dumping his rubbish below it. The wheel ground it with a crunch—sand, stones, plants, all into powder that sifted away somewhere. While we watched, others filed in, repeating the process, and that seemed to be all. No rhyme nor reason to the whole thing—but that's characteristic of this crazy planet. And there was another fact that's almost too bizarre to believe.

"One of the creatures, having dumped his load, pushed his cart aside with a crash and calmly shoved himself under the wheel! I watched him being crushed, too stupefied to make a sound, and a moment later, another followed him! They were perfectly methodical about it, too; one of the cartless creatures took the abandoned pushcart.

"Tweel didn't seem surprised; I pointed out the next suicide to him, and he just gave the most human-like shrug imaginable, as much as to say, 'What can I do about it?' He must have known more or less about these creatures.

"Then I saw something else. There was something beyond the wheel, something shining on a sort of low pedestal. I walked over; there was a little crystal about the size of an egg, fluorescing to beat Tophet. The light from it stung my hands and face, almost like a static discharge, and then I noticed another funny thing. Remember that wart I had on my left thumb? Look!" Jarvis extended his hand. "It dried up and fell off—just like that! And my abused nose—say, the pain went out of it like magic! The thing had the property of hard ex-rays or gamma radiations, only more so; it destroyed diseased tissue and left healthy tissue unharmed!

"I was thinking what a present *that'd* be to take back to Mother Earth when a lot of racket interrupted. We dashed back to the other side of the wheel in time to see one of the pushcarts ground up. Some suicide had been careless, it seems.

"Then suddenly the creatures were booming and drumming all around us and their noise was decidedly menacing. A crowd of them advanced toward us; we backed out of what I thought was the passage we'd entered by, and they came rumbling after us, some pushing carts and some not. Crazy brutes! There was a whole chorus of 'We are v-r-r-riends! Ouch!' I didn't like the 'ouch'; it was rather suggestive.

"Tweel had his glass gun out and I dumped my water tank for greater freedom and got mine. We backed up the corridor with the barrel-beasts following—about twenty of them. Queer thing—the ones coming in with loaded carts moved past us inches away without a sign.

"Tweel must have noticed that. Suddenly, he snatched out that glowing coal cigar-lighter of his and touched a cart-load of plant limbs. Puff! The whole load was burning—and the crazy beast pushing it went right along without a change of pace! It created some disturbance among our 'v-r-r-riends,' however—and then I noticed the smoke eddying and swirling past us, and sure enough, there was the entrance!

"I grabbed Tweel and out we dashed and after us our twenty pursuers. The daylight felt like Heaven, though I saw at first glance that the sun was all but set, and that was bad, since I couldn't live outside my thermo-skin bag in a Martian night—at least, without a fire.

"And things got worse in a hurry. They cornered us in an angle between two mounds, and there we stood. I hadn't fired nor had Tweel; there wasn't any use in irritating the brutes. They stopped a little distance away and began their booming about friendship and ouches.

"Then things got still worse! A barrel-brute came out with a pushcart and they all grabbed into it and came out with handfuls of foot-long copper darts—sharp-looking ones—and all of a sudden one sailed past my ear—zing! And it was shoot or die then.

"We were doing pretty well for a while. We picked off the ones next to the pushcart and managed to keep the darts at a minimum, but suddenly there was a thunderous booming of 'v-r-r-riends' and 'ouches,' and a whole army of 'em came out of their hole.

"Man! We were through and I knew it! Then I realized that Tweel wasn't. He could have leaped the mound behind us as easily as not. He was staying for me!

"Say, I could have cried if there'd been time! I'd liked Tweel from the first, but whether I'd have had gratitude to do what he was doing—suppose I *had* saved him from the first dream-beast—he'd done as much for me, hadn't he? I grabbed his arm, and said 'Tweel,' and pointed up, and he understood. He said, 'No—no—no, Tick!' and popped away with his glass pistol.

"What could I do? I'd be a goner anyway when the sun set, but I couldn't explain that to him. I said, 'Thanks, Tweel. You're a man!' and felt that I wasn't paying him any compliment at all. A man! There are mighty few men who'd do that.

"So I went 'bang' with my gun and Tweel went 'puff' with his, and the barrels were throwing darts and getting ready to rush us, and booming about being friends. I had given up hope. Then suddenly an angel dropped right down from Heaven in the shape of Putz, with his under-jets blasting the barrels into very small pieces!

"Wow! I let out a yell and dashed for the rocket; Putz opened the door and in I went, laughing and crying and shouting! It was a moment or so before I remembered Tweel; I looked around in time to see him rising in one of his nosedives over the mound and away.

"I had a devil of a job arguing Putz into following! By the time we got the rocket aloft, darkness was down; you know how it comes here—like turning off a light. We sailed out over the desert and put down once or twice. I yelled 'Tweel!' and yelled it a hundred times,

I guess. We couldn't find him; he could travel like the wind and all I got—or else I imagined it—was a faint trilling and twittering drifting out of the south. He'd gone, and damn it! I wish—I wish he hadn't!"

The four men of the *Ares* were silent—even the sardonic Harrison. At last little Leroy broke the stillness.

"I should like to see," he murmured.

"Yeah," said Harrison. "And the wart-cure. Too bad you missed that; it might be the cancer cure they've been hunting for a century and a half."

"Oh, that!" muttered Jarvis gloomily. "That's what started the fight!" He drew a glistening object from his pocket.

"Here it is."

YOUTH

ISAAC ASIMOV

There was a spatter of pebbles against the window and the youngster stirred in his sleep. Another, and he was awake.

He sat up stiffly in bed. Seconds passed while he interpreted his strange surroundings. He wasn't in his own home, of course. This was out in the country. It was colder than it should be and there was green at the window.

"Slim!"

The call was a hoarse, urgent whisper, and the youngster bounded to the open window.

Slim wasn't his real name, but the new friend he had met the day before had needed only one look at his slight figure to say, "You're Slim." He added, "I'm Red."

Red wasn't his real name, either, but its appropriateness was obvious. They were friends instantly with the quick unquestioning friendship of young ones not yet quite in adolescence, before even the first stains of adulthood began to make their appearance.

Slim cried, "Hi, Red!" and waved cheerfully, still blinking the sleep out of himself.

Red kept to his croaking whisper, "Quiet! You want to wake somebody?"

Slim noticed all at once that the sun scarcely topped the low hills in the east that the shadows were long and soft and that the grass was wet.

Slim said, more softly, "What's the matter?"

Red only waved for him to come out.

Slim dressed quickly, gladly confining his morning wash to the momentary sprinkle of a little luke-warm water. He let the air dry the exposed portions of his body as he ran out, while bare skin grew wet against the dewy grass.

Red said, "You've got to be quiet. If Mom wakes up or Dad or your Dad or even any of the hands then it'll be 'Come on in or you'll catch your death of cold.'"

He mimicked voice and tone faithfully, so that Slim laughed and thought that there had never been so funny a fellow as Red.

Slim said, eagerly, "Do you come out here every day like this, Red? Real early? It's like the whole world is just yours, isn't it, Red? No one else around and all like that." He felt proud at being allowed entrance into this private world.

Red stared at him sidelong. He said carelessly, "I've been up for hours. Didn't you hear it last night?"

"Hear what?"

"Thunder."

"Was there a thunderstorm?" Slim never slept through a thunderstorm.

"I guess not. But there was thunder. I heard it, and then I went to the window and it wasn't raining. It was all stars and the sky was just getting sort of almost gray. You know what I mean?"

Slim had never seen it so, but he nodded.

"So I just thought I'd go out," said Red.

They walked along the grassy side of the concrete road that split the panorama right down the middle all the way down to where it vanished among the hills. It was so old that Red's father couldn't tell Red when it had been built. It didn't have a crack or a rough spot in it.

Red said, "Can you keep a secret?"

"Sure, Red. What kind of a secret?"

"Just a secret. Maybe I'll tell you and maybe I won't. I don't know yet." Red broke a long, supple stem from a fern they passed, methodically stripped it of its leaflets and swung what was left whip-fashion. For a moment, he was on a wild charger, which reared and champed under his iron control. Then he got tired, tossed the whip aside and stowed the charger away in a corner of his imagination for future use.

He said, "There'll be a circus around."

Slim said, "That's no secret. I knew that. My Dad told me even before we came here—"

"That's not the secret. Fine secret! Ever see a circus?"

"Oh, sure. You bet."

"Like it?"

"Say, there isn't anything I like better."

Red was watching out of the corner of his eyes again. "Ever think you would like to be with a circus? I mean, for good?"

Slim considered, "I guess not. I think I'll be an astronomer like my Dad. I think he wants me to be."

"Huh! Astronomer!" said Red.

Slim felt the doors of the new, private world closing on him and astronomy became a thing of dead stars and black, empty space.

He said, placatingly, "A circus *would* be more fun."

"You're just saying that."

"No, I'm not. I mean it."

Red grew argumentative. "Suppose you had a chance to join the circus right now. What would you do?"

"I—I—"

"See!" Red affected scornful laughter.

Slim was stung. "I'd join up."

"Go on."

"Try me."

Red whirled at him, strange and intense. "You meant that? You want to go in with me?"

"What do you mean?" Slim stepped back a bit, surprised by the unexpected challenge.

"I got something that can get us into the circus. Maybe some-day we can even have a circus of our own. We could be the biggest circus-fellows in the world. That's if you want to go in with me. Otherwise—Well, I guess I can do it on my own. I just thought: Let's give good old Slim a chance."

The world was strange and glamorous, and Slim said, "Sure thing, Red. I'm in! What is it, huh, Red? Tell me what it is."

"Figure it out. What's the most important thing in circuses?"

Slim thought desperately. He wanted to give the right answer. Finally, he said, "Acrobats?"

"Holy Smokes! I wouldn't go five steps to look at acrobats."

"I don't know then."

"Animals, that's what! What's the best side-show? Where are the biggest crowds? Even in the main rings the best acts are animal acts." There was no doubt in Red's voice.

"Do you think so?"

"Everyone thinks so. You ask anyone. Anyway, I found animals this morning. Two of them."

"And you've got them?"

"Sure. That's the secret. Are you telling?"

"Of course not."

"Okay. I've got them in the barn. Do you want to see them?"

They were almost at the barn; its huge open door black. Too black. They had been heading there all the time. Slim stopped in his tracks.

He tried to make his words casual. "Are they big?"

"Would I fool with them if they were big? They can't hurt you. They're only about so long. I've got them in a cage."

They were in the barn now and Slim saw the large cage suspended from a hook in the roof. It was covered with stiff canvas.

Red said, "We used to have some bird there or something. Anyway, they can't get away from there. Come on, let's go up to the loft."

They clambered up the wooden stairs and Red hooked the cage toward them.

Slim pointed and said, "There's sort of a hole in the canvas."

Red frowned. "How'd that get there?" He lifted the canvas, looked in, and said, with relief, "They're still there."

"The canvas appeared to be burned," worried Slim.

"You want to look, or don't you?"

Slim nodded slowly. He wasn't sure he wanted to, after all. They might be—

But the canvas had been jerked off and there they were. Two of them, the way Red said. They were small, and sort of disgusting-looking. The animals moved quickly as the canvas lifted and were on the side toward the youngsters. Red poked a cautious finger at them.

"Watch out," said Slim, in agony.

"They don't hurt you," said Red. "Ever see anything like them?"

"No."

"Can't you see how a circus would jump at a chance to have these?"

"Maybe they're too small for a circus."

Red looked annoyed. He let go the cage which swung back and forth pendulum-fashion. "You're just trying to back out, aren't you?"

"No, I'm not. It's just—"

"They're not too small, don't worry. Right now, I've only got one worry."

"What's that?"

"Well, I've got to keep them till the circus comes, don't I? I've got to figure out what to feed them meanwhile."

The cage swung and the little trapped creatures clung to its bars, gesturing at the youngsters with queer, quick motions—almost as though they were intelligent.

II

The Astronomer entered the dining room with decorum. He felt very much the guest.

He said, "Where are the youngsters? My son isn't in his room."

The Industrialist smiled. "They've been out for hours. However, breakfast was forced into them among the women some time ago, so there is nothing to worry about. Youth, Doctor, youth!"

"Youth!" The word seemed to depress the Astronomer.

They ate breakfast in silence. The Industrialist said once, "You really think they'll come. The day looks so—*normal.*"

The Astronomer said, "They'll come."

That was all.

Afterward the Industrialist said, "You'll pardon me. I can't conceive your playing so elaborate a hoax. You really spoke to them?"

"As I speak to you. At least, in a sense. They can project thoughts."

"I gathered that must be so from your letter. How, I wonder."

"I could not say. I asked them and, of course, they were vague. Or perhaps it was just that I could not understand. It involves a projector for the focussing of thought and, even more than that, conscious attention on the part of both projector and receptor. It was quite a while before I realized they were trying to think at me. Such thought-projectors may be part of the science they will give us."

"Perhaps," said the Industrialist. "Yet think of the changes it would bring to society. A thought-projector!"

"Why not? Change would be good for us."

"I don't think so."

"It is only in old age that change is unwelcome," said the Astronomer, "and races can be old as well as individuals."

The Industrialist pointed out the window. "You see that road. It was built Beforethewars. I don't know exactly when. It is as good now as the day it was built. We couldn't possibly duplicate it now. The race was young when that was built, eh?"

"Then? Yes! At least they weren't afraid of new things."

"No. I wish they had been. Where is the society of Beforethewars? Destroyed, Doctor! What good were youth and new things? We are better off now. The world is peaceful and jogs along. The race goes nowhere but after all, there is nowhere to go. *They* proved that. The men who built the road. I will speak with your visitors as I agreed, if they come. But I think I will only ask them to go."

"The race is not going nowhere," said the Astronomer, earnestly. "It is going toward final destruction. My university has a smaller student body each year. Fewer books are written. Less work is done. An old man sleeps in the sun and his days are peaceful and unchanging, but each day finds him nearer death all the same."

"Well, well," said the Industrialist.

"No, don't dismiss it. Listen. Before I wrote you, I investigated your position in the planetary economy."

"And you found me solvent?" interrupted the Industrialist, smiling.

"Why, yes. Oh, I see, you are joking. And yet—perhaps the joke is not far off. You are less solvent than your father and he was less solvent than his father. Perhaps your son will no longer be solvent. It becomes too troublesome for the planet to support even the industries that still exist, though they are toothpicks to the oak trees of Beforethewars. We will be back to village economy and then to what? The caves?"

"And the infusion of fresh technological knowledge will be the changing of all that?"

"Not just the new knowledge. Rather the whole effect of change, of a broadening of horizons. Look, sir, I chose you to approach in this matter not only because you were rich and influential with government officials, but because you had an unusual reputation, for these days, of daring to break with tradition. Our people will resist change and you would know how to handle them, how to see to it that—that—"

"That the youth of the race is revived?"

"Yes."

"With its atomic bombs?"

"The atomic bombs," returned the Astronomer, "need not be the end of civilization. These visitors of mine had their atomic bomb, or whatever their equivalent was on their own worlds, and survived it, because they didn't give up. Don't you see? It wasn't the bomb that defeated us, but our own shellshock. This may be the last chance to reverse the process."

"Tell me," said the Industrialist, "what do these friends from space want in return?"

The Astronomer hesitated. He said, "I will be truthful with you. They come from a denser planet. Ours is richer in the lighter atoms."

"They want magnesium? Aluminum?"

"No, sir. Carbon and hydrogen. They want coal and oil."

"Really?"

The Astronomer said, quickly, "You are going to ask why creatures who have mastered space travel, and therefore atomic power, would want coal and oil. I can't answer that."

The Industrialist smiled, "But I can. This is the best evidence yet of the truth of your story. Superficially, atomic power would seem to preclude the use of coal and oil. However, quite apart from the energy gained by their combustion they remain, and always will remain, the basic raw material for all organic chemistry. Plastics, dyes, pharmaceuticals, solvents. Industry could not exist without them, even in an atomic age. Still, if coal and oil are the low price for which they would sell us the troubles and tortures of racial youth, my answer is that the commodity would be dear if offered gratis."

The Astronomer sighed and said, "There are the boys!"

They were visible through the open window, standing together in the grassy field and lost in animated conversation. The Industrialist's son pointed imperiously and the Astronomer's son nodded and made off at a run toward the house.

The Industrialist said, "There is the Youth you speak of. Our race has as much of it as it ever had."

"Yes, but we age them quickly and pour them into the mold."

Slim scuttled into the room, the door banging behind him.

The Astronomer said, in mild disapproval, "What's this?"

Slim looked up in surprise and came to a halt. "I beg your pardon. I didn't know anyone was here. I am sorry to have interrupted." His enunciation was almost painfully precise.

The Industrialist said, "It's all right, youngster."

But the Astronomer said, "Even if you had been entering an empty room, son, there would be no cause for slamming a door."

"Nonsense," insisted the Industrialist. "The youngster has done no harm. You simply scold him for being young. You, with your views!"

He said to Slim, "Come here, lad."

Slim advanced slowly.

"How do you like the country, eh?"

"Very much, sir, thank you."

"My son has been showing you about the place, has he?"

"Yes, sir. Red—I mean—"

"No, no. Call him Red. I call him that myself. Now tell me, what are you two up to, eh?"

Slim looked away. "Why—just exploring, sir."

The Industrialist turned to the Astronomer. "There you are, youthful curiosity and adventure-lust. The race has not yet lost it."

Slim said, "Sir?"

"Yes, lad."

The youngster took a long time in getting on with it. He said, "Red sent me in for something good to eat, but I don't exactly know what he meant. I didn't like to say so."

"Why, just ask cook. She'll have something good for young'uns to eat."

"Oh, no, sir. I mean for animals."

"For animals?"

"Yes, sir. What do animals eat?"

The Astronomer said, "I am afraid my son is city-bred."

"Well," said the Industrialist, "there's no harm in that. What kind of an animal, lad?"

"A small one, sir."

"Then try grass or leaves, and if they don't want that, nuts or berries would probably do the trick."

"Thank you, sir." Slim ran out again, closing the door gently behind him.

The Astronomer said, "Do you suppose they've trapped an animal alive?" He was obviously perturbed.

"That's common enough. There's no shooting on my estate and it's tame country, full of rodents and small creatures. Red is always coming home with pets of one sort or another. They rarely maintain his interest for long."

He looked at the wall clock. "Your friends should have been here by now, shouldn't they?"

III

The swaying had come to a halt and it was dark. The Explorer was not comfortable in the alien air. It felt as thick as soup and he had to breath shallowly. Even so—

He reached out in a sudden need for company. The Merchant was warm to the touch. His breathing was rough, he moved in an occasional spasm, and was obviously asleep. The Explorer hesitated and decided not to wake him. It would serve no real purpose.

There would be no rescue, of course. That was the penalty paid for the high profits which unrestrained competition could lead to. The Merchant who opened a new planet could have a ten year monopoly if its trade, which he might hug to himself or, more likely, rent out to all comers at a stiff price. It followed that planets were searched for in secrecy and, preferably, away from the usual trade routes. In a case such as theirs, then, there was little or no chance that another ship would come within range of their subetherics except for the most improbable of coincidences. Even if they were in their ship, that is, rather than in this—this—*cage*.

The Explorer grasped the thick bars. Even if they blasted those away, as they could, they would be stuck too high in open air for leaping.

It was too bad. They had landed twice before in the scout-ship. They had established contact with the natives who were grotesquely huge, but mild and unaggressive. It was obvious that they had once owned a flourishing technology, but hadn't faced up to the consequences of such a technology. It would have been a wonderful market.

And it was a tremendous world. The Merchant, especially, had been taken aback. He had known the figures that expressed the planet's diameter, but from a distance of two light-seconds, he had stood at the visi-plate and muttered, "Unbelievable!"

"Oh, there are larger worlds," the Explorer said. It wouldn't do for an Explorer to be too easily impressed.

"Inhabited?"

"Well, no."

"Why, you could drop your planet into that large ocean and drown it."

The Explorer smiled. It was a gentle dig at his Arcturian homeland, which was smaller than most planets. He said, "Not quite."

The Merchant followed along the line of his thoughts. "And the inhabitants are large in proportion to their world?" He sounded as though the news struck him less favorably now.

"Nearly ten times our height."

"Are you sure they are friendly?"

"That is hard to say. Friendship between alien intelligences is an imponderable. They are not dangerous, I think. We've come across other groups that could not maintain equilibrium after the atomic war stage and you know the results. Introversion. Retreat. Gradual decadence and increasing gentleness."

"Even if they are such monsters?"

"The principle remains."

It was about then that the Explorer felt the heavy throbbing of the engines.

He frowned and said, "We are descending a bit too quickly."

There had been some speculation on the dangers of landing some hours before. The planetary target was a huge one for an oxygen-water world. Though it lacked the size of the uninhabitable hydrogen-ammonia planets and its low density made its surface gravity fairly normal, its gravitational forces fell off but slowly with distance. In short, its gravitational potential was high and the ship's Calculator was a run-of-the-mill model not designed to plot landing trajectories at that potential range. That meant the Pilot would have to use manual controls.

It would have been wiser to install a more high-powered model, but that would have meant a trip to some outpost of civilization; lost time; perhaps a lost secret. The Merchant demanded an immediate landing.

The Merchant felt it necessary to defend his position now. He said angrily to the Explorer, "Don't you think the Pilot knows his job? He landed you safely twice before."

Yes, thought the Explorer, in a scoutship, not in this unmaneuverable freighter. Aloud, he said nothing.

He kept his eye on the visi-plate. They were descending too quickly. There was no room for doubt. Much too quickly.

The Merchant said, peevishly, "Why do you keep silence?"

"Well, then, if you wish me to speak, I would suggest that you strap on your Floater and help me prepare the Ejector."

The Pilot fought a noble fight. He was no beginner. The atmosphere, abnormally high and thick in the gravitational potential of this world whipped and burned about the ship, but to the very last it looked as though he might bring it under control despite that.

He even maintained course, following the extrapolated line to the point on the northern continent toward which they were headed. Under other circumstances, with a shade more luck, the story would eventually have been told and retold as a heroic and masterly reversal of a lost situation. But within sight of victory, tired body and tired nerves clamped a control bar with a shade too much pressure. The ship, which had almost levelled off, dipped down again.

There was no room to retrieve the final error. There was only a mile left to fall. The Pilot remained at his post to the actual landing, his only thought that of breaking the force of the crash, of maintaining the spaceworthiness of the vessel. He did not survive. With the ship bucking madly in a soupy atmosphere, few Ejectors could be mobilized and only one of them in time.

When afterwards, the Explorer lifted out of unconsciousness and rose to his feet, he had the definite feeling that but for himself and the Merchant, there were no survivors. And perhaps that was an overcalculation. His Floater had burnt out while still sufficiently distant from the surface to have the fall stun him. The Merchant might have had less luck, even, than that.

He was surrounded by a world of thick, ropy stalks of grass, and in the distance were trees that reminded him vaguely of similar structures on his native Arcturian world except that their lowest branches were high above what he would consider normal treetops.

He called, his voice sounding basso in the thick air and the Merchant answered. The Explorer made his way toward him, thrusting violently at the coarse stalks that barred his path.

"Are you hurt?" he asked.

The Merchant grimaced, "I've sprained something. It hurts to walk."

The Explorer probed gently. "I don't think anything is broken. You'll have to walk despite the pain."

"Can't we rest first?"

"It's important to try to find the ship. If it is space-worthy or if it can be repaired, we may live. Otherwise, we won't."

"Just a few minutes. Let me catch my breath."

The Explorer was glad enough for those few minutes. The Merchant's eyes were already closed. He allowed his to do the same.

He heard the trampling and his eyes snapped open. Never sleep on a strange planet, he told himself futilely.

The Merchant was awake too and his steady screaming was a rumble of terror.

The Explorer called, "It's only a native of this planet. It won't harm you."

But even as he spoke, the giant had swooped down and in a moment they were in its grasp being lifted closer to its monstrous ugliness.

The Merchant struggled violently and, of course, quite futilely. "Can't you talk to it?" he yelled.

The Explorer could only shake his head. "I can't reach it with the Projector. It won't be listening."

"Then blast it. Blast it down."

"We can't do that." The phrase "you fool" had almost been added. The Explorer struggled to keep his self-control. They were swallowing space as the monster moved purposefully away.

"Why not?" cried the Merchant. "You can reach your blaster. I see it in plain sight. Don't be afraid of falling."

"It's simpler than that. If this monster is killed, you'll never trade with this planet. You'll never even leave it. You probably won't live the day out."

"Why? Why?"

"Because this is one of the young of the species. You should know what happens when a trader kills a native young, even accidentally. What's more, if this is the target-point, then we are on the estate of a powerful native. This might be one of his brood."

That was how they entered their present prison. They had carefully burnt away a portion of the thick, stiff covering and it was obvious that the height from which they were suspended was a killing one.

Now, once again, the prison-cage shuddered and lifted in an upward arc. The Merchant rolled to the lower rim and startled awake. The cover lifted and light flooded in. As was the case the time before, there were two specimens of the young. They were not very different in appearance from adults of the species, reflected the Explorer, though, of course, they were considerably smaller.

A handful of reedy green stalks was stuffed between the bars. Its odor was not unpleasant but it carried clods of soil at its ends.

The Merchant drew away and said, huskily, "What are they doing?"

The Explorer said, "Trying to feed us, I should judge. At least this seems to be the native equivalent of grass."

The cover was replaced and they were set swinging again, alone with their fodder.

IV

Slim started at the sound of footsteps and brightened when it turned out to be only Red.

He said, "No one's around. I had my eye peeled, you bet."

Red said, "Ssh. Look. You take this stuff and stick it in the cage. I've got to scoot back to the house."

"What is it?" Slim reached reluctantly.

"Ground meat. Holy Smokes, haven't you ever seen ground meat? That's what you should've got when I sent you to the house instead of coming back with that stupid grass."

Slim was hurt. "How'd I know they don't eat grass. Besides, ground meat doesn't come loose like that. It comes in cellophane and it isn't that color."

"Sure—in the city. Out here we grind our own and it's always this color till it's cooked."

"You mean it isn't cooked?" Slim drew away quickly.

Red looked disgusted. "Do you think animals eat *cooked* food. Come on, take it. It won't hurt you. I tell you there isn't much time."

"Why? What's doing back at the house?"

"I don't know. Dad and your father are walking around. I think maybe they're looking for me. Maybe the cook told them I took the meat. Anyway, we don't want them coming here after me."

"Didn't you ask the cook before you took this stuff?"

"Who? That crab? Shouldn't wonder if she only let me have a drink of water because Dad makes her. Come on. Take it."

Slim took the large glob of meat though his skin crawled at the touch. He turned toward the barn and Red sped away in the direction from which he had come.

He slowed when he approached the two adults, took a few deep breaths to bring himself back to normal, and then carefully and nonchalantly sauntered past. (They were walking in the general direction of the barn, he noticed, but not dead on.)

He said, "Hi, Dad. Hello, sir."

The Industrialist said, "Just a moment, Red. I have a question to ask you?"

Red turned a carefully blank face to his father. "Yes, Dad?"

"Mother tells me you were out early this morning."

"Not real early, Dad. Just a little before breakfast."

"She said you told her it was because you had been awakened during the night and didn't go back to sleep."

Red waited before answering. Should he have told Mom that?

Then he said, "Yes, sir."

"What was it that awakened you?"

Red saw no harm in it. He said, "I don't know, Dad. It sounded like thunder, sort of, and like a collision, sort of."

"Could you tell where it came from?"

"It *sounded* like it was out by the hill." That was truthful, and useful as well, since the direction was almost opposite that in which the barn lay.

The Industrialist looked at his guest. "I suppose it would do no harm to walk toward the hill."

The Astronomer said, "I am ready."

Red watched them walk away and when he turned he saw Slim peering cautiously out from among the briars of a hedge.

Red waved at him. "Come on."

Slim stepped out and approached. "Did they say anything about the meat?"

"No. I guess they don't know about that. They went down to the hill."

"What for?"

"Search me. They kept asking about the noise I heard. Listen, did the animals eat the meat?"

"Well," said Slim, cautiously, "they were sort of *looking* at it and smelling it or something."

"Okay," Red said, "I guess they'll eat it. Holy Smokes, they've got to eat *something*. Let's walk along toward the hill and see what Dad and your father are going to do."

"What about the animals?"

"They'll be all right. A fellow can't spend all his time on them. Did you give them water?"

"Sure. They drank that."

"See. Come on. We'll look at them after lunch. I tell you what. We'll bring them fruit. Anything'll eat fruit."

Together they trotted up the rise, Red, as usual, in the lead.

V

The Astronomer said, "You think the noise was their ship landing?"

"Don't you think it could be?"

"If it were, they may all be dead."

"Perhaps not." The Industrialist frowned.

"If they have landed, and are still alive, where are they?"

"Think about that for a while." He was still frowning.

The Astronomer said, "I don't understand you."

"They may not be friendly."

"Oh, no. I've spoken with them. They've—"

"You've spoken with them. Call that reconnaissance. What would their next step be? Invasion?"

"But they only have one ship, sir."

"You know that only because they say so. They might have a fleet."

"I've told you about their size. They—"

"Their size would not matter, if they have handweapons that may well be superior to our artillery."

"That is not what I meant."

"I had this partly in mind from the first." The Industrialist went on. "It is for that reason I agreed to see them after I received your letter. Not to agree to an unsettling and impossible trade, but to judge their real purposes. I did not count on their evading the meeting."

He sighed. "I suppose it isn't our fault. You are right in one thing, at any rate. The world has been at peace too long. We are losing a healthy sense of suspicion."

The Astronomer's mild voice rose to an unusual pitch and he said, "I *will* speak. I tell you that there is no reason to suppose they can possibly be hostile. They are small, yes, but that is only important because it is a reflection of the fact that their native worlds are small. Our world has what is for them a normal gravity, but because of our much higher gravitational potential, our atmosphere is too dense to support them comfortably over sustained periods. For a similar reason the use of the world as a base for interstellar travel, except for trade in certain items, is uneconomical. And there are important differences in chemistry of life due to the basic differences in soils. They couldn't eat our food or we theirs."

"Surely all this can be overcome. They can bring their own food, build domed stations of lowered air pressure, devise specially designed ships."

"They can. And how glibly you can describe feats that are easy to a race in its youth. It is simply that they don't have to do any of that. There are millions of worlds suitable for them in the Galaxy. They don't need this one which isn't."

"How do you know? All this is their information again."

"This I was able to check independently. I am an astronomer, after all."

"That is true. Let me hear what you have to say then, while we walk."

"Then, sir, consider that for a long time our astronomers have believed that two general classes of planetary bodies existed? First, the planets which formed at distances far enough from their stellar nucleus to become cool enough to capture hydrogen. These would be large planets rich in hydrogen, ammonia and methane. We have examples of these in the giant outer planets. The second class would include those planets formed so near the stellar center that the high temperature would make it impossible to capture much hydrogen. These would be smaller planets, comparatively poorer in hydrogen and richer in oxygen. We know that type very well since we live on one. Ours is the only solar system we know in detail, however, and it has been reasonable for us to assume that these were the *only* two planetary classes."

"I take it then that there is another."

"Yes. There is a super-dense class, still smaller, poorer in hydrogen, than the inner planets of the solar system. The ratio of occurrence of hydrogen-ammonia planets and these super-dense water-oxygen worlds of theirs over the entire Galaxy—and remember that they have actually conducted a survey of significant sample volumes of the Galaxy which we, without interstellar travel, cannot do—is about 3 to 1. This leaves them seven million superdense worlds for exploration and colonization."

The Industrialist looked at the blue sky and the green-covered trees among which they were making their way. He said, "And worlds like ours?"

The Astronomer said, softly, "Ours is the first solar system they have found which contains them. Apparently the development of our solar system was unique and did not follow the ordinary rules."

The Industrialist considered that. "What it amounts to is that these creatures from space are asteroid-dwellers."

"No, no. The asteroids are something else again. They occur, I was told, in one out of eight stellar systems, but they're completely different from what we've been discussing."

"And how does your being an astronomer change the fact that you are still only quoting their unsupported statements?"

"But they did not restrict themselves to bald items of information. They presented me with a theory of stellar evolution which I had to accept and which is more nearly valid than anything our own astronomy has ever been able to devise, if we except possible lost theories dating from Beforethewars. Mind you, their theory had a rigidly mathematical development and it predicted just such a Galaxy as they describe. So you see, they have all the worlds they wish. They are not land-hungry. Certainly not for our land."

"Reason would say so, if what you say is true. But creatures may be intelligent and not reasonable. Our forefathers were presumably intelligent, yet they were certainly not reasonable. Was it reasonable to destroy almost all their tremendous civilization in atomic warfare over causes our historians can no longer accurately determine?" The Industrialist brooded over it. "From the dropping of the first atom bomb over those islands—I forget the ancient name—there was only one end in sight, and in plain sight. Yet events were allowed to proceed to that end."

He looked up, said briskly, "Well, where are we? I wonder if we are not on a fool's errand after all."

But the Astronomer was a little in advance and his voice came thickly. "No fool's errand, sir. Look there."

VI

Red and Slim had trailed their elders with the experience of youth, aided by the absorption and anxiety of their fathers. Their view of the final object of the search was somewhat obscured by the underbrush behind which they remained.

Red said, "Holy Smokes. Look at that. It's all shiny silver or something."

But it was Slim who was really excited. He caught at the other. "I know what this is. It's a space-ship. That must be why my father came here. He's one of the biggest astronomers in the world and your father would have to call him if a spaceship landed on his estate."

"What are you talking about? Dad didn't even know that thing was there. He only came here because I told him I heard the thunder from here. Besides, there isn't any such thing as a spaceship."

"Sure, there is. Look at it. See those round things. They are ports. And you can see the rocket tubes."

"How do you know so much?"

Slim was flushed. He said, "I read about them. My father has books about them. Old books. From Beforethewars."

"Huh. Now I know you're making it up. Books from Beforethewars!"

"My father *has* to have them. He teaches at the University. It's his job."

His voice had risen and Red had to pull at him. "You want them to hear us?" he whispered indignantly.

"Well, it is, too, a spaceship."

"Look here, Slim, you mean that's a ship from another world."

"It's *got* to be. Look at my father going round and round it. He wouldn't be so interested if it was anything else."

"Other worlds! Where are there other worlds?"

"Everywhere. How about the planets? They're worlds just like ours, some of them. And other stars probably have planets. There's probably zillions of planets."

Red felt outweighed and outnumbered. He muttered, "You're crazy!"

"All right, then. I'll show you."

"Hey! Where are you going?"

"Down there. I'm going to ask my father. I suppose you'll believe it if *he* tells you. I suppose you'll believe a Professor of Astronomy knows what—"

He had scrambled upright.

Red said, "Hey. You don't want them to see us. We're not supposed to be here. Do you want them to start asking questions and find out about our animals?"

"I don't care. You said I was crazy."

"Snitcher! You promised you wouldn't tell."

"I'm *not* going to tell. But if they find out themselves, it's your fault, for starting an argument and saying I was crazy."

"I take it back, then," grumbled Red.

"Well, all right. You better."

In a way, Slim was disappointed. He wanted to see the space-ship at closer quarters. Still, he could not break his vow of secrecy even in spirit without at least the excuse of personal insult.

Red said, "It's awfully small for a space-ship."

"Sure, because it's probably a scout-ship."

"I'll bet Dad couldn't even get into the old thing."

So much Slim realized to be true. It was a weak point in his argument and he made no answer. His interest was absorbed by the adults.

Red rose to his feet; an elaborate attitude of boredom all about him. "Well, I guess we better be going. There's business to do and I can't spend all day here looking at some old space-ship or whatever it is. We've got to take care of the animals if we're going to be circus-folks. That's the first rule with circus-folks. They've got to take care of the animals. And," he finished virtuously, "that's what I aim to do, anyway."

Slim said, "What for, Red? They've got plenty of meat. Let's watch."

"There's no fun in watching. Besides Dad and your father are going away and I guess it's about lunch time."

Red became argumentative. "Look, Slim, we can't start acting suspicious or they're going to start investigating. Holy Smokes, don't you ever read any detective stories? When you're trying to work a big deal without being caught, it's practically the main thing to keep on acting just like always. Then they don't suspect anything. That's the first law—"

"Oh, all right."

Slim rose resentfully. At the moment, the circus appeared to him a rather tawdry and shoddy substitute for the glories of astronomy, and he wondered how he had come to fall in with Red's silly scheme.

Down the slope they went, Slim, as usual, in the rear.

VII

The Industrialist said, "It's the workmanship that gets me. I never saw such construction."

"What good is it now?" said the Astronomer, bitterly. "There's nothing left. There'll be no second landing. This ship detected life on our planet through accident. Other exploring parties would come no closer than necessary to establish the fact that there were no super-dense worlds existing in our solar system."

"Well, there's no quarreling with a crash landing."

"The ship hardly seems damaged. If only some had survived, the ship might have been repaired."

"If they had survived, there would be no trade in any case. They're too different. Too disturbing. In any case—it's over."

They entered the house and the Industrialist greeted his wife calmly. "Lunch about ready, dear?"

"I'm afraid not. You see—" She looked hesitantly at the Astronomer.

"Is anything wrong?" asked the Industrialist. "Why not tell me? I'm sure our guest won't mind a little family discussion."

"Pray don't pay any attention whatever to me," muttered the Astronomer. He moved miserably to the other end of the living room.

The woman said, in low, hurried tones, "Really, dear, cook's that upset. I've been soothing her for hours and honestly, I don't know why Red should have done it."

"Done what?" The Industrialist was more amused than otherwise. It had taken the united efforts of himself and his son months to argue his wife into using the name "Red" rather than the perfectly ridiculous (viewed youngster fashion) name which was his real one.

She said, "He's taken most of the chopped meat."

"He's eaten it?"

"Well, I hope not. It was raw."

"Then what would he want it for?"

"I haven't the slightest idea. I haven't seen him since breakfast. Meanwhile cook's just furious. She caught him vanishing out the kitchen door and there was the bowl of chopped meat just about empty and she was going to use it for lunch. Well, you know cook. She had to change the lunch menu and that means she won't be worth living with for a week. You'll just have to speak to Red, dear, and make him promise not to do things in the kitchen any more. And it wouldn't hurt to have him apologize to cook."

"Oh, come. She works for us. If we don't complain about a change in lunch menu, why should she?"

"Because she's the one who has double-work made for her, and she's talking about quitting. Good cooks aren't easy to get. Do you remember the one before her?"

It was a strong argument.

The Industrialist looked about vaguely. He said, "I suppose you're right. He isn't here, I suppose. When he comes in, I'll talk to him."

"You'd better start. Here he comes."

Red walked into the house and said cheerfully, "Time for lunch, I guess." He looked from one parent to the other in quick speculation at their fixed stares and said, "Got to clean up first, though," and made for the other door.

The Industrialist said, "One moment, son."

"Sir?"

"Where's your little friend?"

Red said, carelessly, "He's around somewhere. We were just sort of walking and I looked around and he wasn't there." This was perfectly true, and Red felt on safe ground. "I told him it was lunch time. I said, 'I suppose it's about lunch time.' I said, 'We got to be getting back to the house.' And he said, 'Yes.' And I just went on and then when I was about at the creek I looked around and—"

The Astronomer interrupted the voluble story, looking up from a magazine he had been sightlessly rummaging through. "I wouldn't worry about my youngster. He is quite self-reliant. Don't wait lunch for him."

"Lunch isn't ready in any case, Doctor." The Industrialist turned once more to his son. "And talking about that, son, the reason for it is that something happened to the ingredients. Do you have anything to say?"

"Sir?"

"I hate to feel that I have to explain myself more fully. Why did you take the chopped meat?"

"The chopped meat?"

"The chopped meat." He waited patiently.

Red said, "Well, I was sort of—"

"Hungry?" prompted his father. "For raw meat?"

"No, sir. I just sort of needed it."

"For what exactly?"

Red looked miserable and remained silent.

The Astronomer broke in again. "If you don't mind my putting in a few words—You'll remember that just after breakfast my son came in to ask what animals ate."

"Oh, you're right. How stupid of me to forget. Look here, Red, did you take it for an animal pet you've got?"

Red recovered indignant breath. He said, "You mean Slim came in here and said I had an animal? He came in here and said that? He said I had an animal?"

"No, he didn't. He simply asked what animals ate. That's all. Now if he promised he wouldn't tell on you, he didn't. It's your own foolishness in trying to take something without permission that gave you away. That happened to be stealing. Now have you an animal? I ask you a direct question."

"Yes, sir." It was a whisper so low as hardly to be heard.

"All right, you'll have to get rid of it. Do you understand?"

Red's mother intervened. "Do you mean to say you're keeping a meat-eating animal, Red? It might bite you and give you blood-poison."

"They're only small ones," quavered Red. "They hardly budge if you touch them."

"They? How many do you have?"

"Two."

"Where are they?"

The Industrialist touched her arm. "Don't chivvy the child any further," he said, in a low voice. "If he says he'll get rid of them, he will, and that's punishment enough."

He dismissed the matter from his mind.

VIII

Lunch was half over when Slim dashed into the dining room. For a moment, he stood abashed, and then he said in what was almost hysteria, "I've got to speak to Red. I've got to say something."

Red looked up in fright, but the Astronomer said, "I don't think, son, you're being very polite. You've kept lunch waiting."

"I'm sorry, Father."

"Oh, don't rate the lad," said the Industrialist's wife. "He can speak to Red if he wants to, and there was no damage done to the lunch."

"I've got to speak to Red alone," Slim insisted.

"Now that's enough," said the Astronomer with a kind of gentleness that was obviously manufactured for the benefit of strangers and which had beneath it an easily-recognized edge. "Take your seat."

Slim did so, but he ate only when someone looked directly upon him. Even then he was not very successful.

Red caught his eyes. He made soundless words, "Did the animals get loose?"

Slim shook his head slightly. He whispered, "No, it's—"

The Astronomer looked at him hard and Slim faltered to a stop.

With lunch over, Red slipped out of the room, with a microscopic motion at Slim to follow.

They walked in silence to the creek.

Then Red turned fiercely upon his companion. "Look here, what's the idea of telling my Dad we were feeding animals?"

Slim said, "I didn't. I asked what you feed animals. That's not the same as saying we were doing it. Besides, it's something else, Red."

But Red had not used up his grievances. "And where did you go anyway? I thought you were coming to the house. They acted like it was my fault you weren't there."

"But I'm trying to tell you about that, if you'd only shut *up* a second and let me talk. You don't give a fellow a chance."

"Well, go on and tell me if you've got so much to say."

"I'm *trying* to. I went back to the space-ship. The folks weren't there anymore and I wanted to see what it was like."

"It isn't a space-ship," said Red, sullenly. He had nothing to lose.

"It is, too. I looked inside. You could look through the ports and I looked inside and they were *dead*." He looked sick. "They were dead."

"*Who* were dead?"

Slim screeched, "Animals! like *our* animals! Only they *aren't* animals. They're people-things from other planets."

For a moment Red might have been turned to stone. It didn't occur to him to disbelieve Slim at this point. Slim looked too genuinely the bearer of just such tidings. He said, finally, "Oh, my."

"Well, what are we going to do? Golly, will we get a whopping if they find out?" He was shivering.

"We better turn them loose," said Red.

"They'll tell on us."

"They can't talk our language. Not if they're from another planet."

"Yes, they can. Because I remember my father talking about some stuff like that to my mother when he didn't know I was in the room. He was talking about visitors who could talk with the mind. Telepathery or something. I thought he was making it up."

"Well, Holy Smokes. I mean—Holy Smokes." Red looked up. "I tell you. My Dad said to get rid of them. Let's sort of bury them somewhere or throw them in the creek."

"He *told* you to do that."

"He made me say I had animals and then he said, 'Get rid of them.' I got to do what he says. Holy Smokes, he's my Dad."

Some of the panic left Slim's heart. It was a thoroughly legalistic way out. "Well, let's do it right now, then, before they find out. Oh, golly, if they find out, will we be in trouble!"

They broke into a run toward the barn, unspeakable visions in their minds.

IX

It was different, looking at them as though they were "people." As animals, they had been interesting; as "people," horrible. Their eyes, which were neutral little objects before, now seemed to watch them with active malevolence.

"They're making noises," said Slim, in a whisper which was barely audible.

"I guess they're talking or something," said Red. Funny that those noises which they had heard before had not had significance earlier. He was making no move toward them. Neither was Slim.

The canvas was off but they were just watching. The ground meat, Slim noticed, hadn't been touched.

Slim said, "Aren't you going to do something?"

"Aren't you?"

"You found them."

"It's your turn, now."

"No, it isn't. You found them. It's your fault, the whole thing. I was watching."

"You joined in, Slim. You know you did."

"I don't care. You found them and that's what I'll say when they come here looking for us."

Red said, "All right for you." But the thought of the consequences inspired him anyway, and he reached for the cage door.

Slim said, "Wait!"

Red was glad to. He said, "Now what's biting you?"

"One of them's got something on him that looks like it might be iron or something."

"Where?"

"Right there. I saw it before but I thought it was just part of him. But if he's 'people,' maybe it's a disintegrator gun."

"What's that?"

"I read about it in the books from Beforethewars. Mostly people with spaceships have disintegrator guns. They point them at you and you get disintegratored."

"They didn't point it at us till now," pointed out Red with his heart not quite in it.

"I don't care. I'm not hanging around here and getting disintegratored. I'm getting my father."

"Cowardy-cat. Yellow cowardy-cat."

"I don't care. You can call all the names you want, but if you bother them now you'll get disintegratored. You wait and see, and it'll be all your fault."

He made for the narrow spiral stairs that led to the main floor of the barn, stopped at its head, then backed away.

Red's mother was moving up, panting a little with the exertion and smiling a tight smile for the benefit of Slim in his capacity as guest.

"Red! You, Red! Are you up there? Now don't try to hide. I know this is where you're keeping them. Cook saw where you ran with the meat."

Red quavered, "Hello, ma!"

"Now show me those nasty animals? I'm going to see to it that you get rid of them right away."

It was over! And despite the imminent corporal punishment, Red felt something like a load fall from him. At least the decision was out of his hands.

"Right there, ma. I didn't do anything to them, ma. I didn't know. They just looked like little animals and I thought you'd let me keep them, ma. I wouldn't have taken the meat only they wouldn't eat grass or leaves and we couldn't find good nuts or berries and cook never lets me have anything or I would have asked her and I didn't know it was for lunch and—"

He was speaking on the sheer momentum of terror and did not realize that his mother did not hear him but, with eyes frozen and popping at the cage, was screaming in thin, piercing tones.

X

The Astronomer was saying, "A quiet burial is all we can do. There is no point in any publicity now," when they heard the screams.

She had not entirely recovered by the time she reached them, running and running. It was minutes before her husband could extract sense from her.

She was saying, finally, "I tell you they're in the barn. I don't know what they are. No, no—"

She barred the Industrialist's quick movement in that direction. She said, "Don't *you* go. Send one of the hands with a shotgun. I tell you I never saw anything like it. Little horrible beasts with—with—I can't describe it. To think that Red was touching them and trying to feed them. He was *holding* them, and feeding them meat."

Red began, "I only—"

And Slim said, "It was not—"

The Industrialist said, quickly, "Now you boys have done enough harm today. March! Into the house! And not a word; not one word! I'm not interested in anything you have to say. After this is all over, I'll hear you out and as for you, Red, I'll see that you're properly punished."

He turned to his wife, "Now whatever the animals are, we'll have them killed." He added quietly once the youngsters were out of hearing, "Come, come. The children aren't hurt and, after all, they haven't done anything really terrible. They've just found a new pet."

The Astronomer spoke with difficulty. "Pardon me, ma'am, but can you describe these animals?"

She shook her head. She was quite beyond words.

"Can you just tell me if they—"

"I'm sorry," said the Industrialist, apologetically, "but I think I had better take care of her. Will you excuse me?"

"A moment. Please. One moment. She said she had never seen such animals before. Surely it is not usual to find animals that are completely unique on an estate such as this."

"I'm sorry. Let's not discuss that now."

"Except that unique animals might have landed during the night."

The Industrialist stepped away from his wife. "What are you implying?"

"I think we had better go to the barn, sir!"

The Industrialist stared a moment, turned and suddenly and quite uncharacteristically began running. The Astronomer followed and the woman's wail rose unheeded behind them.

XI

The Industrialist stared, looked at the Astronomer, turned to stare again.

"Those?"

"Those," said the Astronomer. "I have no doubt we appear strange and repulsive to them."

"What do they say?"

"Why, that they are uncomfortable and tired and even a little sick, but that they are not seriously damaged, and that the youngsters treated them well."

"Treated them well! Scooping them up, keeping them in a cage, giving them grass and raw meat to eat? Tell me how to speak to them."

"It may take a little time. Think *at* them. Try to listen. It will come to you, but perhaps not right away."

The Industrialist tried. He grimaced with the effort of it, thinking over and over again, "The youngsters were ignorant of your identity."

And the thought was suddenly in his mind: "We were quite aware of it and because we knew they meant well by us according to their own view of the matter, we did not attempt to attack them."

"Attack them?" thought the Industrialist, and said it aloud in his concentration.

"Why, yes," came the answering thought. "We are armed."

One of the revolting little creatures in the cage lifted a metal object and there was a sudden hole in the top of the cage and another in the roof of the barn, each hole rimmed with charred wood.

"We hope," the creatures thought, "it will not be too difficult to make repairs."

The Industrialist found it impossible to organize himself to the point of directed thought. He turned to the Astronomer. "And with that weapon in their possession they let themselves be handled and caged? I don't understand it."

But the calm thought came, "We would not harm the young of an intelligent species."

XII

It was twilight. The Industrialist had entirely missed the evening meal and remained unaware of the fact.

He said, "Do you really think the ship will fly?"

"If they say so," said the Astronomer, "I'm sure it will. They'll be back, I hope, before too long."

"And when they do," said the Industrialist, energetically, "I will keep my part of the agreement. What is more I will move sky and earth to have the world accept them. I was entirely wrong, Doctor. Creatures that would refuse to harm children under such provocation as they received, are admirable. But you know—I almost hate to say this—"

"Say what?"

"The kids. Yours and mine. I'm almost proud of them. Imagine seizing these creatures, feeding them or trying to, and keeping them hidden. The amazing gall of it. Red told me it was his idea to get a job in a circus on the strength of them. Imagine!"

The Astronomer said, "Youth!"

XIII

The Merchant said, "Will we be taking off soon?"

"Half an hour," said the Explorer.

It was going to be a lonely trip back. All the remaining seventeen of the crew were dead and their ashes were to be left on a strange planet. Back they would go with a limping ship and the burden of the controls entirely on himself.

The Merchant said, "It was a good business stroke, not harming the young ones. We will get very good terms; *very* good terms."

The Explorer thought: Business!

The Merchant then said, "They've lined up to see us off. All of them. You don't think they're too close, do you? It would be bad to burn any of them with the rocket blast at this stage of the game."

"They're safe."

"Horrible looking things, aren't they?"

"Pleasant enough, inside. Their thoughts are perfectly friendly."

"You wouldn't believe it of them. That immature one, the one that first picked us up—"

"They call him Red," provided the Explorer.

"That's a queer name for a monster. Makes me laugh. He actually feels *bad* that we're leaving. Only I can't make out exactly why. The nearest I can come to it is something about a lost opportunity with some organization or other that I can't quite interpret."

"A circus," said the Explorer, briefly.

"What? Why, the impertinent monstrosity."

"Why not? What would you have done if you had found *him* wandering on *your* native world; found him sleeping on a field on Earth, red tentacles, six legs, pseudopods and all?"

XIV

Red watched the ship leave. His red tentacles, which gave him his nickname, quivered their regret at lost opportunity to the very last, and the eyes at their tips filled with drifting yellowish crystals that were the equivalent of Earthly tears.

WARRIOR RACE

ROBERT SHECKLEY

They never did discover whose fault it was. Fannia pointed out that
if Donnaught had had the brains of an ox, as well as the build, he
would have remembered to check the tanks. Donnaught, although
twice as big as him, wasn't quite as fast with an insult. He intimated,
after a little thought, that Fannia's nose might have obstructed his
reading of the fuel guage.

This still left them twenty light-years from Thetis, with a cupful of
transformer fuel in the emergency tank.

"All right," Fannia said presently. "What's done is done. We can
squeeze about three light-years out of the fuel before we're back on
atomics. Hand me *The Galactic Pilot*—unless you forgot that, too."

Donnaught dragged the bulky microfilm volume out of its locker,
and they explored its pages.

The Galactic Pilot told them they were in a sparse, seldom-visited
section of space, which they already knew. The nearest planetary
system was Hatterfield; no intelligent life there. Sersus had a native
population, but no refueling facilities. The same with Illed, Hung
and Porderai.

"Ah-ha!" Fannia said. "Read that, Donnaught. If you can read,
that is."

"Cascella," Donnaught read, slowly and clearly, following the
line with a thick forefinger. "Type M sun. Three planets, intelligent (AA3C) human-type life on second. Oxygen-breathers. Non-
mechanical. Religious. Friendly. Unique social structure, described

63

in Galactic Survey Report 33877242. Population estimate: stable at three billion. Basic Cascellan vocabulary taped under Cas33b2. Scheduled for resurvey 2375A.D. Cache of transformer fuel left, beam coordinate 8741 kgl. Physical descript: Unocc. flatland."

"Transformer fuel, boy!" Fannia said gleefully. "I believe we will get to Thetis, after all." He punched the new direction on the ship's tape. "If that fuel's still there."

"Should we read up on the unique social structure?" Donnaught asked, still poring over *The Galactic Pilot*.

"Certainly," Fannia said. "Just step over to the main galactic base on Earth and buy me a copy."

"I forgot," Donnaught admitted slowly.

"Let me see," Fannia said, dragging out the ship's language library. "Cascellan, Cascellan . . . Here it is. Be good while I learn the language." He set the tape in the hypnophone and switched it on. "Another useless tongue in my overstuffed head," he murmured, and then the hypnophone took over.

Coming out of transformer drive with at least a drop of fuel left, they switched to atomics. Fannia rode the beam right across the planet, locating the slender metal spire of the Galactic Survey cache. The plain was no longer unoccupied, however. The Cascellans had built a city around the cache, and the spire dominated the crude wood-and-mud buildings.

"Hang on," Fannia said, and brought the ship down on the outskirts of the city, in a field of stubble.

"Now look," Fannia said, unfastening his safety belt. "We're just here for fuel. No souvenirs, no side-trips, no fraternizing."

Through the port, they could see a cloud of dust from the city. As it came closer, they made out figures running toward their ship.

"What do you think this unique social structure is?" Donnaught asked, pensively checking the charge in a needler gun.

"I know not and care less," Fannia said, struggling into space armor. "Get dressed."

"The air's breathable."

"Look, pachyderm, for all we know, these Cascellans think the proper way to greet visitors is to chop off their heads and stuff them with green apples. If Galactic says unique, it probably means unique."

"Galactic said they were friendly."

"That means they haven't got atomic bombs. Come on, get dressed." Donnaught put down the needler and struggled into an oversize suit of space armor. Both men strapped on needlers, paralyzers, and a few grenades.

"I don't think we have anything to worry about," Fannia said, tightening the last nut on his helmet. "Even if they get rough, they can't crack space armor. And if they're not rough, we won't have any trouble. Maybe these gewgaws will help." He picked up a box of trading articles—mirrors, toys and the like.

Helmeted and armored, Fannia slid out the port and raised one hand to the Cascellans. The language, hypnotically placed in his mind, leaped to his lips.

"We come as friends and brothers. Take us to the chief."

The natives clustered around, gaping at the ship and the space armor. Although they had the same number of eyes, ears and limbs as humans, they completely missed looking like them.

"If they're friendly," Donnaught asked, climbing out of the port, "why all the hardware?" The Cascellans were dressed predominantly in a collection of knives, swords and daggers. Each man had at least five, and some had eight or nine.

"Maybe Galactic got their signals crossed," Fannia said, as the natives spread out in an escort. "Or maybe the natives just use the knives for mumblypeg."

The city was typical of a non-mechanical culture. Narrow, packed-dirt streets twisted between ramshackle huts. A few two-story buildings threatened to collapse at any minute. A stench filled the air, so strong that Fannia's filter couldn't quite eradicate it. The Cascellans bounded ahead of the heavily laden Earthmen, dashing around like a pack of playful puppies. Their knives glittered and clanked.

The chief's house was the only three-story building in the city. The tall spire of the cache was right behind it.

"If you come in peace," the chief said when they entered, "you are welcome." He was a middle-aged Cascellan with at least fifteen knives strapped to various parts of his person. He squatted cross-legged on a raised dais.

"We are privileged," Fannia said. He remembered from the hypnotic language lesson that "chief" on Cascella meant more than it usually did on Earth. The chief here was a combination of king, high priest, deity and bravest warrior.

"We have a few simple gifts here," Fannia added, placing the gew-gaws at the king's feet. "Will his majesty accept?"

"No," the king said. "We accept no gifts." Was that the unique social structure? Fannia wondered. It certainly was not human. "We are a warrior race. What we want, we take."

Fannia sat cross-legged in front of the dais and exchanged conversation with the king while Donnaught played with the spurned toys. Trying to overcome the initial bad impression, Fannia told the chief about the stars and other worlds, since simple people usually liked fables. He spoke of the ship, not mentioning yet that it was out of fuel. He spoke of Cascella, telling the chief how its fame was known throughout the Galaxy.

"That is as it should be," the chief said proudly. "We are a race of warriors, the like of which has never been seen. Every man of us dies fighting."

"You must have fought some great wars," Fannia said politely, wondering what idiot had written up the galactic report.

"I have not fought a war for many years," the chief said. "We are united now, and all our enemies have joined us."

Bit by bit, Fannia led up to the matter of the fuel.

"What is this 'fuel?'" the chief asked, haltingly because there was no equivalent for it in the Cascellan language.

"It makes our ship go."

"And where is it?"

"In the metal spire," Fannia said. "If you would just allow us—"

"In the holy shrine?" the chief exclaimed, shocked. "The tall metal church which the gods left here long ago?"

"Yeah," Fannia said sadly, knowing what was coming. "I guess that's it."

"It is sacrilege for an outworlder to go near it," the chief said. "I forbid it."

"We need the fuel." Fannia was getting tired of sitting cross-legged. Space armor wasn't built for complicated postures. "The spire was put here for such emergencies."

"Strangers, know that I am god of my people, as well as their leader. If you dare approach the sacred temple, there will be war."

"I was afraid of that," Fannia said, getting to his feet.

"And since we are a race of warriors," the chief said, "at my command, every fighting man of the planet will move against you. More will come from the hills and from across the rivers."

Abruptly, the chief drew a knife. It must have been a signal, because every native in the room did the same.

Fannia dragged Donnaught away from the toys. "Look, lummox. These friendly warriors can't do a damn thing to us. Those knives can't cut space armor, and I doubt if they have anything better. Don't let them pile up on you, though. Use the paralyzer first, the needler if they really get thick."

"Right." Donnaught whisked out and primed a paralyzer in a single coordinated movement. With weapons, Donnaught was fast and reliable, which was virtue enough for Fannia to keep him as a partner.

"We'll cut around this building and grab the fuel. Two cans ought to be enough. Then we'll beat it fast."

They walked out the building, followed by the Cascellans. Four carriers lifted the chief, who was barking orders. The narrow street outside was suddenly jammed with armed natives. No one tried to touch them yet, but at least a thousand knives were flashing in the sun.

In front of the cache was a solid phalanx of Cascellans. They stood behind a network of ropes that probably marked the boundary between sacred and profane ground.

"Get set for it," Fannia said, and stepped over the ropes.

Immediately the foremost temple guard raised his knife. Fannia brought up the paralyzer, not firing it yet, still moving forward.

The foremost native shouted something, and the knife swept across in a glittering arc. The Cascellan gurgled something else, staggered and fell. Bright blood oozed from his throat.

"I *told* you not to use the needler yet!" Fannia said.

"I didn't," Donnaught protested. Glancing back, Fannia saw that Donnaught's needler was still holstered.

"Then I don't get it," said Fannia bewilderedly.

Three more natives bounded forward, their knives held high. They tumbled to the ground also. Fannia stopped and watched as a platoon of natives advanced on them.

Once they were within stabbing range of the Earthmen, the natives were slitting their own throats!

Fannia was frozen for a moment, unable to believe his eyes. Donnaught halted behind him.

Natives were rushing forward by the hundreds now, their knives poised, screaming at the Earthmen. As they came within range, each native stabbed himself, tumbling on a quickly growing pile of bodies. In minutes the Earthmen were surrounded by a heap of bleeding Cascellan flesh, which was steadily growing higher.

"All right!" Fannia shouted. "Stop it." He yanked Donnaught back with him, to profane ground. "Truce!" he yelled in Cascellan.

The crowd parted and the chief was carried through. With two knives clenched in his fists, he was panting from excitement.

"We have won the first battle!" he said proudly. "The might of our warriors frightens even such aliens as yourselves. You shall not profane our temple while a man is alive on Cascella!"

The natives shouted their approval and triumph.

The two aliens dazedly stumbled back to their ship.

"So that's what Galactic meant by 'a unique social structure,'" Fannia said morosely. He stripped off his armor and lay down on his bunk. "Their way of making war is to suicide their enemies into capitulation."

"They must be nuts," Donnaught grumbled. "That's no way to fight."

"It works, doesn't it?" Fannia got up and stared out a porthole. The sun was setting, painting the city a charming red in its glow. The beams of light glistened off the spire of the Galactic cache. Through the open doorway they could hear the boom and rattle of drums. "Tribal call to arms," Fannia said.

"I still say it's crazy." Donnaught had some definite ideas on fighting. "It ain't human."

"I'll buy that. The idea seems to be that if enough people slaughter themselves, the enemy gives up out of sheer guilty conscience."

"What if the enemy doesn't give up?"

"Before these people united, they must have fought it out tribe to tribe, suiciding until someone gave up. The losers probably joined the victors; the tribe must have grown until it could take over the planet by sheer weight of numbers." Fannia looked carefully at Donnaught, trying to see if he understood. "It's anti-survival, of course; if someone didn't give up, the race would probably kill themselves." He shook his head. "But war of any kind is anti-survival. Perhaps they've got rules."

"Couldn't we just barge in and grab the fuel quick?" Donnaught asked. "And get out before they all killed themselves?"

"I don't think so," Fannia said. "They might go on committing suicide for the next ten years, figuring they were still fighting us." He looked thoughtfully at the city. "It's that chief of theirs. He's their god and he'd probably keep them suiciding until he was the only man left. Then he'd grin, say, 'We are great warriors,' and kill himself."

Donnaught shrugged his big shoulders in disgust. "Why don't we knock him off?"

"They'd just elect another god." The sun was almost below the horizon now. "I've got an idea, though," Fannia said. He scratched his head. "It might work. All we can do is try."

At midnight, the two men sneaked out of the ship, moving silently into the city. They were both dressed in space armor again. Donnaught carried two empty fuel cans. Fannia had his paralyzer out.

The streets were dark and silent as they slid along walls and around posts, keeping out of sight. A native turned a corner suddenly, but Fannia paralyzed him before he could make a sound.

They crouched in the darkness, in the mouth of an alley facing the cache.

"Have you got it straight?" Fannia asked. "I paralyze the guards. You bolt in and fill up those cans. We get the hell out of here, quick. When they check, they find the cans still there. Maybe they won't commit suicide then."

The men moved across the shadowy steps in front of the cache. There were three Cascellans guarding the entrance, their knives stuck in their loincloths. Fannia stunned them with a medium charge, and Donnaught broke into a run.

Torches instantly flared, natives boiled out of every alleyway, shouting, waving their knives.

"We've been ambushed!" Fannia shouted. "Get back here, Donnaught!"

Donnaught hurriedly retreated. The natives had been waiting for them. Screaming, yowling, they rushed at the Earthmen, slitting their own throats at five-foot range. Bodies tumbled in front of Fannia, almost tripping him as he backed up. Donnaught caught him by an arm and yanked him straight. They ran out of the sacred area.

"Truce, damn it!" Fannia called out. "Let me speak to the chief. Stop it! Stop it! I want a truce!"

Reluctantly, the Cascellans stopped their slaughter.

"This is war," the chief said, striding forward. His almost human face was stern under the torchlight. "You have seen our warriors. You know now that you cannot stand against them. The word has spread to all our lands. My entire people are prepared to do battle."

He looked proudly at his fellow-Cascellans, then back to the Earthmen. "I myself will lead my people into battle now. There will be no stopping us. We will fight until you surrender yourselves completely, stripping off your armor."

"Wait, chief," Fannia panted, sick at the sight of so much blood. The clearing was a scene out of the Inferno. Hundreds of bodies were sprawled around. The streets were muddy with blood.

"Let me confer with my partner tonight. I will speak with you tomorrow."

"No." the chief said. "You started the battle. It must go to its conclusion. Brave men wish to die in battle. It is our fondest wish. You are the first enemy we have had in many years, since we subdued the mountain tribes."

"Sure," Fannia said. "But let's talk about it—"

"I myself will fight you," the chief said, holding up a dagger. "I will die for my people, as a warrior must!"

"Hold it!" Fannia shouted. "Grant us a truce. We are allowed to fight only by sunlight. It is a tribal taboo."

The chief thought for a moment, then said, "Very well. Until tomorrow."

The beaten Earthmen walked slowly back to their ship amid the jeers of the victorious populace.

Next morning, Fannia still didn't have a plan. He knew that he had to have fuel; he wasn't planning on spending the rest of his life on Cascella, or waiting until the Galactic Survey sent another ship, in fifty years or so. On the other hand, he hesitated at the idea of being responsible for the death of anywhere up to three billion people. It wouldn't be a very good record to take to Thetis. The Galactic Survey might find out about it. Anyway, he just wouldn't do it.

He was stuck both ways.

Slowly, the two men walked out to meet the chief. Fannia was still searching wildly for an idea while listening to the drums booming.

"If there was only someone we could fight," Donnaught mourned, looking at his useless blasters.

"That's the deal," Fannia said. "Guilty conscience is making sinners of us all, or something like that. They expect us to give in before the carnage gets out of hand." He considered for a moment. "It's not so crazy, actually. On Earth, armies don't usually fight until every last man is slaughtered on one side. Someone surrenders when they've had enough."

"If they'd just fight *us*!"

"Yeah, if they only—" He stopped. "We'll fight each other!" he said. "These people look at suicide as war. Wouldn't they look upon war—real fighting—as suicide?"

"What good would that do us?" Donnaught asked.

They were coming into the city now and the streets were lined with armed natives. Around the city there were thousands more. Natives were filling the plain, as far as the eye could see. Evidently they had responded to the drums and were here to do battle with the aliens.

Which meant, of course, a wholesale suicide.

"Look at it this way," Fannia said. "If a guy plans on suiciding on Earth, what do we do?"

"Arrest him?" Donnaught asked.

"Not at first. We offer him anything he wants, if he just won't do it. People offer the guy money, a job, their daughters, anything, just so he won't do it. It's taboo on Earth."

"So?"

"So," Fannia went on, "maybe fighting is just as taboo here. Maybe they'll offer us fuel, if we'll just stop."

Donnaught looked dubious, but Fannia felt it was worth a try.

They pushed their way through the crowded city, to the entrance of the cache. The chief was waiting for them, beaming on his people like a jovial war god.

"Are you ready to do battle?" he asked. "Or to surrender?"

"Sure," Fannia said. "Now, Donnaught!"

He swung, and his mailed fist caught Donnaught in the ribs. Donnaught blinked.

"Come on, you idiot, hit me back."

Donnaught swung, and Fannia staggered from the force of the blow. In a second they were at it like a pair of blacksmiths, mailed blows ringing from their armored hides.

"A little lighter," Fannia gasped, picking himself up from the ground. "You're denting my ribs." He belted Donnaught viciously on the helmet.

"Stop it!" the chief cried. "This is disgusting!"

"It's working," Fannia panted. "Now let me strangle you. I think that might do it."

Donnaught obliged by falling to the ground. Fannia clamped both hands around Donnaught's armored neck, and squeezed.

"Make believe you're in agony, idiot," he said.

Donnaught groaned and moaned as convincingly as he could.

"You must stop!" the chief screamed. "It is terrible to kill another!"

"Then let me get some fuel," Fannia said, tightening his grip on Donnaught's throat.

The chief thought it over for a little while. Then he shook his head.

"No."

"What?"

"You are aliens. If you want to do this disgraceful thing, do it. But you shall not profane our religious relics."

Donnaught and Fannia staggered to their feet. Fannia was exhausted from fighting in the heavy space armor; he barely made it up.

"Now," the chief said, "surrender at once. Take off your armor or do battle with us."

The thousands of warriors—possibly millions, because more were arriving every second—shouted their blood-wrath. The cry was taken up on the outskirts and echoed to the hills, where more fighting men were pouring down into the crowded plain.

Fannia's face contorted. He couldn't give himself and Donnaught up to the Cascellans. They might be cooked at the next church supper. For a moment he considered going after the fuel and letting the damned fools suicide all they pleased.

His mind an angry blank, Fannia staggered forward and hit the chief in the face with a mailed glove.

The chief went down, and the natives backed away in horror. Quickly, the chief snapped out a knife and brought it up to his throat. Fannia's hands closed on the chief's wrists.

"Listen to me," Fannia croaked. "We're going to take that fuel. If any man makes a move—if anyone kills himself—I'll kill your chief."

The natives milled around uncertainly. The chief was struggling wildly in Fannia's hands, trying to get a knife to his throat, so he could die honorably.

"Get it," Fannia told Donnaught, "and hurry it up."

The natives were uncertain just what to do. They had their knives poised at their throats, ready to plunge if battle was joined.

"Don't do it," Fannia warned. "I'll kill the chief and then he'll never die a warrior's death."

The chief was still trying to kill himself. Desperately, Fannia held on, knowing he had to keep him from suicide in order to hold the threat of death over him.

"Listen, Chief," Fannia said, eying the uncertain crowd. "I must have your promise there'll be no more war between us. Either I get it or I kill you."

"Warriors!" the chief roared. "Choose a new ruler. Forget me and do battle!"

The Cascellans were still uncertain, but knives started to lift.

"If you do it," Fannia shouted in despair, "I'll kill your chief. *I'll kill all of you!*"

That stopped them.

"I have powerful magic in my ship. I can kill every last man, and then you won't be able to die a warrior's death. *Or* get to heaven!"

The chief tried to free himself with a mighty surge that almost tore one of his arms free, but Fannia held on, pinning both arms behind his back.

"Very well," the chief said, tears springing into his eyes. "A warrior must die by his own hand. You have won, alien."

The crowd shouted curses as the Earthmen carried the chief and the cans of fuel back to the ship. They waved their knives and danced up and down in a frenzy of hate.

"Let's make it fast," Fannia said, after Donnaught had fueled the ship.

He gave the chief a push and leaped in. In a second they were in the air, heading for Thetis and the nearest bar at top speed.

The natives were hot for blood—their own. Every man of them pledged his life to wiping out the insult to their leader and god, and to their shrine.

But the aliens were gone. There was nobody to fight.

YEAR OF THE BIG THAW

MARION ZIMMER BRADLEY

You say that Matthew is your own son, Mr. Emmett?

Yes, Rev'rend Doane, and a better boy never stepped, if I do say it as shouldn't. I've trusted him to drive team for me since he was eleven, and you can't say more than that for a farm boy. Way back when he was a little shaver so high, when the war came on, he was bounden he was going to sail with this Admiral Farragut. You know boys that age—like runaway colts. I couldn't see no good in his being cabin boy on some tarnation Navy ship and I told him so. If he'd wanted to sail out on a whaling ship, I 'low I'd have let him go. But Marthy—that's the boy's Ma—took on so that Matt stayed home. Yes, he's a good boy and a good son.

We'll miss him a powerful lot if he gets this scholarship thing. But I 'low it'll be good for the boy to get some learnin' besides what he gets in the school here. It's right kind of you, Rev'rend, to look over this application thing for me.

Well, if he is your own son, Mr. Emmett, why did you write 'birth-place unknown' on the line here?

Rev'rend Doane, I'm glad you asked me that question. I've been turnin' it over in my mind and I've jest about come to the conclusion it wouldn't be nohow fair to hold it back. I didn't lie when I said Matt was my son, because he's been a good son to me and Marthy. But I'm not his Pa and Marthy ain't his Ma, so could be I stretched the truth jest a mite. Rev'rend Doane, it's a tarnal funny yarn but I'll walk into the meetin' house and swear to it on a stack o'Bibles as thick as a cord of wood.

You know I've been farming the old Corning place these past seven year? It's good flat Connecticut bottom-land, but it isn't like our land up in Hampshire where I was born and raised. My Pa called it the Hampshire Grants and all that was King's land when *his* Pa came in there and started farming at the foot of Scuttock Mountain. That's Injun for fires, folks say, because the Injuns used to build fires up there in the spring for some of their heathen doodads. Anyhow, up there in the mountains we see a tarnal power of quare things.

You call to mind the year we had the big thaw, about twelve years before the war? You mind the blizzard that year? I heard tell it spread down most to York. And at Fort Orange, the place they call Albany now, the Hudson froze right over, so they say. But those York folks do a sight of exaggerating, I'm told.

Anyhow, when the ice went out there was an almighty good thaw all over, and when the snow run off Scuttock mountain there was a good-sized hunk of farmland in our valley went under water. The crick on my farm flowed over the bank and there was a foot of water in the cowshed, and down in the swimmin' hole in the back pasture wasn't nothing but a big gully fifty foot and more across, rushing through the pasture, deep as a lake and brown as the old cow. You know freshet-floods? Full up with sticks and stones and old dead trees and somebody's old shed floatin' down the middle. And I swear to goodness, Parson, that stream was running along so fast I saw four-inch cobblestones floating and bumping along.

I tied the cow and the calf and Kate—she was our white mare; you mind she went lame last year and I had to shoot her, but she was just a young mare then and skittish as all get-out—but she was a good little mare.

Anyhow, I tied the whole kit and caboodle of them in the wood-shed up behind the house, where they'd be dry, then I started to get the milkpail. Right then I heard the gosh-awfullest screech I ever heard in my life. Sounded like thunder and a freshet and a forest-fire all at once. I dropped the milkpail as I heard Marthy scream inside the house, and I run outside. Marthy was already there in the yard and she points up in the sky and yelled, "Look up yander!"

We stood looking up at the sky over Shattuck mountain where there was a great big—shoot now, I d'no as I can call its name but it was like a trail of fire in the sky, and it was makin' the dangdest racket you ever heard, Rev'rend. Looked kind of like one of them Fourth-of-July skyrockets, but it was big as a house. Marthy was screaming and she grabbed me and hollered, "Hez! Hez, what in tunket is it?" And when Marthy cusses like that, Rev'rend, she don't know what she's saying, she's so scared.

I was plumb scared myself. I heard Liza—that's our young-un, Liza Grace, that got married to the Taylor boy. I heard her crying on the stoop, and she came flying out with her pinny all black and hollered to Marthy that the pea soup was burning. Marthy let out another screech and ran for the house. That's a woman for you. So I quietened Liza down some and I went in and told Marthy it weren't no more than one of them shooting stars. Then I went and did the milking.

But you know, while we were sitting down to supper there came the most awful grinding, screeching, pounding crash I ever heard. Sounded if it were in the back pasture but the house shook as if somethin' had hit it.

Marthy jumped a mile and I never saw such a look on her face.

"Hez, what was that?" she asked.

"Shoot, now, nothing but the freshet," I told her.

But she kept on about it. "You reckon that shooting star fell in our back pasture, Hez?"

"Well, now, I don't 'low it did nothing like that," I told her. But she was jittery as an old hen and it weren't like her nohow. She said it sounded like trouble and I finally quietened her down by saying I'd saddle Kate up and go have a look. I kind of thought, though I didn't tell Marthy, that somebody's house had floated away in the freshet and run aground in our back pasture.

So I saddled up Kate and told Marthy to get some hot rum ready in case there was some poor soul run aground back there. And I rode Kate back to the back pasture.

It was mostly uphill because the top of the pasture is on high ground, and it sloped down to the crick on the other side of the rise.

Well, I reached the top of the hill and looked down. The crick were a regular river now, rushing along like Niagary. On the other side of it was a stand of timber, then the slope of Shattuck mountain. And I saw right away the long streak where all the timber had been cut out in a big scoop with roots standing up in the air and a big slide of rocks down to the water.

It was still raining a mite and the ground was sloshy and squanchy under foot. Kate scrunched her hooves and got real balky, not likin' it a bit. When we got to the top of the pasture she started to whine and whicker and stamp, and no matter how loud I whoa-ed she kept on a-stamping and I was plumb scared she'd pitch me off in the mud. Then I started to smell a funny smell, like somethin' burning. Now, don't ask me how anything could burn in all that water, because I don't know.

When we came up on the rise I saw the contraption.

Rev'rend, it was the most tarnal crazy contraption I ever saw in my life. It was bigger nor my cowshed and it was long and thin and as shiny as Marthy's old pewter pitcher her Ma brought from England. It had a pair of red rods sticking out behind and a crazy globe fitted up where the top ought to be. It was stuck in the mud, turned half-way over on the little slide of roots and rocks, and I could see what had happened, all right.

The thing must have been—now, Rev'rend, you can say what you like but that thing must have *flew* across Shattuck and landed on the slope in the trees, then turned over and slid down the hill. That must have been the crash we heard. The rods weren't just red, they were *red-hot*. I could hear them sizzle as the rain hit 'em.

In the middle of the infernal contraption there was a door, and it hung all to-other as if every hinge on it had been wrenched half-way off. As I pushed old Kate alongside it I heared somebody hollering alongside the contraption. I didn't nohow get the words but it must have been for help, because I looked down and there was a man a-flopping along in the water.

He was a big fellow and he wasn't swimming, just thrashin' and hollering. So I pulled off my coat and boots and dove in after him. The stream was running fast but he was near the edge and I managed to catch on to an old tree-root and hang on, keeping his head out of the water till I got my feet aground. Then I hauled him onto the bank. Up above me Kate was still whinnying and raising Ned and I shouted at her as I bent over the man.

Wal, Rev'rend, he sure did give me a surprise—weren't no proper man I'd ever seed before. He was wearing some kind of red clothes, real shiny and sort of stretchy and not wet from the water, like you'd expect, but dry and it felt like that silk and India-rubber stuff mixed together. And it was such a bright red that at first I didn't see the blood on it. When I did I knew he were a goner. His chest were all stove in, smashed to pieces. One of the old tree-roots must have jabbed him as the current flung him down. I thought he were dead already, but then he opened up his eyes.

A funny color they were, greeny yellow. And I swear, Rev'rend, when he opened them eyes I *felt* he was readin' my mind. I thought maybe he might be one of them circus fellers in their flying contraptions that hang at the bottom of a balloon.

He spoke to me in English, kind of choky and stiff, not like Joe the Portygee sailor or like those tarnal dumb Frenchies up Canady way, but—well, funny. He said, "My baby—in ship. Get—baby . . ." He tried to say more but his eyes went shut and he moaned hard.

I yelped, "Godamighty!" Scuse me, Rev'rend, but I was so blame upset that's just what I did say, "Godamighty, man, you mean there's a baby in that there dingfol contraption?" He just moaned so after spreadin' my coat around the man a little bit I just plunged in that there river again.

Rev'rend, I heard tell once about some tomfool idiot going over Niagary in a barrel, and I tell you it was like that when I tried crossin' that freshet to reach the contraption.

I went under and down, and was whacked by floating sticks and whirled around in the freshet. But somehow, I d'no how except by the pure grace of God, I got across that raging torrent and clumb up to where the crazy dingfol machine was sitting.

Ship, he'd called it. But that were no ship, Rev'rend, it was some flying dragon kind of thing. It was a real scarey lookin' thing but I clumb up to the little door and hauled myself inside it. And, sure enough, there was other people in the cabin, only they was all dead.

There was a lady and a man and some kind of an animal looked like a bobcat only smaller, with a funny-shaped rooster-comb thing on its head. They all—even the cat-thing—was wearing those shiny, stretchy clo'es. And they all was so battered and smashed I didn't even bother to hunt for their heart beats. I could see by a look they was dead as a doornail.

Then I heard a funny little whimper, like a kitten, and in a funny, rubber-cushioned thing there's a little boy baby, looked about six months old. He was howling lusty enough, and when I lifted him out of the cradle kind of thing, I saw why. That boy baby, he was wet, and his little arm was twisted under him. That there flying contraption must have smashed down awful hard, but that rubber hammock was so soft and cushiony all it did to him was jolt him good.

I looked around but I couldn't find anything to wrap him in. And the baby didn't have a stitch on him except a sort of spongy paper diaper, wet as sin. So I finally lifted up the lady, who had a long cape thing around her, and I took the cape off her real gentle. I knew she was dead and she wouldn't be needin' it, and that boy baby would catch his death if I took him out bare-naked like that. She was probably the baby's Ma; a right pretty woman she was but smashed up something shameful.

So anyhow, to make a long story short, I got that baby boy back across that Niagary falls somehow, and laid him down by his Pa. The man opened his eyes kind, and said in a choky voice, "Take care— baby."

I told him I would, and said I'd try to get him up to the house where Marthy could doctor him. The man told me not to bother.

"I dying," he says. "We come from planet—star up there—crash here—" His voice trailed off into a language I couldn't understand, and he looked like he was praying.

I bent over him and held his head on my knees real easy, and I said, "Don't worry, mister, I'll take care of your little fellow until your folks come after him. Before God I will."

So the man closed his eyes and I said, *Our Father which art in Heaven,* and when I got through he was dead.

I got him up on Kate, but he was cruel heavy for all he was such a tall skinny fellow. Then I wrapped that there baby up in the cape thing and took him home and give him to Marthy. And the next day I buried the fellow in the south medder and next meetin' day we had the baby baptized Matthew Daniel Emmett, and brung him up just like our own kids. That's all.

All? Mr. Emmett, didn't you ever find out where that ship really came from?

Why, Rev'rend, he said it come from a star. Dying men don't lie, you know that. I asked the Teacher about them planets he mentioned and she says that on one of the planets—can't rightly remember the name, March or Mark or something like that—she says some big scientist feller with a telescope saw canals on that planet, and they'd hev to be pretty near as big as this-here Erie canal to see them so far off. And if they could build canals on that planet I d'no why they couldn't build a flying machine.

I went back the next day when the water was down a little, to see if I couldn't get the rest of them folks and bury them, but the flying machine had broke up and washed down the crick.

Marthy's still got the cape thing. She's a powerful saving woman. We never did tell Matt, though. Might make him feel funny to think he didn't really b'long to us.

But—but—Mr. Emmett, didn't anybody ask questions about the baby—where you got it?

Well, now, I'll 'low they was curious, because Marthy hadn't been in the family way and they knew it. But up here folks minds their own business pretty well, and I jest let them wonder. I told Liza Grace I'd found her new little brother in the back pasture, and o'course it was the truth. When Liza Grace growed up she thought it was jest one of those yarns old folks tell the little shavers.

And has Matthew ever shown any differences from the other children that you could see?

Well, Rev'rend, not so's you could notice it. He's powerful smart, but his real Pa and Ma must have been right smart too to build a flying contraption that could come so far.

O'course, when he were about twelve years old he started reading folks' minds, which didn't seem exactly right. He'd tell Marthy what I was thinkin' and things like that. He was just at the pesky age. Liza Grace and Minnie were both a-courtin' then, and he'd drive their boy friends crazy telling them what Liza Grace and Minnie were a-thinking and tease the gals by telling them what the boys were thinking about.

There weren't no harm in the boy, though, it was all teasing. But it just weren't decent, somehow. So I tuk him out behind the woodshed and give his britches a good dusting just to remind him that that kind of thing weren't polite nohow. And Rev'rend Doane, he ain't never done it sence.

RASTIGNAC THE DEVIL

PHILIP JOSÉ FARMER

*After the apocalyptic war, the decimated remnants of the French hud-
dled in the Loire Valley were gradually squeezed between two new
and growing nations. The Colossus to the north was unfriendly and
obviously intended to absorb the little New France. The Colossus to the
south was friendly and offered to take the weak state into its confeder-
ation of republics as a full partner.*

*A number of proud and independent French citizens feared that
even the latter alternative meant the eventual transmutation of their
tongue, religion and nationality into those of their southern neighbor.
Seeking a way of salvation, they built six huge space-ships that would
hold thirty thousand people, most of whom would be in deep freeze
until they reached their destination. The six vessels then set off into
interstellar space to find a planet that would be as much like Earth as
possible.*

*That was in the 22nd Century. Over three hundred and fifty years
passed before Earth heard of them again. However, we are not here
concerned with the home world but with the story of a man of that
pioneer group who wanted to leave the New Gaul and sail again to the
stars . . .*

Rastignac had no Skin. He was, nevertheless, happier than he had
been since the age of five.

He was as happy as a man can be who lives deep under the ground.
Underground organizations are often under the ground. They are

84

formed into cells. Cell Number One usually contains the leader of the underground.

Jean-Jacques Rastignac, chief of the Legal Underground of the Kingdom of L'Bawpfey, was literally in a cell beneath the surface of the earth. He was in jail.

For a dungeon, it wasn't bad. He had two cells. One was deep inside the building proper, built into the wall so that he could sit in it when he wanted to retreat from the sun or the rain. The adjoining cell was at the bottom of a well whose top was covered with a grille of thin steel bars. Here he spent most of his waking hours. Forced to look upwards if he wanted to see the sky or the stars, Rastignac suffered from a chronic stiff neck.

Several times during the day he had visitors. They were allowed to bend over the grille and talk down to him. A guard, one of the King's mucketeers,* stood by as a censor.

When night came, Rastignac ate the meal let down by ropes on a platform. Then another of the King's mucketeers stood by with drawn épée until he had finished eating. When the tray was pulled back up and the grille lowered and locked, the mucketeer marched off with the turnkey.

Rastignac sharpened his wit by calling a few choice insults to the night guard, then went into the cell inside the wall and lay down to take a nap. Later, he would rise and pace back and forth like a caged tiger. Now and then he would stop and look upwards, scan the stars, hunch his shoulders and resume his savage circuit of the cell. But the time would come when he would stand statue-still. Nothing moved except his head, which turned slowly.

"Some day I'll ride to the stars with you."

He said it as be watched the Six Flying Stars speed across the night sky—six glowing stars that moved in a direction opposite to the march of the other stars. Bright as Sirius seen from Earth, strung

---

* Mucketeer is the best translation of the 26th century French noun *foutri-quet*, pronounced *vfeutwikey.*

.out one behind the other like jewels on a velvet string, they hurtled across the heavens.

They were the six ships on which the original Loire Valley Frenchmen had sailed out into space, seeking a home on a new planet. They had been put into an orbit around New Gaul and left there while their thirty thousand passengers had descended to the surface in chemical-fuel rockets. Mankind, once on the fair and fresh earth of the new planet, had never again ascended to re-visit the great ships.

For three hundred years the six ships had circled the planet known as New Gaul, nightly beacons and glowing reminders to Man that he was a stranger on this planet.

When the Earthmen landed on the new planet they had called the new land *Le Beau Pays,* or, as it was now pronounced, *L'Bawpfey*— The Beautiful Country. They had been delighted, entranced with the fresh new land. After the burned, war-racked Earth they had just left, it was like coming to Heaven.

They found two intelligent species living on the planet, and they found that the species lived in peace and that they had no conception of war or of poverty. And they were quite willing to receive the Terrans into their society.

Provided, that is, they became integrated, or—as they phrased it—natural. The Frenchmen from Earth had been given their choice. They were told:

"You can live with the people of the Beautiful Land on our terms— war with us, or leave to seek another planet."

The Terrans conferred. Half of them decided to stay; the other half decided to remain only long enough to mine uranium and other chemicals. Then they would voyage onwards.

But nobody from that group of Earthmen ever again stepped into the ferry-rockets and soared up to the six ion-beam ships circling about Le Beau Pays. All succumbed to the Philosophy of the Natural. Within a few generations a stranger landing upon the planet would not have known without previous information that the Terrans were not aboriginal.

He would have found three species. Two were warm-blooded egglayers who had evolved directly from reptiles without becoming mammals—the Ssassarors and the Amphibs. Somewhere in their dim past—like all happy nations, they had no history—they had set up their society and been very satisfied with it since.

It was a peaceful quiet world, largely peasant, where nobody had to scratch for a living and where a superb manipulation of biological forces ensured very long lives, no disease, and a social lubrication that left little to desire—from their viewpoint, anyway.

The government was, nominally, a monarchy. The Kings were elected by the people and were a different species than the group each ruled. Ssassaror ruled Human, and vice versa, each assisted by foster-brothers and sisters of the race over which they reigned. These were the so-called Dukes and Duchesses.

The Chamber of Deputies—*L'Syawp t' Tapfuti*—was half Human and half Ssassaror. The so-called Kings took turns presiding over the Chamber for forty day intervals. The Deputies were elected for ten-year terms by constituents who could not be deceived about their representatives' purposes because of the sensitive Skins which allowed them to determine their true feelings and worth.

In one custom alone did the ex-Terrans differ from their neighbors. This was in carrying arms. In the beginning, the Ssassaror had allowed the Men to wear their short rapiers, so they would feel safe even though in the midst of aliens.

As time went on, only the King's mucketeers—and members of the official underground—were allowed to carry épées. These men, it might be noticed, were the congenital adventurers, men who needed to swashbuckle and revel in the name of individualist.

Like the egg-stealers, they needed an institution in which they could work off anti-social steam.

From the beginning the Amphibians had been a little separate from the Ssassaror and when the Earthmen came they did not get any more neighborly. Nevertheless, they preserved excellent relations and they, too, participated in the Changeling-custom.

This Changeling-custom was another social device set up millennia ago to keep a mutual understanding between all species on the planet. It was a peculiar institution, one that the Earthmen had found hard to understand and even more difficult to adopt. Nevertheless, once the Skins had been accepted they had changed their attitude, forgot their speculations about its origin and threw themselves into the custom of stealing babies—or eggs—from another race and raising the children as their own.

You rob my cradle; I'll rob yours. Such was their motto, and it worked.

A Guild of Egg Stealers was formed. The Human branch of it guaranteed, for a price, to bring you a Ssassaror child to replace the one that had been stolen from you. Or, if you lived on the seashore, and an Amphibian had crept into your nursery and taken your baby—always under two years old, according to the rules—then the Guildsman would bring you an Amphib or, perhaps, the child of a Human Changeling reared by the Seafolk.

You raised it and loved it as your own. How could you help loving it?

Your Skin told you that it was small and helpless and needed you and was, despite appearances, as Human as any of your babies. Nor did you need to worry about the one that had been abducted. It was getting just as good care as you were giving this one.

It had never occurred to anyone to quit the stealing and voluntary exchange of babies. Perhaps that was because it would strain even the loving nature of the Skin-wearers to give away their own flesh and blood. But once the transfer had taken place, they could, adapt.

Or perhaps the custom was kept because tradition is stronger than law in a peasant-monarchy society and also because egg-and-baby stealing gave the more naturally aggressive and daring citizens a chance to work off anti-social behavior.

Nobody but a historian would have known, and there were no historians in The Beautiful Land.

Long ago the Ssassaror had discovered that if they lived meatless, they had a much easier time curbing their belligerency, obeying the Skins and remaining cooperative. So they induced the Earthmen to put a taboo on eating flesh. The only drawback to the meatless diet was that both Ssassaror and Man became as stunted in stature as they did in aggressiveness, the former so much so that they barely came to the chins of the Humans. These, in turn, would have seemed short to a Western European.

But Rastignac, an Earthman, and his good friend, Mapfarity, the Ssassaror Giant, became taboo-breakers when they were children and played together on the beach where they first ate seafood out of curiosity, then continued because they liked it. And due to their protein diet the Terran had grown well over six feet in height and the Ssassaror seemed to have touched off a rocket of expansion in his body with his protein-eating. Those Ssassarors who shared his guilt—became meat-eaters—became ostracized and eventually moved off to live by themselves. They were called Ssassaror-Giants and were pointed to as an object lesson to the young of the normal Ssassarors and Humans on the land.

If a stranger had landed shortly before Rastignac was born, however, he would have noticed that all was not as serene as it was supposed to be among the different species. The cause for the flaw in the former Eden might have puzzled him if he had not known the previous history of L'Bawpfey and the fact that the situation had not changed for the worst until the introduction of Human Changelings among the Amphibians.

Then it had been that blood-drinking began among them, that Amphibians began seducing Humans to come live with them by their tales of easy immortality, and that they started the system of leaving savage little carnivores in the Human nurseries.

When the Land-dwellers protested, the Amphibs replied that these things were carried out by unnaturals or outlaws, and that the

Sea-King could not be held responsible. Permission was given to Chalice those caught in such behavior.

Nevertheless, the suspicion remained that the Amphib monarch had, in accordance with age-old procedure, given his unofficial official blessing and that he was preparing even more disgusting and outrageous and unnatural moves. Through his control of the populace by the Master Skin, he would be able to do as he pleased with their minds.

It was the Skins that had made the universal peace possible on the planet of New Gaul. And it would be the custom of the Skins that would make possible the change from peace to conflict among the populace.

Through the artificial Skins that were put on all babies at birth— and which grew with them, attached to their body, feeding from their bloodstreams, their nervous systems—the Skins, controlled by a huge Master Skin that floated in a chemical vat in the palace of the rulers, fed, indoctrinated and attended day and night by a crew of the most brilliant scientists of the planet, gave the Kings complete control of the minds and emotions of the inhabitants of the planet.

Originally the rulers of New Gaul had desired only that the populace live in peace and enjoy the good things of their planet equally. But the change that had been coming gradually—the growth of conflict between the Kings of the different species for control of the whole populace—was beginning to be generally felt. Uneasiness, distrust of each other was growing among the people. Hence the legalizing of the Underground, the Philosophy of Violence by the government, an effort to control the revolt that was brewing.

Yet, the Land-dwellers had managed to take no action at all and to ignore the growing number of vicious acts.

But not all were content to drowse. One man was aroused. He was Rastignac.

They were Rastignac's hope, those Six Stars, the gods to which he prayed. When they passed quickly out of his sight he would continue his pacing, meditating for the twenty-thousandth time on a means for reaching one of those ships and using it to visit the stars. The end of his fantasies was always a curse because of the futility of such hopes. He was doomed! Mankind was doomed!

And it was all the more maddening because Man would not admit that he was through. Ended, that is, as a human being.

Man was changing into something not quite *homo sapiens*. It might be a desirable change, but it would mean the finish of his climb upwards. So it seemed to Rastignac. And he, being the man he was, had decided to do something about it even if it meant violence.

That was why he was now in the well-dungeon. He was an advocator of violence against the status quo.

II

There was another cell next to his. It was also at the bottom of a well and was separated from his by a thin wall of cement. A window had been set into it so that the prisoners could talk to each other. Rastignac did not care for the woman who had been let down into the adjoining cell, but she was somebody to talk to.

"Amphib-changelings" was the name given to those human beings who had been stolen from their cradles and raised among the non-humanoid Amphibians as their own. The girl in the adjoining cell, Lusine, was such a person. It was not her fault that she was a blood-drinking Amphib. Yet he could not help disliking her for what she had done and for the things she stood for.

She was in prison because she had been caught in the act of stealing a Man child from its cradle. This was no crime, but she had left in the cradle, under the covers, a savage and blood-thirsty little monster that had leaped up and slashed the throat of the unsuspecting baby's mother.

Her cell was lit by a cageful of glowworms. Rastignac, peering through the grille, could see her shadowy shape in the inner cell inside the wall. She rose langorously and stepped into the circle of dim orange light cast by the insects.

"*B'zhu, m'fweh*," she greeted him.

It annoyed him that she called him her brother, and it annoyed him even more to know that she knew it. It was true that she had some excuse for thus addressing him. She did resemble him. Like him, she had straight glossy blue-black hair, thick bracket-shaped eyebrows, brown eyes, a straight nose and a prominent chin. And where his build was superbly masculine, hers was magnificently feminine.

Nevertheless, this was not her reason for so speaking to him. She knew the disgust the Land-walker had for the Amphib-changeling, and she took a perverted delight in baiting him.

He was proud that he seldom allowed her to see that she annoyed him. "*B'zhu, fam tey zafeep*," he said. "Good evening, woman of the Amphibians."

Mockingly she said, "Have you been watching the Six Flying Stars, Jean-Jacques?"

"*Vi.* I do so every time they come over."

"Why do you eat your heart out because you cannot fly up to them and then voyage among the stars on one of them?"

He refused to give her the satisfaction of knowing his real reason. He did not want her to realize how little he thought of Mankind and its chances for surviving—as humanity—upon the face of this planet, L'Bawpfey.

"I look at them because they remind me that Man was once captain of his soul."

"Then you admit that the Land-walker is weak?"

"I think he is on the way to becoming non-human, which is to say that he is weak, yes. But what I say about Landman goes for Seaman, too. You Changelings are becoming more Amphibian every day and less Human. Through the Skins the Amphibs are gradually changing you completely. Soon you will be completely sea-people."

She laughed scornfully, exposing perfect white teeth as she did so.

"The Sea will win out against the Land. It launches itself against the shore and shakes it with the crash of its body. It eats away the rock and the dirt and absorbs it into its own self. It can't be worn away nor caught and held in a net. It is elusive and all-powerful and never-tiring."

Lusine paused for breath. He said, "That is a very pretty analogy, but it doesn't apply. You Seafolk are as much flesh and blood as we Landfolk. What hurts us hurts you."

She put a hand around one bar. The glow-light fell upon it in such a way that it showed plainly the webbing of skin between her fingers. He glanced at it with a faint repulsion under which was a counter-current of attraction. This was the hand that had, indirectly, shed blood.

She glanced at him sidewise, challenged him in trembling tones. "You are not one to throw stones, Jean-Jacques. I have heard that you eat meat."

"Fish, not meat. That is part of my Philosophy of Violence," he retorted. "I maintain that one of the reasons man is losing his power and strength is that he has so long been upon a vegetable diet. He is as cowed and submissive as the grass-eating beast of the fields."

Lusine put her face against the bars.

"That is interesting," she said. "But how did you happen to begin eating fish? I thought we Amphibs alone did that."

What Lusine had just said angered him. He had no reply.

Rastignac knew he should not be talking to a Sea-changeling. They were glib and seductive and always searching for ways to twist your thoughts. But being Rastignac, he had to talk. Moreover, it was so difficult to find anybody who would listen to his ideas that he could not resist the temptation.

"I was given fish by the Ssassaror, Mapfarity, when I was a child. We lived along the seashore. Mapfarity was a child, too, and we played together. 'Don't eat fish!' my parents said. To me that meant 'Eat it!' So, despite my distaste at the idea, and my squeamish stomach, I did eat fish. And I liked it. And as I grew to manhood I adopted the Philosophy of Violence and I continued to eat fish although I am not a Changeling."

"What did your Skin do when it detected you?" Lusine asked. Her eyes were wide and luminous with wonder and a sort of glee as if she relished the confession of his sins. Also, he knew, she was taunting him about the futility of his ideas of violence so long as he was a prisoner of the Skin.

He frowned in annoyance at the reminder of the Skin. Much thought had he given, in a weak way, to the possibility of life without the Skin.

Ashamed now of his weak resistance to the Skin, he blustered a bit in front of the teasing Amphib girl.

"Mapfarity and I discovered something that most people don't know," he answered boastfully. "We found that if you can stand the shocks your Skin gives you when you do something wrong, the Skin gets tired and quits after a while. Of course your Skin recharges itself and the next time you eat fish it shocks you again. But after very many shocks it becomes accustomed, forgets its conditioning, and leaves you alone."

Lusine laughed and said in a low conspirational tone, "So your Ssassaror pal and you adopted the Philosophy of Violence because you remained fish and meat eaters?"

"Yes, we did. When Mapfarity reached puberty he became a Giant and went off to live in a castle in the forest. But we have remained friends through our connection in the underground."

"Your parents must have suspected that you were a fish eater when you first proposed your Philosophy of Violence?" she said.

"Suspicion isn't proof," he answered. "But I shouldn't be telling you all this, Lusine. I feel it is safe for me to do so only because you will never have a chance to tell on me. You will soon be taken to Chalice and there you will stay until you have been cured."

She shivered and said, "This Chalice? What is it?"

"It is a place far to the north where both Terrans and Ssassarors send their incorrigibles. It is an extinct volcano whose steep-sided interior makes an inescapable prison. There those who have persisted in unnatural behavior are given special treatment."

"They are bled?" she asked, her eyes widening as her tongue flicked over her lips again hungrily.

"No. A special breed of Skin is given them to wear. These Skins shock them more powerfully than the ordinary ones, and the shocks are associated with the habit they are trying to cure. The shocks effect a cure. Also, these special Skins are used to detect hidden unnatural emotions. They re-condition the deviate. The result is that when the Chaliced Man is judged able to go out and take his place in society again, he is thoroughly re-conditioned. Then his regular Skin is given back to him and it has no trouble keeping him in line from then on. The Chaliced Man is a very good citizen."

"And what if a revolter doesn't become Chaliced?"

"Then he stays in Chalice until he decides to become so."

Her voice rose sharply as she said, "But if I go there, and I am not fed the diet of the Amphibs, I will grow old and die!"

"No. The government will feed you the diet you need until you are re-conditioned. Except . . ." He paused.

"Except I won't get blood," she wailed. Then, realizing she was acting undignified before a Landman, she firmed her voice.

"The King of the Amphibians will not allow them to do this to me," she said. "When he hears of it he will demand my return. And if the King of Men refuses, my King will use violence to get me back."

Rastignac smiled and said, "I hope he does. Then perhaps my people will wake up and get rid of their Skins and make war upon your people."

"So that is what you Philosophers of Violence want, is it? Well, you will not get it. My father, the Amphib King, will not be so stupid as to declare a war."

"I suppose not," replied Rastignac. "He will send a band to rescue you. If they're caught they'll claim to be criminals and say they are *not* under the King's orders."

Lusine looked upwards to see if a guard was hanging over the well's mouth listening. Perceiving no one, she nodded and said, "You have guessed it correctly. And that is why we laugh so much at you stupid Humans. You know as well as we do what's going on, but you are afraid to tell us so. You keep clinging to the idea that your turn-the-other-cheek policy will soften us and insure peace."

"Not I," said Rastignac. "I know perfectly well there is only one solution to man's problems. That is—"

"That is Violence," she finished for him. "That is what you have been preaching. And that is why you are in this cell, waiting for trial."

"You don't understand," he said. "Men are not put into the Chalice for *proposing* new philosophies. As long as they behave naturally they may say what they wish. They may even petition the King that the new philosophy be made a law. The King passes it on to the Chamber of Deputies. They consider it and put it up to the people. If the people like it, it becomes a law. The only trouble with that procedure is that it may take ten years before the law is considered by the Chamber of Deputies."

"And in those ten years," she mocked him, "the Amphibs and the Amphibian-changelings will have won the planet."

"That is true," he said.

"The King of the Humans is a Ssassaror and the King of the Ssassarors is a Man," said Lusine. "Our King can't see any reason for changing the status quo. After all, it is the Ssassarors who are responsible for the Skins and for Man's position in the sentient society of this planet. Why should he be favorable to a policy of Violence? The Ssassarors loathe violence.

"And so you have preached Violence without waiting for it to become a law? And for that you are now in this cell?"

"Not exactly. The Ssassarors have long known that to suppress too much of Man's naturally belligerent nature only results in an explosion. So they have legalized illegality—up to a point. Thus the King officially made me the Chief of the Underground and gave me a state license to preach—but not practice—Violence. I am even allowed to advocate overthrow of the present system of government—as long as I take no action that is too productive of results.

"I am in jail now because the Minister of Ill-Will put me here. He had my Skin examined, and it was found to be 'unhealthy.' He thought I'd be better off locked up until I became 'healthy' again. But the King . . ."

III

Lusine's laughter was like the call of a silverbell bird. Whatever her unhuman appetites, she had a beautiful voice. She said, "How comical! And how do you, with your brave ideas, like being regarded as a harmless figure of fun, or as a sick man?"

"I like it as well as you would," he growled.

She gripped the bars of her window until the tendons on the back of her long thin hands stood out and the membranes between her fingers stretched like windblown tents. Face twisted, she spat at him, "Coward! Why don't you kill somebody and break out of this ridiculous mold—that Skin that the Ssassarors have poured you into?"

Rastignac was silent. That was a good question. Why didn't he? Killing was the logical result of his philosophy. But the Skin kept him docile. Yes, he could vaguely see that he had purposely shut his eyes to the destination towards which his ideas were slowly but inevitably traveling.

And there was another facet to the answer to her question—if he had to kill, he would not kill a Man. His philosophy was directed towards the Amphibians and the Sea-changelings.

He said, "Violence doesn't necessarily mean the shedding of blood, Lusine. My philosophy urges that we take a more vigorous action, that we overthrow some of the bio-social institutions which have imprisoned Man and stripped him of his dignity as an individual."

"Yes, I have heard that you want Man to stop wearing the Skin. That is what has horrified your people, isn't it?"

"Yes," he said. "And I understand it has had the same effect among the Amphibians."

She bridled, her brown eyes flashing in the feeble glowworms' light. "Why shouldn't it? What would we be without our Skins?"

"What, indeed?" he said, laughing derisively afterwards.

Earnestly she said, "You don't understand. We Amphibians—our Skins are not like yours. We do not wear them for the same reason you do. You are imprisoned by your Skins—they tell you how to feel, what to think. Above all, they keep you from getting ideas about non-cooperation or non-integration with Nature as a whole.

"That, to us individualistic Amphibians, is false. The purpose of our Skins is to make sure that our King's subjects understand what he wants so that we may all act as one unit and thus further the progress of the Seafolk."

The first time Rastignac had heard this statement he had howled with laughter. Now, however, knowing that she could not see the fallacy, he did not try to argue the point. The Amphibs were, in their way, as hidebound—no pun intended—as the Land-walkers.

"Look, Lusine," he said, "there are only three places where a Man may take off his Skin. One is in his own home, when he may hang it upon the halltree. Two is when he is, like us, in jail and therefore may not harm anybody. The third is when a man is King. Now you and I have been without our Skins for a week. We have gone longer without them than anybody, except the King. Tell me true, don't you feel free for the first time in your life?

"Don't you feel as if you belong to nobody but yourself, that you are accountable to no one but yourself, and that you love that feeling? And don't you dread the day we will be let out of prison and made to wear our Skins again? That day which, curiously enough, will be the very day that we will lose our freedom."

Lusine looked as if she didn't know what he was talking about.

"You'll see what I mean when we are freed and the Skins are put back upon us," he said. Immediately after, he was embarrassed. He remembered that she would go to the Chalice where one of the heavy and powerful Skins used for unnaturals would be fastened to her shoulders.

Lusine did not notice. She was considering the last but most telling point in her argument "You cannot win against us," she said, watching him narrowly for the effect of her words. "We have a weapon that is irresistible. We have immortality."

His face did not lose its imperturbability.

She continued, "And what is more, we can give immortality to anyone who casts off his Skin and adopts ours. Don't think that your people don't know this. For instance, during the last year more than two thousand Humans living along the beaches deserted and went over to us, the Amphibs."

He was a little shocked to hear this, but he did not doubt her. He remembered the mysterious case of the schooner *Le Pauvre Pierre* which had been found drifting and crewless, and he remembered a conversation he had had with a fisherman in his home port of Marrec.

He put his hands behind his back and began pacing. Lusine continued staring at him through the bars. Despite the fact that her face was in the shadows, he could see—or feel—her smile. He had humiliated her, but she had won in the end.

Rastignac quit his limited roving and called up to the guard.

"*Shoo l'footyay, kal u ay tee?*"

The guard leaned over the grille. His large hat with its tall wings sticking from the peak was green in the daytime. But now, illuminated only by a far off torchlight and by a glowworm coiled around the band, it was black.

"*Ah, shoo Zhaw-Zhawk W'stenyek*" he said, loudly. "What time is it? What do you care what time it is?" And he concluded with the stock phrase of the jailer, unchanged through millennia and over light-years. "You're not going any place, are you?"

Rastignac threw his head back to howl at the guard but stopped to wince at the sudden pain in his neck. After uttering, "*Sek Ploo!*" and "*S'pweestee!*" both of which were close enough to the old Terran

French so that a language specialist might have recognized them, he said, more calmly, "If you would let me out on the ground, *monsieur le foutriquet*, and give me a good épée, I would show you where I am going. Or, at least, where my sword is going. I am thinking of a nice sheath for it."

Tonight he had a special reason for keeping the attention of the King's mucketeer directed towards himself. So, when the guard grew tired of returning insults—mainly because his limited imagination could invent no new ones—Rastignac began telling jokes. They were broad and aimed at the mucketeer's narrow intellect.

"Then," said Rastignac, "there was the itinerant salesman whose *s'fel* threw a shoe. He knocked on the door of the hut of the nearest peasant and said . . ." What was said by the salesman was never known.

A strangled gasp had come from above.

IV

Rastignac saw something enormous blot out the smaller shadow of the guard. Then both figures disappeared. A moment later a silhouette cut across the lines of the grille. Unoiled hinges screeched; the bars lifted. A rope uncoiled from above to fall at Rastignac's feet. He seized it and felt himself being drawn powerfully upwards.

When he came over the edge of the well, he saw that his rescuer was a giant Ssassaror. The light from the glowworm on the guard's hat lit up feebly his face, which was orthagnathous and had quite humanoid eyes and lips. Large canine teeth stuck out from the mouth, and its huge ears were tipped with feathery tufts. The forehead down to the eyebrows looked as if it needed a shave, but Rastignac knew that more light would show the blue-black shade came from many small feathers, not stubbled hair.

"Mapfarity!" Rastignac said. "It's good to see you after all these years!"

The Ssassaror giant put his hand on his friend's shoulder. Clenched, it was almost as big as Rastignac's head. He spoke with a voice like a lion coughing at the bottom of a deep well.

"It is good to see you again, my friend."

"What are you doing here?" said Rastignac, tears running down his face as he stroked the great fingers on his shoulder.

Mapfarity's huge ears quivered like the wings of a bat tied to a rock and unable to fly off. The tufts of feathers at their ends grew stiff and suddenly crackled with tiny sparks.

The electrical display was his equivalent of the human's weeping. Both creatures discharged emotion; their bodies chose different avenues and manifestations. Nevertheless, the sight of the other's joy affected each deeply.

"I have come to rescue you," said Mapfarity. "I caught Archambaud here,"—he indicated the other man—"stealing eggs from my golden goose. And . . ."

Raoul Archambaud—pronounced Wawl Shebvo—interrupted excitedly, "I showed him my license to steal eggs from Giants who were raising counterfeit geese, but he was going to lock me up anyway. He was going to take my Skin off and feed me on meat . . ."

"Meat!" said Rastignac, astonished and revolted despite himself. "Mapfarity, what have you been doing in that castle of yours?"

Mapfarity lowered his voice to match the distant roar of a cataract. "I haven't been very active these last few years," he said, "because I am so big that it hurts my feet if I walk very much. So I've had much time to think. And I, being logical, decided that the next step after eating fish was eating meat. It couldn't make me any larger. So, I ate meat. And while doing so, I came to the same conclusion that you, apparently, have done independently. That is, the Philosophy of . . ."

"Of Violence," interrupted Archambaud. "Ah, Jean-Jacques, there must be some mystic bond that brings two Humans of such different backgrounds as yours and the Ssassaror together, giving you both the same philosophy. When I explained what you had been doing and that you were in jail because you had advocated getting rid of the Skins, Mapfarity petitioned . . ."

"The King to make an official jail-break," said Mapfarity with an impatient glance at the roly-poly egg-stealer. "And . . ."

"The King agreed," broke in Archambaud, "provided Mapfarity would turn in his counterfeit goose and provided you would agree to say no more about abandoning Skins, but . . ."

The Giant's basso profundoredundo pushed the egg-stealer's high pitch aside. "If this squeaker will quit interrupting, perhaps we can get on with the rescue. We'll talk later, if you don't mind."

At that moment Lusine's voice floated up from the bottom of her cell. "Jean-Jacques, my love, my brave, my own, would you abandon me to the Chalice? Please take me with you! You will need somebody to hide you when the Minister of Ill-Will sends his mucketeers after you. I can hide you where no one will ever find you." Her voice was mocking, but there was an undercurrent of anxiety to it.

Mapfarity muttered, "She will hide us, yes, at the bottom of a sea-cave where we will eat strange food and suffer a change. Never . . ."

"Trust an Amphib," finished Archambaud for him.

Mapfarity forgot to whisper. "*Bey-t'cul, vu nu fez yey! Fe'm sa!*" he roared.

A shocked hush covered the courtyard. Only Mapfarity's wrathful breathing could be heard. Then, disembodied, Lusine's voice floated from the well.

"Jean-Jacques, do not forget that I am the foster-daughter of the King of the Amphibians! If you were to take me with you, I could assure you of safety and a warm welcome in the halls of the Sea-King's Palace!"

"Pah!" said Mapfarity. "That web-footed witch!"

Rastignac did not reply to her. He took the broad silk belt and the sheathed épée from Archambaud and buckled them around his waist. Mapfarity handed him a mucketeer's hat; he clapped that on firmly. Last of all, he took the Skin that the fat egg-stealer had been holding out to him.

For the first time he hesitated. It was his Skin, the one he had been wearing since he was six. It had grown with him, fed off his blood for twenty-two years, clung to him as clothing, censor, and castigator, and parted from him only when he was inside the walls of his own house, went swimming, or, as during the last seven days, when he laid in jail.

A week ago, after they had removed his second Skin, he had felt naked and helpless and cut off from his fellow creatures. But that was a week ago. Since then, as he had remarked to Lusine, he had experienced the birth of a strange feeling. It was, at first, frightening. It made him cling to the bars as if they were the only stable thing in the center of a whirling universe.

Later, when that first giddiness had passed, it was succeeded by another intoxication—the joy of being an individual, the knowledge that he was separate, not a part of a multitude. Without the Skin he could think as he pleased. He did not have a censor.

Now, he was on level ground again, out of the cell. But as soon as he had put that prison-shaft behind him he was faced with the old second Skin.

Archambaud held it out like a cloak in his hands. It looked much like a ragged garment. It was pale and limp and roughly rectangular with four extensions at each corner. When Rastignac put it on his back, it would sink four tiny hollow teeth into his veins and the suckers on the inner surface of its flat body would cling to him. Its long upper extensions would wrap themselves around his shoulders and over his chest; the lower, around his loins and thighs. Soon it would lose its paleness and flaccidity, become pink and slightly convex, pulsing with Rastignac's blood.

V

Rastignac hesitated for a few seconds. Then he allowed the habit of a lifetime to take over. Sighing, he turned his back. In a moment he felt the cold flesh descend over his shoulders and the little bite of the four teeth as they attached the Skin to his shoulders. Then, as his blood poured into the creature he felt it grow warm and strong. It spread out and followed the passages it had long ago been conditioned to follow, wrapped him warmly and lovingly and comfortably. And he knew, though he couldn't feel it, that it was pushing nerves into the grooves along the teeth. Nerves to connect with his.

A minute later he experienced the first of the expected *rapport*. It was nothing that you could put a mental finger on. It was just a diffused tingling and then the sudden consciousness of how the others around him *felt*.

They were ghosts in the background of his mind. Yet, pale and ectoplasmic as they were, they were easily identifiable. Mapfarity loomed above the others, a transparent Colossus radiating streamers of confidence in his clumsy strength. A meat-eater, uncertain about the future, with a hope and trust in Rastignac to show him the right way. And with a strong current of anger against the conqueror who had inflicted the Skin upon him.

Archambaud was a shorter phantom, rolypoly even in his psychic manifestations, emitting bursts of impatience because other people did not talk fast enough to suit him, his mind leaping on ahead of their tongues, his fingers wriggling to wrap themselves around something valuable—preferably the eggs of the golden goose—and a general eagerness to be up and about and onwards. He was one round fidget on two legs, yet a good man for any project requiring action.

Faintly, Rastignac detected the slumbering guard as if he were the tendrils of some plant at the sea-bottom, floating in the green twilight, at peace and unconscious.

And even more faintly he felt Lusine's presence, shielded by the walls of the shaft. Hers was a pale and light hand, one whose fingers tapped a barely heard code of impotent rage and voiceless screaming fear. Yet beneath that anguish was a base of confidence and mockery at others. She might be temporarily upset, but when the chance came for her to do something she would seize it with every ability at her command.

Another radiation dipped into the general picture and out. A wild glowworm had swooped over them and disturbed the smooth reflection built up by the Skins.

This was the way the Skins worked. They penetrated into you and found out what you were feeling and emoting, and then they broadcast it to other closeby Skins, which then projected their hosts' psychosomatic responses. The whole was then integrated so that each Skin-wearer could detect the group-feeling and at the same time, though in a much duller manner, the feeling of the individuals of the *gestalt*.

That wasn't the only function of the Skin. The parasite, created in the bio-factories, had several other social and biological uses.

Rastignac almost fell into a reverie at that point. It was nothing unusual. The effect of the Skins was a slowing-down one. The wearer thought more slowly, acted more leisurely, and was much more contented.

But now, by a deliberate wrenching of himself from the feeling-pattern, Rastignac woke up. There were things to do, and standing around and drinking in the lotus of the group-rapport was not one of them.

He gestured at the prostrate form of the mucketeer. "You didn't hurt him?"

The Ssassaror rumbled, "No. I scratched him with a little venom of the dream-snake. He will sleep for an hour or so. Besides, I would not be allowed to hurt him. You forget that all this is carefully staged by the King's Official Jail-breaker."

"*Me'dt!*" swore Rastignac.

Alarmed, Archambaud said, "What's the matter, Jean-Jacques?"

"Can't we do anything on our own? Must the King meddle in everything?"

"You wouldn't want us to take a chance and have to shed *blood*, would you?" breathed Archambaud.

"What are you carrying those swords for? As a decoration?" Rastignac snarled.

"*Seelahs, m'fweh,*" warned Mapfarity. "If you alarm the other guards, you will embarrass them. They will be forced to do their duty and recapture you. And the Jail-breaker would be reprimanded because he had fallen down on his job. He might even get a demotion."

Rastignac was so upset that his Skin, reacting to the negative fields racing over the Skin and the hormone imbalance of his blood, writhed away from his back.

"What are we, a bunch of children playing war?"

Mapfarity growled, "We are all God's children, and we mustn't hurt anyone if we can help it."

"Mapfarity, you eat meat!"

"*Voo zavf w'zaw m'fweh,*" admitted the Giant. "But it is the flesh of unintelligent creatures. I have not yet shed the blood of any being that can talk with the tongue of Man."

Rastignac snorted and said, "If you stick with me you will some day do that, *m'fweh* Mapfarity. There is no other course. It is inevitable."

"Nature spare me the day! But if it comes it will find Mapfarity unafraid. They do not call me Giant for nothing."

Rastignac sighed and walked ahead. Sometimes he wondered if the members of his underground—or anybody else for that matter—ever realized the grim conclusions formed by the Philosophy of Violence.

The Amphibians, he was sure, did. And they were doing something positive about it. But it was the Amphibians who had driven Rastignac to adopt a Philosophy of Violence.

"*Law,*" he said again, "Let's go."

The three of them walked out of the huge courtyard and through the open gate. Nearby stood a short man whose Skin gleamed black-red in the light shed by the two glowworms attached to his shoulders. The Skin was oversized and hung to the ground.

The King's man, however, did not think he was a comic figure. He sputtered, and the red of his face matched the color of the skin on his back.

"You took long enough," he said accusingly and then, when Rastignac opened his mouth to protest, the Jail-breaker said, "Never mind, never mind. *Sa n'apawt.* The thing is that we get you away fast. The Minister of Ill-Will has doubtless by now received word that an official jail-break is planned for tonight. He will send a company of his mucketeers to intercept you. By coming in advance of the appointed time we shall have time to escape before the official rescue party arrives."

"How much time do we have?" asked Rastignac.

The King's man said, "Let's see. After I escort you through the rooms of the Duke, the King's foster-brother—he is most favorable to the Violent Philosophy, you know, and has petitioned the King to become your official patron, which petition will be considered at the next meeting of the Chamber of Deputies in three months—let's see, where was I? Ah, yes, I escort you through the rooms of the King's brother. You will be disguised as His Majesty's mucketeers, ostensibly looking for the escaped prisoners. From the rooms of the Duke you will be let out through a small door in the wall of the palace itself. A car will be waiting.

"From then on it will be up to you. I suggest, however, that you make a dash for Mapfarity's castle. Follow the *Rue des Nues;* that is your best chance. The mucketeers have been pulled off that boulevard. However, it is possible that Auverpin, the Ill-Will Minister, may see that order and will rescind it, realizing what it means. If he does, I suppose I will see you back in your cell, Rastignac."

He bowed to the Ssassaror and Archambaud and said, "And you two gentlemen will then be with him."

"And then what?" rumbled Mapfarity.

"According to the law, you will be allowed one more jail-break. Any more after that will, of course, be illegal. That is, unthinkable."

Rastignac unsheathed his épée and slashed it at the air. "Let the mucketeers stand in my way," he said fiercely. "I will cut them down with this!"

The Jail-breaker staggered back, hands outthrust.

"Please, Monsieur Rastignac! Please! Don't even talk about it! You know that your philosophy is, as yet, illegal. The shedding of blood is an act that will be regarded with horror throughout the sentient planet. People would think you are an Amphibian!"

"The Amphibians know what they're doing far better than we do," answered Rastignac. "Why do you think they're winning against us Humans?"

Suddenly, before anybody could answer, the sound of blaring horns came from somewhere on the ramparts. Shouts went up; drums began to beat, calling the mucketeers to alert.

And above it all came the roar of a giant Ssassaror voice: "*An Earthship has landed in the sea! And the pilot of the ship is in the hands of the Amphibians!*"

As the meaning of the words seeped into Rastignac's consciousness he made a sudden violent movement—and began to tear the Skin from his body!

VI

Rastignac ran down the steps, out into the courtyard. He seized the Jail-breaker's arm and demanded the key to the grilles. Dazed, the white-faced official meekly and silently handed it to him. Without his Skin Rastignac was no longer fearfully inhibited. If you were forceful enough and did not behave according to the normal pattern you could get just about anything you wanted. The average Man or Ssassaror did not know how to react to his violence. By the time they had recovered from their confusion he could be miles away.

Such a thought flashed through his head as he ran towards the prison wells. At the same time he heard the horn-blasts of the king's mucketeers and knew that he shortly would have a different type of

Man to deal with. The mucketeers, closest approach to soldiers in this pacifistic land, wore Skins that conditioned them to be more belligerent than the common citizen. They carried épées and, while it was true that their points were dull and their wielders had never engaged in serious swordsmanship, the mucketeers could be dangerous from a viewpoint of numbers alone.

Mapfarity bellowed, "Jean-Jacques, what are you doing?"

He called back over his shoulder, "I'm taking Lusine with us! She can help us get the Earthman from the Amphibians!"

The Giant lumbered up behind him, threw a rope down to the eager hands of Lusine and pulled her up without effort to the top of the well. A second later, Rastignac leaped upon Mapfarity's back, dug his hands under the upper fringe of the huge Skin and, ignoring its electrical blasts, ripped downwards.

Mapfarity cried out with shock and surprise as his skin flopped on the stones like a devilfish on dry land.

Archambaud ran up then and, without bothering to explain, the Ssassaror and the Man seized him and peeled off *his* artificial hide.

"Now we're all free men!" panted Rastignac. "And the mucketeers have no way of locating us if we hide, nor can they punish us with shocks."

He put the Giant on his right side, Lusine on his left, and the egg-stealer behind him. He removed the Jail-breaker's rapier from his sheath. The official was too astonished to protest.

"*Law, m'zawfa!*" cried Rastignac, parodying in his grotesque French the old Gallic war cry of "*Allons, mes enfants!*"

The King's official came to life and screamed orders at the group of mucketeers who had poured into the courtyard. They halted in confusion. They could not hear him above the roar of horns and thunder of drums and the people sticking their heads out of windows and shouting.

Rastignac scooped up with his épée one of the abandoned Skins flopping on the floor and threw it at the foremost guard. It descended upon the man's head, knocking off his hat and wrapping itself around the head and shoulders. The guard dropped his sword and staggered backwards into the group. At the same time the escapees charged and bowled over their feeble opposition.

It was here that Rastignac drew first blood. The tip of his épée drove past a bewildered mucketeer's blade and entered the fellow's throat just below the chin. It did not penetrate very far because of the dullness of the point. Nevertheless, when Rastignac withdrew his sword he saw blood spurt.

It was the first flower of violence, this scarlet blossom set against the whiteness of a Man's skin.

It would, if he had worn his Skin, have sickened him. Now, he exulted with a shout of triumph.

Lusine swooped up from behind him, bent over the fallen man. Her fingers dipped into the blood and went to her mouth. Greedily, she sucked her fingers.

Rastignac struck her cheek hard with the flat of his hand. She staggered back, her eyes narrow, but she laughed.

The next moments were busy as they entered the castle, knocked down two mucketeers who tried to prevent their passage to the Duke's rooms, then filed across the long suite.

The Duke rose from his writing-desk to greet them. Rastignac, determined to sever all ties and impress the government with the fact that he meant a real violence, snarled at his benefactor, "*Va t'feh fout!*"

The Duke was disconcerted at this harsh command, so obviously impossible to carry out. He blinked and said nothing. The escapees hurried past him to the door that gave exit to the outside. They pushed it open and stepped out into the car that waited for them. A chauffeur leaned against its thin wooden body.

Mapfarity pushed him aside and climbed in. The others followed. Rastignac was the last to get in. He examined in a glance the vehicle they were supposed to make their flight in.

It was as good a car as you could find in the realm. A Renault of the large class, it had a long boat-shaped scarlet body. There wasn't a scratch on it. It had seats for six. And that it had the power to out-run most anything was indicated by the two extra pairs of legs stick-ing out from the bottom. There were twelve pairs of legs, equine in form and shod with the best steel. It was the kind of vehicle you wanted when you might have to take off across the country. Wheeled cars could go faster on the highway, but this Renault would not be daunted by water, plowed fields, or steep hillsides.

Rastignac climbed into the driver's seat, seized the wheel and pressed his foot down on the accelerator. The nerve-spot beneath the pedal sent a message to the muscles hidden beneath the hood and the legs projecting from the body. The Renault lurched for-ward, steadied, and began to pick up speed. It entered a broad paved highway. Hooves drummed; sparks shot out from the steel shoes.

Rastignac guided the brainless, blind creature concealed within the body. He was helped by the somatically-generated radar it employed to steer it past obstacles. When he came to the *Rue des Nues,* he slowed it down to a trot. There was no use tiring it out. Halfway up the gentle slope of the boulevard, however, a Ford gal-loped out from a side-street. Its seats bristled with tall peaked hats with outspread glowworm wings and with drawn épées.

Rastignac shoved the accelerator to the floor. The Renault broke into a gallop. The Ford turned so that it would present its broad side. As there was a fencework of tall shrubbery growing along the boule-vard, the Ford was thus able to block most of the passage.

But, just before his vehicle reached the Ford, Rastignac pressed the Jump button. Few cars had this; only sportsmen or the royalty could afford to have such a neural circuit installed. And it did not allow for gradations in leaping. It was an all-or-none reaction; the legs spumed the ground in perfect unison and with every bit of the power in them. There was no holding back.

The nose lifted, the Renault soared into the air. There was a shout, a slight swaying as the trailing hooves struck the heads of mucketeers who had been stupid enough not to duck, and the vehicle landed with a screeching lurch, upright, on the other side of the Ford. Nor did it pause.

Half an hour later Rastignac reined in the car under a large tree whose shadow protected them. "We're well out in the country," he said.

"What do we do now?" asked impatient Archambaud.

"First we must know more about this Earthman," Rastignac answered. "Then we can decide."

VII

Dawn broke through night's guard and spilled a crimson swath on the hills to the East, and the Six Flying Stars faded from sight like a necklace of glowing jewels dipped into an ink bottle.

Rastignac halted the weary Renault on the top of a hill, looked down over the landscape spread out for miles below him. Mapfarity's castle—a tall rose-colored tower of flying buttresses—flashed in the rising sun. It stood on another hill by the sea shore. The country around was a madman's dream of color. Yet to Rastignac every hue sickened the eye. That bright green, for instance, was poisonous; that flaming scarlet was bloody; that pale yellow, rheumy; that velvet black, funeral; that pure white, maggotty.

"Rastignac!" It was Mapfarity's bass, strumming irritation deep in his chest.

"What?"

"What do we do now?"

Jean-Jacques was silent. Archambaud spoke plaintively.

"I'm not used to going without my Skin. There are things I miss. For one thing, I don't know what you're thinking, Jean-Jacques. I don't know whether you're angry at me or love me or are indifferent to me. I don't know where other people *are*. I don't feel the joy of the little animals playing, the freedom of the flight of birds, the ghostly plucking of the growing grass, the sweet stab of the mating lust of the wild-horned apigator, the humming of bees working to build a hive, and the sleepy stupid arrogance of the giant cabbage-eating *deuxnez*. I can feel nothing without the Skin I have worn so long. I feel alone."

Rastignac replied, "You are not alone. I am with you."

Lusine spoke in a low voice, her large brown eyes upon his.

"I, too, feel alone. My Skin is gone, the Skin by which I knew how to act according to the wisdom of my father, the Amphib King. Now that it is gone and I cannot hear his voice through the vibrating tympanum, I do not know what to do."

"At present," replied Rastignac, "you will do as I tell you."

Mapfarity repeated, "What now?"

Rastignac became brisk. He said, "We go to your castle, Giant. We use your smithy to put sharp points on our swords, points to slide through a man's body from front to back. Don't pale! That is what we must do. And then we pick up your goose that lays the golden eggs, for we must have money if we are to act efficiently. After that, we buy—or steal—a boat and we go to wherever the Earthman is held captive. And we rescue him."

"And then?" said Lusine, her eyes shining with emotion.

"What you do then will be up to you. But I am going to leave this planet and voyage with the Earthman to other worlds."

Silence. Then Mapfarity said, "Why leave here?"

"Because there is no hope for this land. Nobody will give up his Skin. *Le Beau Pays* is doomed to a lotus-life. And that is not for me."

Archambaud jerked a thumb at the Amphib girl. "What about her people?"

"They may win, the water-people. What's the difference? It will be just the exchange of one Skin for another. Before I heard of the landing of the Earthman I was going to fight no matter what the cost to me or inevitable defeat. But not now."

Mapfarity's rumble was angry. "Ah, Jean-Jacques, this is not my comrade talking. Are you sure you haven't swallowed your Skin? You talk as if you were inside-out. What is the matter with your brain? Can't you see that it will indeed make a difference if the Amphibs get the upper hand? Can't you see *who* is making the Amphibs behave the way they have been?"

Rastignac urged the Renault towards the rose-colored lacy castle high upon a hill. The vehicle trotted tiredly along the rough and narrow forest path.

"What do you mean?" he said

"I mean the Amphibs got along fine with the Ssassaror until a new element entered their lives—the Earthmen. Then the antagonising began. What is this new element? It's the Changelings—the mixture of Earthmen and Amphibs or Ssassaror and Terran. Add it up. Turn it around. Look at it from any angle. It is the Changelings who are behind this restlessness—the Human element.

"Another thing. The Amphibs have always had Skins different from ours. Our factories create our Skins to set up an affinity and communication between their wearers and all of Nature. They are designed to make it easier for every Man to love his neighbor.

"Now, the strange thing about the Amphibs' Skin is that they, too, were once designed to do such things. But in the past thirty or forty years new Skins have been created for one primary purpose—to establish a communication between the Sea-King and his subjects. Not only that, the Skins can be operated at long distances so that the King may punish any disobedient subject. And they are set so that they establish affinity only among the Waterfolk, not between them and all of Nature."

"I had gathered some of that during my conversations with Lusine," said Rastignac. "But I did not know it had gone to such lengths."

"Yes, and you may safely bet that the Changelings are behind it."

"Then it is the human element that is corrupting?"

"What else?"

Rastignac said, "Lusine, what do you say to this?"

"I think it is best that you leave this world. Or else turn Changeling-Amphib."

"Why should I join you Amphibians?"

"A man like you could become a Sea-King."

"And drink blood?"

"I would rather drink blood than mate with a Man. Almost, that is. But I would make an exception with you, Jean-Jacques."

If it had been a Land-woman who made such a blunt proposal he would have listened with equanimity. There was no modesty, false or otherwise, in the country of the Skin-wearers. But to hear such a thing from a woman whose mouth had drunk the blood of a living man filled him with disgust.

Yet, he had to admit Lusine was beautiful. If she had not been a blood-drinker . . .

Though he lacked his receptive Skin, Mapfarity seemed to sense Rastignac's emotions. He said, "You must not blame her too much, Jean-Jacques. Sea-changelings are conditioned from babyhood to love blood. And for a very definite purpose, too, unnatural though it is. When the time comes for hordes of Changelings to sweep out of the sea and overwhelm the Landfolk, they will have no compunctions about cutting the throats of their fellow-creatures."

Lusine laughed. The rest of them shifted uneasily but did not comment. Rastignac changed the subject.

"How did you find out about the Earthman, Mapfarity?" he said.

The Ssassaror smiled. Two long yellow canines shone wetly; the nose, which had nostrils set in the sides, gaped open; blue sparks shot out from it; at the same time the feathered tufts on the ends of the elephantine ears stiffened and crackled with red-and-blue sparks.

"I have been doing something besides breeding geese to lay golden eggs," he said. "I have set traps for Waterfolk, and I have caught two. These I caged in a dungeon in my castle, and I experimented with them. I removed their Skins and put them on me, and I found out many interesting facts."

He leered at Lusine, who was no longer laughing, and he said, "For instance, I discovered that the Sea-King can locate, talk to, and punish any of his subjects anywhere in the sea or along the coast. He has booster Skins planted all over his realm so that any message he sends will reach the receiver, no matter how far away he is. Moreover, he has conditioned each and every Skin so that, by uttering a certain codeword to which only one particular Skin will respond, he may stimulate it to shock or even to kill its carrier."

Mapfarity continued, "I analyzed those two Skins in my lab and then, using them as models, made a number of duplicates in my fleshforge. They lacked only the nerves that would enable the Sea-King to shock us."

Rastignac smiled his appreciation of this coup. Mapfarity's ears crackled blue sparks of joy, his equivalent of blushing.

"Ah, then you have doubtless listened in to many broadcasts. And you know where the Earthman is located?"

"Yes," said the Giant. "He is in the palace of the Amphib King, upon the island of Kataproimnoin. That is only thirty miles out to the sea."

Rastignac did not know what he would do, but he had two advantages in the Amphibs' Skins and in Lusine. And he burned to get off this doomed planet, this land of men too sunk in false happiness, sloth, and stupidity to see that soon death would come from the water.

He had two possible avenues of escape. One was to use the newly arrived Earthman's knowledge so that the fuels necessary to propel the ferry-rockets could be manufactured. The rockets themselves still stood in a museum. Rastignac had not planned to use them because neither he nor any one else on this planet knew how to make fuel for them. Such secrets had long ago been forgotten.

But now that science was available through the newcomer from Earth, the rockets could be equipped and taken up to one of the Six Flying Stars. The Earthman could study the rocket, determine what was needed in the way of supplies, then it could be outfitted for the long voyage.

An alternative was the Terran's vessel. Perhaps he might invite him to come along in it . . .

The huge gateway to Mapfarity's castle interrupted his thoughts.

VIII

He halted the Renault, told Archambaud to find the Giant's servant and have him feed their vehicle, rub its legs down with liniment, and examine the hooves for defective shoes.

Archambaud was glad to look up Mapfabvisheen, the Giant's servant, because he had not seen him for a long time. The little Ssassaror had been an active member of the Egg-stealer's Guild until the night three years ago when he had tried to creep into Mapfarity's strongroom. The crafty guildsman had avoided the Giant's traps and there found the two geese squatting upon their bed of minerals.

These fabulous geese made no sound when he picked them up with lead-lined gloves and put them in his bag, also lined with lead-leaf. They were not even aware of him. Laboratory-bred, retort-shaped, their protoplasm a blend of silicon-carbon, unconscious even that they lived, they munched upon lead and other elements, ruminated, gastated, transmuted, and every month, regular as the clockwork march of stars or whirl of electrons, each laid an octagonal egg of pure gold.

Mapfabvisheen had trodden softly from the strongroom and thought himself safe. And then, amazingly, frighteningly, and totally unethically, from his viewpoint, the geese had begun honking loudly!

He had run, but not fast enough. The Giant had come stumbling from his bed in response to the wild clamor and had caught him. And, according to the contract drawn up between the Guild of Egg-stealers and the League of Giants, a guildsman seized within the precints of a castle must serve the goose's owner for two years. Mapfabvisheen had been greedy; he had tried to take both geese. Therefore, he must wait upon the Giant for a double term.

Afterwards, he found out how he'd been trapped. The egg-layers themselves hadn't been honking. Mouthless, they were utterly incapable of that. Mapfarity had fastened a so-called "goose-tracker" to the strongroom's doorway. This device clicked loudly whenever a goose was nearby. It could smell out one even through a lead-leaf-lined bag. When Mapfabvisheen passed underneath it, its clicks woke up a small Skin beside it. The Skin, mostly lung-sac and voice organs, honked its warning. And the dwarf, Mapfabvisheen, began his servitude to the Giant, Mapfarity.

Rastignac knew the story. He also knew that Mapfarity had infected the fellow with the philosophy of Violence and that he was now a good member of his Underground. He was eager to tell him his servitor days were over, that he could now take his place in their band as an equal. Subject, of course, to Rastignac's order.

Mapfabvisheen was stretched out upon the floor and snoring a sour breath. A grey-haired man was slumped on a nearby table. His head, turned to one side, exhibited the same slack-jawed look that the Ssassaror's had, and he flung the ill-smelling gauntlet of his breath at the visitors. He held an empty bottle in one loose hand. Two other bottles lay on the stone floor, one shattered.

Besides the bottles lay the men's Skins. Rastignac wondered why they had not crawled to the hall-tree and hung themselves up.

"What ails them? What is that smell?" said Mapfarity.

"I don't know," replied Archambaud, "but I know the visitor. He is Father Jules, priest of the Guild of Egg-stealers."

Rastignac raised his queer, bracket-shaped eyebrows, picked up a bottle in which there remained a slight residue, and drank.

"Mon Dieu, it is the sacrament wine!" he cried.

Mapfarity said, "Why would they be drinking that?"

"I don't know. Wake Mapfabvisheen up, but let the good father sleep. He seems tired after his spiritual labors and doubtless deserves a rest."

Doused with a bucket of cold water the little Ssassaror staggered to his feet. Seeing Archambaud, he embraced him. "Ah, Archambaud, old baby-abductor, my sweet goose-bagger, my ears tingle to see you again!"

They did. Red and blue sparks flew off his ear-feathers.

"What is the meaning of this?" sternly interrupted Mapfarity. He pointed at the dirt swept into the corners.

Mapfabvisheen drew himself up to his full dignity, which wasn't much. "Good Father Jules was making his circuits," he said. "You know he travels around the country and hears confession and sings Mass for us poor egg-stealers who have been unlucky enough to fall into the clutches of some rich and greedy and anti-social Giant who is too stingy to hire servants, but captures them instead, and who won't allow us to leave the premises until our servitude is over . . ."

"Cut it!" thundered Mapfarity. "I can't stand around all day, listening to the likes of you. My feet hurt too much. Anyway, you know I've allowed you to go into town every week-end. Why don't you see a priest then?"

Mapfabvisheen said, "You know very well the closest town is ten kilometers away and it's full of Pantheists. There's not a priest to be found there."

Rastignac groaned inwardly. Always it was thus. You could never hurry these people or get them to regard anything seriously.

Take the case they were wasting their breath on now. Everybody knew the Church had been outlawed a long time ago because it opposed the use of the Skins and certain other practices that went along with it. So, no sooner had that been done than the Ssassarors, anxious to establish their check-and-balance system, had made arrangements through the Minister of Ill-Will to give the Church unofficial legal recognizance.

Then, though the aborigines had belonged to that pantheistical organization known as the Sons of Good And Old Mother Nature, they had all joined the Church of the Terrans. They operated under the theory that the best way to make an institution innocuous was for everybody to sign up for it. Never persecute. That makes it thrive.

Much to the Church's chagrin, the theory worked. How can you fight an enemy who insists on joining you and who will also agree to everything you teach him and then still worship at the other service? Supposedly driven underground, the Church counted almost every Landsman among its supporters from the Kings down.

Every now and then a priest would forget to wear his Skin out-of-doors and be arrested, then released later in an official jail-break. Those who refused to cooperate were forcibly kidnapped, taken to another town and there let loose. Nor did it do the priest any good to proclaim boldly who he was. Everybody pretended not to know he was a fugitive from justice. They insisted on calling him by his official pseudonym.

However, few priests were such martyrs. Generations of Skin-wearing had sapped the ecclesiastical vigor.

The thing that puzzled Rastignac about Father Jules was the sacrament wine. Neither he nor anybody else in L'Bawpfey, as far as he knew, had ever tasted the liquid outside of the ceremony. Indeed, except for certain of the priests, nobody even knew how to make wine.

He shook the priest awake, said, "What's the matter, Father?"

Father Jules burst into tears. "Ah, my boy, you have caught me in my sin. I am a drunkard."

Everybody looked blank. "What does that word *drunkard* mean?"

"It means a man who's damned enough to fill his Skin with alcohol, my boy, fill it until he's no longer a man but a beast."

"Alcohol? What is that?"

"The stuff that's in the wine, my boy. You don't know what I'm talking about because the knowledge was long ago forbidden except to us of the cloth. Cloth, he says! Bah! We go around like everybody, naked except for these extradermal monstrosities which reveal rather than conceal, which not only serve us as clothing but as mentors, parents, censors, interpreters, and, yes, even as priests. Where's a bottle that's not empty? I'm thirsty."

Rastignac stuck to the subject. "Why was the making of this alcohol forbidden?"

"How should I know?" said Father Jules. "I'm old, but not so ancient that I came with the Six Flying Stars ... Where is that bottle?"

Rastignac was not offended by his crossness. Priests were notorious for being the most ill-tempered, obstreperous, and unstable of men. They were not at all like the clerics of Earth, whom everybody knew from legend had been sweet-tempered, meek, humble, and obedient to authority. But on L'Bawpfey these men of the Church had reason to be out of sorts. Everybody attended Mass, paid their tithes, went to confession, and did not fall asleep during sermons. Everybody believed what the priests told them and were as good as it was possible for human beings to be. So, the priests had no real incentive to work, no evil to fight.

Then why the prohibition against alcohol?

"*Sacre Bleu!*" groaned Father Jules. "Drink as much as I did last night and you'll find out. Never again, I say. Ah, there's another bottle, hidden by a providential fate under my traveling robe. Where's that corkscrew?"

Father Jules swallowed half of the bottle, smacked his lips, picked up his Skin from the floor, brushed off the dirt and said, "I must be going, my sons. I've a noon appointment with the bishop, and I've a good twelve kilometers to travel. Perhaps one of you gentlemen has a car?"

Rastignac shook his head and said he was sorry but their car was tired and had, besides, thrown a shoe. Father Jules shrugged philosophically, put on his Skin and reached out again for the bottle.

Rastignac said, "Sorry, Father. I'm keeping this bottle."

"For what?" asked Father Jules.

"Never mind. Say I'm keeping you from temptation."

"Bless you, my son, and may you have a big enough hangover to show you the wickedness of your ways."

Smiling, Rastignac watched the Father walk out. He was not disappointed. The priest had no sooner reached the huge door than his Skin fell off and lay motionless upon the stone.

"Ah," breathed Rastignac. "The same thing happened to Mapfabvisheen when he put his on. There must be something about the wine that deadens the Skins, makes them fall off."

After the padre had left, Rastignac handed the bottle to Mapfarity. "We're dedicated to breaking the law most illegally, brother. So I'm asking you to analyze this wine and find out how to make it."

"Why not ask Father Jules?"

"Because priests are pledged never to' reveal the secret. That was one of the original agreements whereby the Church was allowed to remain on L'Bawpfey. Or, at least that's what my parish priest told me. He said it was a good thing, as it removed an evil from man's temptation. He never did say why it was so evil. Maybe he didn't know.

"That doesn't matter. What does matter is that the Church has inadvertently given us a weapon whereby we may free Man from his bondage to the Skins and it has also given itself once again a chance to be really persecuted and to flourish on the blood of its martyrs."

"Blood?" said Lusine, licking her lips. "The Churchmen drink blood?"

Rastignac did not explain. He could be wrong. If so, he'd feel less like a fool if they didn't know what he thought.

Meanwhile, there were the first steps to be taken for the unskinning of an entire planet.

IX

Later that day the mucketeers surrounded the castle but they made no effort to storm it. The following day one of them knocked on the huge front door and presented Mapfarity with a summons requiring them to surrender. The Giant laughed, put the document in his mouth and ate it. The server fainted and had to be revived with a bucket of cold water before he could stagger back to report this tradition-shattering reception.

Rastignac set up his underground so it could be expanded in a hurry. He didn't worry about the blockade because, as was well known, Giants' castles had all sorts of subterranean tunnels and secret exits. He contacted a small number of priests who were willing to work for him. These were congenital rebels who became quite enthusiastic when he told them their activities would result in a fierce persecution of the Church.

The majority, however, clung to their Skins and said they would have nothing to do with this extradermal-less devil. They took pride and comfort in that term. The vulgar phrase for the man who refused to wear his Skin was "devil," and, by law and logic, the Church could not be associated with a devil. As everybody knew, the priests have always been on the side of the angels.

Meanwhile, the Devil's band slipped out of the tunnels and made raids. Their targets were Giants' castles and government treasuries; their loot, the geese. So many raids did they make that the president of the League of Giants and the Business Agent for the Guild of Egg-stealers came to plead with them. And remained to denounce. Rastignac was delighted with their complaints, and, after listening for a while, threw them out.

Rastignac had, like all other Skin-wearers, always accepted the monetary system as a thing of reason and steady balance. But, without his Skin he was able to think objectively and saw its weaknesses.

For some cause buried far in history, the Giants had always had control of the means for making the hexagonal golden coins called *oeufs*. But the Kings, wishing to get control of the golden eggs, had set up that élite branch of the Guild which specialized in abducting the half-living 'geese.' Whenever a thief was successful he turned the goose over to his King. The monarch, in turn, sent a note to the robbed Giant informing him that the government intended to keep the goose to make its own currency. But even though the Giant was making counterfeit geese, the King, in his generosity, would ship to the Giant one out of every thirty eggs laid by the kidnappee.

The note was a polite and well-recognized lie. The Giants made the only genuine gold-egg-laying geese on the planet because the Giants' League alone knew the secret. And the King gave back one-thirtieth of his loot so the Giant could accumulate enough money to buy the materials to create another goose. Which would, possibly, be stolen later on.

Rastignac, by his illegal rape of geese, was making money scarce. Peasants were hanging on to their produce and waiting to sell until prices were at their highest. The government, merchants, the league, the guild, all saw themselves impoverished.

Furthermore, the Amphibs, taking note of the situation, were making raids of their own and blaming them on Rastignac.

He did not care. He was intent on trying to find a way to reach Kataproimnoin and rescue the Earthman so he could take off in the spaceship floating in the harbor. But he knew that he would have to take things slowly, to scout out the land and plan accordingly.

Furthermore, Mapfarity had made him promise he would do his best to set up the Landsmen so they would be able to resist the Waterfolk when the day for war came.

Rastignac made his biggest raid when he and his band stole one moonless night into the capital itself to rob the big Goose House, only an egg's throw away from the Palace and the Ministry of Ill-Will. They put the Goose House guards to sleep with little arrows smeared with dream-snake venom, filled their lead-leaf-lined bags with gold eggs, and sneaked out the back door.

As they left, Rastignac saw a cloaked figure slinking from the back door of the Ministry. Seized with intuition, he tackled the figure. It was an Amphib-changeling. Rastignac struck the Amphib with a venomous arrow before the Water-human could cry out or stab back.

Mapfarity grabbed up the limp Amphib and they raced for the safety of the castle.

They questioned the Amphib, Pierre Pusipremnoos, in the castle. At first silent, he later began talking freely when Mapfarity got a heavy Skin from his flesh-forge and put it on the fellow. It was a Skin modeled after those worn by the Water-people, but it differed in that the Giant could control, through another Skin, the powerful neural shocks.

After a few shocks Pierre admitted he was the foster-son of the Amphibian King and that, incidentally, Lusine was his foster-sister. He further stated he was a messenger between the Amphib King and the Ssassaror's Ill-Will Minister.

More shocks extracted the fact that the Minister of Ill-Will, Auverpin, was an Amphib-changeling who was passing himself off as a born Landsman. Not only that, the Human hostages among the Amphibs were about to stage a carefully planned revolt against the born Amphibs. It would kill off about half of them. The rest would then be brought under control of the Master Skin.

When the two stepped from the lab they were attacked by Lusine, knife in hand. She gashed Rastignac in the arm before he knocked her out with an uppercut. Later, while Mapfarity applied a little jelly-like creature called a *scar-jester* to the wound, Rastignac complained:

"I don't know if I can endure much more of this. I thought the way of Violence would not be hard to follow because I hated the Skins and the Amphibs so much. But it is easier to attack a faceless, hypothetical enemy, or torture him, than the individual enemy. Much easier."

"My brother," boomed the Giant, "if you continue to dwell upon the philosophical implications of your actions you will end up as helpless and confused as the leg-counting centipede. Better not think. Warriors are not supposed to. They lose their keen fighting edge when they think. And you need all of that now."

"I would suppose that thought would sharpen them."

"When issues are simple, yes. But you must remember that the system on this planet is anything but uncomplicated. It was set up to confuse, to keep one always off balance. Just try to keep one thing in mind—the Skins are far more of an impediment to Man than they are a help. Also, that if the Skins don't come off the Amphibs will soon be cutting our throats. The only way to save ourselves is to kill them first. Right?"

"I suppose so," said Rastignac. He stooped and put his hands under the unconscious Lusine's armpits. "Help me put her in a room. We'll keep her locked up until she cools off. Then we'll use her to guide us when we get to Kataproimnoin. Which reminds me—how many gallons of the wine have you made so far?"

X

A week later Rastignac summoned Lusine. She came in frowning, and with her lower lip protruding in a pretty pout.

He said, "Day after tomorrow is the day on which the new Kings are crowned, isn't it?"

Tonelessly she said, "Supposedly. Actually, the present Kings will be crowned again."

Rastignac smiled. "I know. Peculiar, isn't it, how the 'people' always vote the same Kings back into power? However, that isn't what I'm getting at. If I remember correctly, the Amphibs give their King exotic and amusing gifts on coronation day. What do you think would happen if I took a big shipload of bottles of wine and passed it out among the population just before the Amphibs begin their surprise massacre?"

Lusine had seen Mapfarity and Rastignac experimenting with the wine and she had been frightened by the results. Nevertheless, she made a brave attempt to hide her fear now. She spit at him and said, "You mud-footed fool! There are priests who will know what it is! They will be in the coronation crowd."

"Ah, not so! In the first place, you Amphibs are almost entirely Aggressive Pantheists. You have only a few priests, and you will now pay for that omission of wine-tasters. Second, Mapfarity's concoction tastes not at all vinous and is twice as strong."

She spat at him again and spun on her heel and walked out.

That night Rastignac's band and Lusine went through a tunnel which brought them up through a hollow tree about two miles west of the castle. There they hopped into the Renault, which had been kept in a camouflaged garage, and drove to the little port of Marrec. Archambaud had paved their way here with golden eggs and a sloop was waiting for them.

Rastignac took the boat's wheel. Lusine stood beside him, ready to answer the challenge of any Amphib patrol that tried to stop them. As the Amphib-King's foster-daughter, she could get the boat through to the Amphib island without any trouble at all.

Archambaud stood behind her, a knife under his cloak, to make sure she did not try to betray them. Lusine had sworn she could be trusted. Rastignac had answered that he was sure she could be, too, as long as the knife point pricked her back to remind her.

Nobody stopped them. An hour before dawn they anchored in the harbor of Kataproimnoin. Lusine was tied hand and foot inside the cabin. Before Rastignac could scratch her with dream-snake venom, she pleaded, "You could not do this to me, Jean-Jacques, if you loved me."

"Who said anything about loving you?"

"Well, I like that! You said so, you cheat!"

"Oh, *then!* Well, Lusine, you've had enough experience to know that such protestations of tenderness and affection are only inevitable accompaniments of the moment's passion."

For the first time since he had known her he saw Lusine's lower lip tremble and tears come in her eyes. "Do you mean you were only using me?" she sobbed.

"You forget I had good reason to think you were just using *me.* Remember, you're an Amphib, Lusine. Your people can't be trusted. You blood-drinkers are as savage as the little sea-monsters you leave in Human cradles."

"Jean-Jacques, take me with you! I'll do anything you say! I'll even cut my foster-father's throat for you!"

He laughed. Unheeding, she swept on. "I want to be with you, Jean-Jacques! Look, with me to guide you in my homeland—with my prestige as the Amphib-King's daughter—you can become King yourself after the rebellion. I'd get rid of the Amphib-King for you so there'll be nobody in your way!"

She felt no more guilt than a tigress. She was naive and terrible, innocent and disgusting.

"No, thanks, Lusine." He scratched her with the dream-snake needle. As her eyes closed he said, "You don't understand. All I want to do is voyage to the stars. Being King means nothing to me. The only person I'd trade places with would be the Earthman the Amphibs hold prisoner."

He left her sleeping in the locked cabin.

Noon found them loafing on the great square in front of the Palace of the Two Kings of the Sea and the Islands. All were disguised as Waterfolk. Before they'd left the castle, they had grafted webs between their fingers and toes—just as Amphib-changelings who weren't born with them, did—and they wore the special Amphib

Skins that Mapfarity had grown in his fleshforge. These were able to tune in on the Amphibs' wavelengths, but they lacked their shock mechanism.

Rastignac had to locate the Earthman, rescue him, and get him to the spaceship that lay anchored between two wharfs, its sharp nose pointing outwards. A wooden bridge had been built from one of the wharfs to a place halfway up its towering side.

Rastignac could not make out any breaks in the smooth metal that would indicate a port, but reason told him there must be some sort of entrance to the ship at that point.

A guard of twenty Amphibs repulsed any attempt on the crowd's part to get on the bridge.

Rastignac had contacted the harbor-master and made arrangements for workmen to unload his cargo of wine. His freehandedness with the gold eggs got him immediate service even on this general holiday. Once in the square, he and his men uncrated the wine but left the two heavy chests on the wagon which was hitched to a powerful little six-legged Jeep.

They stacked the bottles of wine in a huge pile while the curious crowd in the square encircled them to watch. Rastignac then stood on a chest to survey the scene, so that he could best judge the time to start. There were perhaps seven or eight thousand of all three races there—the Ssassarors, the Amphibs, the Humans—with an unequal portioning of each.

Rastignac, looking for just such a thing, noticed that every non-human Amphib had at least two Humans tagging at his heels.

It would take two Humans to handle an Amphib or a Ssassaror. The Amphibs stood upon their seal-like hind flippers at least six and a half feet tall and weighed about three hundred pounds. The Giant Ssassarors, being fisheaters, had reached the same enormous height as Mapfarity. The Giants were in the minority, as the Amphibs had always preferred stealing Human babies from the Terrans. These were marked for death as much as the Amphibs.

Rastignac watched for signs of uneasiness or hostility between the three groups. Soon he saw the signs. They were not plentiful, but they were enough to indicate an uneasy undercurrent. Three times the guards had to intervene to break up quarrels. The Humans eyed the non-human quarrelers, but made no move to help their Amphib fellows against the Giants. Not only that, they took them aside afterwards and seemed to be reprimanding them. Evidently the order was that everyone was to be on his best behavior until the time to revolt.

Rastignac glanced at the great tower-clock. "It's an hour before the ceremonies begin," he said to his men. "Let's go."

XI

Mapfarity, who had been loitering in the crowd some distance away, caught Archambaud's signal and slowly, as befit a Giant whose feet hurt, limped towards them. He stopped, scrutinized the pile of bottles, then, in his lion's-roar-at-the-bottom-of-a-well voice said, "Say, what's in these bottles?"

Rastignac shouted back, "A drink which the new Kings will enjoy very much."

"What's that?" replied Mapfarity. "Sea-water?"

The crowd laughed.

"No, it's not water," Rastignac said, "as anybody but a lumbering Giant should know. It is a delicious drink that brings a rare ecstacy upon the drinker. I got the formula for it from an old witch who lives on the shores of far off Apfelabvidanahyew. He told me it had been in his family since the coming of Man to L'Bawpfey. He parted with the formula on condition I make it only for the Kings."

"Will only Their Majesties get to taste this exquisite drink?" bellowed Mapfarity.

"That depends upon whether it pleases Their Majesties to give some to their subjects to celebrate the result of the elections."

Archambaud, also planted in the crowd, shrilled, "I suppose if they do, the big-paunched Amphibs and Giants will get twice as much as us Humans. They always do, it seems."

There was a mutter from the crowd; approbation from the Amphibs, protest from the others.

"That will make no difference," said Rastignac, smiling. "The fascinating thing about this is that an Amphib can drink no more than a Human. That may be why the old man who revealed his secret to me called the drink Old Equalizer."

"Ah, you're skinless," scoffed Mapfarity, throwing the most deadly insult known. "I can out-drink, out-eat, and out-swim any Human here. Here, Amphib, give me a bottle, and we'll see if I'm bragging."

An Amphib captain pushed himself through the throng, waddling clumsily on his flippers like an upright seal.

"No, you don't!" he barked. "Those bottles are intended for the Kings. No commoner touches them, least of all a Human and a Giant."

Rastignac mentally hugged himself. He couldn't have planned a better intervention himself! "Why can't I?" he replied. "Until I make an official presentation, these bottles are mine, not the Kings'. I'll do what I want with them."

"Yeah," said the Amphibs. "That's telling him!"

The Amphib's big brown eyes narrowed and his animal-like face wrinkled, but he couldn't think of a retort. Rastignac at once handed a bottle apiece to each of his comrades. They uncorked and drank and then assumed an ecstatic expression which was a tribute to their acting, for these three bottles held only fruit juice.

"Look here, captain," said Rastignac, "why don't you try a swig yourself? Go ahead. There's plenty. And I'm sure Their Majesties would be pleased to contribute some of it on this joyous occasion. Besides, I can always make more for the Kings.

"As a matter of fact," he added, winking, "I expect to get a pension from the courts as the Kings' Old Equalizer-maker."

The crowd laughed. The Amphib, afraid of losing face, took the bottle—which contained wine rather than fruit juice. After a few long swallows the Amphib's eyes became red and a silly grin curved his thin, black-edged lips. Finally, in a thickening voice, he asked for another bottle.

Rastignac, in a sudden burst of generosity, not only gave him one, but began passing out bottles to the many eager reaching hands. Mapfarity and the two egg-thieves helped him. In a short time, the pile of bottles had dwindled to a fourth of its former height. When a mixed group of guards strode up and demanded to know what the commotion was about, Rastignac gave them some of the bottles.

Meanwhile, Archambaud slipped off into the mob. He lurched into an Amphib, said something nasty about his ancestors, and pulled his knife. When the Amphib lunged for the little man, Archambaud jumped back and shoved a Human-Amphib into the giant flipper-like arms.

Within a minute the square had erupted into a fighting mob. Staggering, red-eyed, slur-tongued, their long-repressed hostility against each other, released by the liquor which their bodies were unaccustomed to, Human, Ssassaror and Amphib fell to with the utmost will, slashing, slugging, fighting with everything they had.

None of them noticed that every one who had drunk from the bottles had lost his Skin. The Skins had fallen off one by one and lay motionless on the pavement where they were kicked or stepped upon. Not one Skin tried to crawl back to its owner because they were all nerve-numbed by the wine.

Rastignac, seated behind the wheel of the Jeep, began driving as best he could through the battling mob. After frequent stops he halted before the broad marble steps that ran like a stairway to heaven, up and up before it ended on the Porpoise Porch of the Palace. He and his gang were about to take the two heavy chests off the wagon when they were transfixed by a scene before them.

A score of dead Humans and Amphibs lay on the steps, evidence of the fierce struggle that had taken place between the guards of the two monarchs. Evidently the King had heard of the riot and hastened outside. There the Amphib-changeling King had apparently realized that the rebellion was way ahead of schedule, but he had attacked the Amphib King anyway.

And he had won, for his guardsmen held the struggling flip-per-footed Amphib ruler down while two others bent his head back over a step. The Changeling-King himself, still clad in the corona-tion robes, was about to draw his long ceremonial knife across the exposed and palpitating throat of the Amphib King.

This in itself was enough to freeze the onlookers. But the sight of Lusine running up the stairway towards the rulers added to their paralysis. She had a knife in her hand and was holding it high as she ran toward her foster-father, the Amphib King.

Mapfarity groaned, but Rastignac said, "It doesn't matter that she has escaped. We'll go ahead with our original plan."

They began unloading the chests while Rastignac kept an eye on Lusine. He saw her run up, stop, say a few words to the Amphib King, then kneel and stab him, burying the knife in his jugular vein. Then, before anybody could stop her she had applied her mouth to the cut in his neck.

The Human-King kicked her in the ribs and sent her rolling down the steps. Rastignac saw correctly that it was not her murderous deed that caused his reaction. It was because she had dared to commit it without his permission and had also drunk the royal blood first.

He further noted with grim satisfaction that when Lusine recov-ered from the blow and ran back up to talk to the King, he ignored her. She pointed at the group around the wagon but he dismissed her with a wave of his hand. He was too busy gloating over his van-quished rival lying at his feet.

The plotters hoisted the two chests and staggered up the steps. The King passed them as he went down with no more than a curious glance. Gifts had been coming up those steps all day for the King, so he undoubtedly thought of them only as more gifts. So Rastignac and his men walked past the knives of the guards as if they had noth-ing to fear.

Lusine stood alone at the top of the steps. She was in a half-crouch, knife ready. "I'll kill the King and I'll drink from his throat!" she cried hoarsely. "No man kicks me except for love. Has he forgotten that I am the foster-daughter of the Amphib King?"

Rastignac felt revulsion but he had learned by now that those who deal in violence and rebellion must march with strange steppers.

"Bear a hand here," he said, ignoring her threat.

Meekly she grabbed hold of a chest's corner. To his further questioning, she replied that the Earthman who had landed in the ship was held in a suite of rooms in the west wing. Their trip thereafter was fast and direct. Unopposed, they carted the chests to the huge room where the Master Skin was kept.

There they found ten frantic bio-technicians excitedly trying to determine why the great extraderm—the Master Skin through which all individual Skins were controlled—was not broadcasting properly. They had no way as yet of knowing that it was operating perfectly but that the little Skins upon the Amphibs and their hostage Humans were not shocking them into submission because they were lying in a wine-stupor on the ground. No one had told them that the Skins, which fed off the bloodstream of their hosts, had become anesthetized from the alcohol and failed any longer to react to their Master Skin.

That, of course, applied only to those Skins in the square that were drunk from the wine. Elsewhere all over the kingdom, Amphibs writhed in agony and Ssassarors and Terrans were taking advantage of their helplessness to cut their throats. But not here, where the crux of the matter was.

XII

The Landsmen rushed the techs and pushed them into the great chemical vat in which the twenty-five hundred foot square Master Skin floated. Then they uncrated the lead-leaf-lined bags filled with stolen geese and emptied them into the nutrient fluid. According to Mapfarity's calculations, the radio-activity from the silicon-carbon geese should kill the big Skin within a few days. When a new one was grown, that, too, would die. Unless the Amphib guessed what was wrong and located the geese on the bottom of the ten-foot deep tank, they would not be able to stop the process. That did not seem likely.

In either case, it was necessary that the Master Skin be put out of temporary commission, at least, so the Amphibs over the Kingdom could have a fighting chance. Mapfarity plunged a hollow harpoon into the isle of floating protoplasm and through a tube connected to that poured into the Skin three gallons of the dream-snake venom. That was enough to knock it out for an hour or two. Meanwhile, if the Amphibs had any sense at all, they'd have rid themselves of their extraderms.

They left the lab and entered the west wing. As they trotted up the long winding corridors Lusine said, "Jean-Jacques, what do you plan on doing now? Will you try to make yourself King of the Terrans and fight us Amphibs?" When he said nothing she went on. "Why don't you kill the Amphib-changeling King and take over here? I could help you do that. You could then have all of L'Bawpfey in your power."

He shot her a look of contempt and cried, "Lusine, can't you get it through that thick little head of yours that everything I've done has been done so that I can win one goal: reach the Flying Stars? If I can get the Earthman to his ship I'll leave with him and not set foot again for years on this planet. Maybe never again."

She looked stricken. "But what about the war here?" she asked.

"There are a few men among the Landfolk who are capable of leading in wartime. It will take strong men, and there are very few like me, I admit, but—oh, oh, opposition!" He broke off at sight of the six guards who stood before the Earthman's suite.

Lusine helped, and within a minute they had slain three and chased away the others. Then they burst through the door—and Rastignac received another shock.

The occupant of the apartment was a tiny and exquisitely formed redhead with large blue eyes and very unmasculine curves!

"I thought you said Earth*man*?" protested Rastignac to the Giant who came lumbering along behind them.

"Oh, I used that in the generic sense," Mapfarity replied. "You didn't expect me to pay any attention to sex, did you? I'm not interested in the gender of you Humans, you know."

There was no time for reproach. Rastignac tried to explain to the Earthwoman who he was, but she did not understand him. However, she did seem to catch on to what he wanted and seemed reassured by his gestures. She picked up a large book from a table and, hugging it to her small, high and rounded bosom, went with him out the door.

They raced from the palace and descended onto the square. Here they found the surviving Amphibs clustered into a solid phalanx and fighting, bloody step by step, towards the street that led to the harbor.

Rastignac's little group skirted the battle and started down the steep avenue toward the harbor. Halfway down he glanced back and saw that nobody as yet was paying any attention to them. Nor was there anybody on the street to bother them, though the pavement was strewn with Skins and bodies. Apparently, those who'd lived through the first savage mêlée had gone to the square.

They ran onto the wharf. The Earthwoman motioned to Rastignac that she knew how to open the spaceship, but the Amphibs didn't. Moreover, if they did get in, they wouldn't know how to operate it. She had the directions for so doing in the book hugged so desperately to her chest. Rastignac surmised she hadn't told the Amphibs about that. Apparently they hadn't, as yet, tried to torture the information from her.

Therefore, her telling him about the book indicated she trusted him.

Lusine said, "Now what, Jean-Jacques? Are you still going to abandon this planet?"

"Of course," he snapped.

"Will you take me with you?"

He had spent most of his life under the tutelage of his Skin, which ensured that others would know when he was lying. It did not come easy to hide his true feelings. So a habit of a lifetime won out.

"I will not take you," he said. "In the first place, though you may have some admirable virtues, I've failed to detect one. In the second place, I could not stand your blood-drinking nor your murderous and totally immoral ways."

"But, Jean-Jacques, I will give them up for you!"

"Can the shark stop eating fish?"

"You would leave Lusine, who loves you as no Earthwoman could, and go with that—that pale little doll I could break with my hands?"

"Be quiet," he said. "I have dreamed of this moment all my life. Nothing can stop me now."

They were on the wharf beside the bridge that ran up the smooth side of the starship. The guard was no longer there, though bodies showed that there had been reluctance on the part of some to leave. They let the Earthwoman precede them up the bridge.

Lusine suddenly ran ahead of him, crying, "If you won't have me, you won't have her, either! Nor the stars!"

Her knife sank twice into the Earthwoman's back. Then, before anybody could reach her, she had leaped off the bridge and into the harbor.

Rastignac knelt beside the Earthwoman. She held out the book to him, then she died. He caught the volume before it struck the wharf.

"My God! My God!" moaned Rastignac, stunned with grief and shock and sorrow. Sorrow for the woman and shock at the loss of the ship and the end of his plans for freedom.

Mapfarity ran up then and took the book from his nerveless hand. "She indicated that this is a manual for running the ship," he said. "All is not lost."

"It will be in a language we don't know," Rastignac whispered.

Archambaud came running up and shrilled, "The Amphibs have broken through and are coming down the street! Let's get to our boat before the whole bloodthirsty mob gets here!"

Mapfarity paid him no attention. He thumbed through the book, then reached down and lifted Rastignac from his crouching position by the corpse.

"There's hope yet, Jean-Jacques," he growled. "This book is printed with the same characters as those I saw in a book owned by a priest I knew. He said it was in Hebrew, and that it was the Holy Book in the original Earth language. This woman must be a citizen of the Republic of Israel, which I understand was rising to be a great power on Earth at the time you French left.

"Perhaps the language of this woman has changed somewhat from the original tongue, but I don't think the alphabet has. I'll bet that if we get this to a priest who can read it—there are only a few left—he can translate it well enough for us to figure out everything."

They walked to the wharf's end and climbed down a ladder to a platform where a dory was tied up. As they rowed out to their sloop Mapfarity said:

"Look, Rastignac, things aren't as bad as they seem. If you haven't the ship nobody else has, either. And you alone have the key to its entrance and operation. For that you can thank the Church, which has preserved the ancient wisdom for emergencies which it couldn't foresee, such as this. Just as it kept the secret of wine, which will eventually be the greatest means for delivering our people from their bondage to the Skins and, thus enable them to fight the Amphibs back instead of being slaughtered.

"Meanwhile, we've a battle to wage. You will have to lead it. Nobody else but the Skinless Devil has the prestige to make the people gather around him. Once we accuse the Minister of Ill-Will of treason and jail him, without an official Breaker to release him, we'll demand a general election. You'll be made King of the Ssassaror; I, of the Terrans. That is inevitable, for we are the only skinless men and, therefore, irresistible. After the war is won, we'll leave for the stars. How do you like that?"

Rastignac smiled. It was weak, but it was a smile. His bracket-shaped eyebrows bent into their old sign of determination.

"You are right," he replied. "I have given it much thought. A man has no right to leave his native land until he's settled his problems here. Even if Lusine hadn't killed the Earthwoman and I had sailed away, my conscience wouldn't have given me any rest. I would have known I had abandoned the fight in the middle of it. But now that I have stripped myself of my Skin—which was a substitute for a conscience—and now that I am being forced to develop my own inward conscience, I must admit that immediate flight to the stars would have been the wrong thing."

The pleased and happy Mapfarity said, "And you must also admit, Rastignac, that things so far have had a way of working out for the best. Even Lusine, evil as she was, has helped towards the general good by keeping you on this planet. And the Church, though it has released once again the old evil of alcohol, has done more good by so doing than..."

But here Rastignac interrupted to say he did not believe in this particular school of thought, and so, while the howls of savage warriors drifted from the wharfs, while the structure of their world crashed around them, they plunged into that most violent and circular of all whirlpools—the Discussion Philosophical.

THE WORLD THAT COULDN'T BE

CLIFFORD D. SIMAK

The tracks went up one row and down another, and in those rows the *vua* plants had been sheared off an inch or two above the ground. The raider had been methodical; it had not wandered about haphazardly, but had done an efficient job of harvesting the first ten rows on the west side of the field. Then, having eaten its fill, it had angled off into the bush—and that had not been long ago, for the soil still trickled down into the great pug marks, sunk deep into the finely cultivated loam.

Somewhere a sawmill bird was whirring through a log, and down in one of the thorn-choked ravines, a choir of chatterers was clicking through a ghastly morning song. It was going to be a scorcher of a day. Already the smell of desiccated dust was rising from the ground and the glare of the newly risen sun was dancing off the bright leaves of the hula-trees, making it appear as if the bush were filled with a million flashing mirrors.

Gavin Duncan hauled a red bandanna from his pocket and mopped his face.

"No, mister," pleaded Zikkara, the native foreman of the farm. "You cannot do it, mister. You do not hunt a Cytha."

"The hell I don't," said Duncan, but he spoke in English and not the native tongue.

He stared out across the bush, a flat expanse of sun-cured grass interspersed with thickets of hula-scrub and thorn and occasional

139

groves of trees, criss-crossed by treacherous ravines and spotted with infrequent waterholes.

It would be murderous out there, he told himself, but it shouldn't take too long. The beast probably would lay up shortly after its pre-dawn feeding and he'd overhaul it in an hour or two. But if he failed to overhaul it, then he must keep on.

"Dangerous," Zikkara pointed out. "No one hunts the Cytha."

"I do," Duncan said, speaking now in the native language. "I hunt anything that damages my crop. A few nights more of this and there would be nothing left."

Jamming the bandanna back into his pocket, he tilted his hat lower across his eyes against the sun.

"It might be a long chase, mister. It is the *skun* season now. If you were caught out there . . ."

"Now listen," Duncan told it sharply. "Before I came, you'd feast one day, then starve for days on end; but now you eat each day. And you like the doctoring. Before, when you got sick, you died. Now you get sick, I doctor you, and you live. You like staying in one place, instead of wandering all around."

"Mister, we like all this," said Zikkara, "but we do not hunt the Cytha."

"If we do not hunt the Cytha, we lose all this," Duncan pointed out. "If I don't make a crop, I'm licked. I'll have to go away. Then what happens to you?"

"We will grow the corn ourselves."

"That's a laugh," said Duncan, "and you know it is. If I didn't kick your backsides all day long, you wouldn't do a lick of work. If I leave, you go back to the bush. Now let's go and get that Cytha."

"But it is such a little one, mister! It is such a young one! It is scarcely worth the trouble. It would be a shame to kill it."

Probably just slightly smaller than a horse, thought Duncan, watching the native closely.

It's scared, he told himself. It's scared dry and spitless.

"Besides, it must have been most hungry. Surely, mister, even a Cytha has the right to eat."

"Not from my crop," said Duncan savagely. "You know why we grow the *vua*, don't you? You know it is great medicine. The berries that it grows cures those who are sick inside their heads. My people need that medicine—need it very badly. And what is more, out there—" he swept his arm toward the sky—"out there they pay very much for it."

"But, mister . . ."

"I tell you this," said Duncan gently, "you either dig me up a bush-runner to do the tracking for me or you can all get out, the kit and caboodle of you. I can get other tribes to work the farm."

"No, mister!" Zikkara screamed in desperation.

"You have your choice," Duncan told it coldly.

He plodded back across the field toward the house. Not much of a house as yet. Not a great deal better than a native shack. But someday it would be, he told himself. Let him sell a crop or two and he'd build a house that would really be a house. It would have a bar and swimming pool and a garden filled with flowers, and at last, after years of wandering, he'd have a home and broad acres and everyone, not just one lousy tribe, would call him mister.

Gavin Duncan, planter, he said to himself, and liked the sound of it. Planter on the planet Layard. But not if the Cytha came back night after night and ate the *vua* plants.

He glanced over his shoulder and saw that Zikkara was racing for the native village.

Called their bluff, Duncan informed himself with satisfaction.

He came out of the field and walked across the yard, heading for the house. One of Shotwell's shirts was hanging on the clothesline, limp in the breathless morning.

Damn the man, thought Duncan. Out here mucking around with those stupid natives, always asking questions, always under foot.

Although, to be fair about it, that was Shotwell's job. That was what the Sociology people had sent him out to do.

Duncan came up to the shack, pushed the door open and entered. Shotwell, stripped to the waist, was at the wash bench.

Breakfast was cooking on the stove, with an elderly native acting as cook.

Duncan strode across the room and took down the heavy rifle from its peg. He slapped the action open, slapped it shut again.

Shotwell reached for a towel.

"What's going on?" he asked.

"Cytha got into the field."

"Cytha?"

"A kind of animal," said Duncan. "It ate ten rows of *vua*."

"Big? Little? What are its characteristics?"

The native began putting breakfast on the table. Duncan walked to the table, laid the rifle across one corner of it and sat down. He poured a brackish liquid out of a big stew pan into their cups.

God, he thought, what I would give for a cup of coffee.

Shotwell pulled up his chair.

"You didn't answer me. What is a Cytha like?"

"I wouldn't know," said Duncan.

"Don't know? But you're going after it, looks like, and how can you hunt it if you don't know—"

"Track it. The thing tied to the other end of the trail is sure to be the Cytha. We'll find out what it's like once we catch up to it."

"We?"

"The natives will send up someone to do the tracking for me. Some of them are better than a dog."

"Look, Gavin. I've put you to a lot of trouble and you've been decent with me. If I can be any help, I would like to go."

"Two make better time than three. And we have to catch this Cytha fast or it might settle down to an endurance contest."

"All right, then. Tell me about the Cytha."

Duncan poured porridge gruel into his bowl, handed the pan to Shotwell. "It's a sort of special thing. The natives are scared to death of it. You hear a lot of stories about it. Said to be unkillable. It's always capitalized, always a proper noun. It has been reported at different times from widely scattered places."

"No one's ever bagged one?"

"Not that I ever heard of." Duncan patted the rifle. "Let me get a bead on it."

He started eating, spooning the porridge into his mouth, munching on the stale corn bread left from the night before. He drank some of the brackish beverage and shuddered.

"Some day," he said, "I'm going to scrape together enough money to buy a pound of coffee. You'd think—"

"It's the freight rates," Shotwell said. "I'll send you a pound when I go back."

"Not at the price they'd charge to ship it out," said Duncan. "I wouldn't hear of it."

They ate in silence for a time. Finally Shotwell said: "I'm getting nowhere, Gavin. The natives are willing to talk, but it all adds up to nothing."

"I tried to tell you that. You could have saved your time."

Shotwell shook his head stubbornly. "There's an answer, a logical explanation. It's easy enough to say you cannot rule out the sexual factor, but that's exactly what has happened here on Layard. It's easy to exclaim that a sexless animal, a sexless race, a sexless planet is impossible, but that is what we have. Somewhere there is an answer and I have to find it."

"Now hold up a minute," Duncan protested. "There's no use blowing a gasket. I haven't got the time this morning to listen to your lecture."

"But it's not the lack of sex that worries me entirely," Shotwell said, "although it's the central factor. There are subsidiary situations deriving from that central fact which are most intriguing."

"I have no doubt of it," said Duncan, "but if you please—"

"Without sex, there is no basis for the family, and without the family there is no basis for a tribe, and yet the natives have an elaborate tribal setup, with taboos by way of regulation. Somewhere there must exist some underlying, basic unifying factor, some common loyalty, some strange relationship which spells out to brotherhood."

"Not brotherhood," said Duncan, chuckling. "Not even sisterhood. You must watch your terminology. The word you want is ithood."

The door pushed open and a native walked in timidly.

"Zikkara said that mister want me," the native told them. "I am Sipar. I can track anything but screamers, stilt-birds, longhorns and donovans. Those are my taboos."

"I am glad to hear that," Duncan replied. "You have no Cytha taboo, then."

"Cytha!" yipped the native. "Zikkara did not tell me Cytha!"

Duncan paid no attention. He got up from the table and went to the heavy chest that stood against one wall. He rummaged in it and came out with a pair of binoculars, a hunting knife and an extra drum of ammunition. At the kitchen cupboard, he rummaged once again, filling a small leather sack with a gritty powder from a can he found.

"Rockahominy," he explained to Shotwell. "Emergency rations thought up by the primitive North American Indians. Parched corn, ground fine. It's no feast exactly, but it keeps a man going."

"You figure you'll be gone that long?"

"Maybe overnight. I don't know. Won't stop until I get it. Can't afford to. It could wipe me out in a few days."

"Good hunting," Shotwell said. "I'll hold the fort."

Duncan said to Sipar: "Quit sniveling and come on."

He picked up the rifle, settled it in the crook of his arm. He kicked open the door and strode out.

Sipar followed meekly.

II

Duncan got his first shot late in the afternoon of that first day.

In the middle of the morning, two hours after they had left the farm, they had flushed the Cytha out of its bed in a thick ravine. But there had been no chance for a shot. Duncan saw no more than a huge black blur fade into the bush.

Through the bake-oven afternoon, they had followed its trail, Sipar tracking and Duncan bringing up the rear, scanning every piece of cover, with the sun-hot rifle always held at ready.

Once they had been held up for fifteen minutes while a massive donovan tramped back and forth, screaming, trying to work up its courage for attack. But after a quarter hour of showing off, it decided to behave itself and went off at a shuffling gallop.

Duncan watched it go with a lot of thankfulness. It could soak up a lot of lead, and for all its awkwardness, it was handy with its feet once it set itself in motion. Donovans had killed a lot of men in the twenty years since Earthmen had come to Layard.

With the beast gone, Duncan looked around for Sipar. He found it fast asleep beneath a hula-shrub. He kicked the native awake with something less than gentleness and they went on again.

The bush swarmed with other animals, but they had no trouble with them.

Sipar, despite its initial reluctance, had worked well at the trailing. A misplaced bunch of grass, a twig bent to one side, a displaced stone, the faintest pug mark were Sipar's stock in trade. It worked like a lithe, well-trained hound. This bush country was its special province; here it was at home.

With the sun dropping toward the west, they had climbed a long, steep hill and as they neared the top of it, Duncan hissed at Sipar. The native looked back over its shoulder in surprise. Duncan made motions for it to stop tracking.

The native crouched and as Duncan went past it, he saw that a look of agony was twisting its face. And in the look of agony he thought he saw as well a touch of pleading and a trace of hatred. It's scared, just like the rest of them, Duncan told himself. But what the native thought or felt had no significance; what counted was the beast ahead.

Duncan went the last few yards on his belly, pushing the gun ahead of him, the binoculars bumping on his back. Swift, vicious insects ran out of the grass and swarmed across his hands and arms and one got on his face and bit him.

He made it to the hilltop and lay there, looking at the sweep of land beyond. It was more of the same, more of the blistering, dusty slogging, more of thorn and tangled ravine and awful emptiness.

He lay motionless, watching for a hint of motion, for the fitful shadow, for any wrongness in the terrain that might be the Cytha.

But there was nothing. The land lay quiet under the declining sun. Far on the horizon, a herd of some sort of animals was grazing, but there was nothing else.

Then he saw the motion, just a flicker, on the knoll ahead—about halfway up.

He laid the rifle carefully on the ground and hitched the binoculars around. He raised them to his eyes and moved them slowly back and forth. The animal was there where he had seen the motion.

It was resting, looking back along the way that it had come, watching for the first sign of its trailers. Duncan tried to make out the size and shape, but it blended with the grass and the dun soil and he could not be sure exactly what it looked like.

He let the glasses down and now that he had located it, he could distinguish its outline with the naked eye.

His hand reached out and slid the rifle to him. He fitted it to his shoulder and wriggled his body for closer contact with the ground. The cross-hairs centered on the faint outline on the knoll and then the beast stood up.

It was not as large as he had thought it might be—perhaps a little larger than Earth lion-size, but it certainly was no lion. It was a

square-set thing and black and inclined to lumpiness and it had an
awkward look about it, but there were strength and ferociousness as
well.

Duncan tilted the muzzle of the rifle so that the cross-hairs centered on the massive neck. He drew in a breath and held it and began
the trigger squeeze.

The rifle bucked hard against his shoulder and the report ham-
mered in his head and the beast went down. It did not lurch or fall; it
simply melted down and disappeared, hidden in the grass.

"Dead center," Duncan assured himself.

He worked the mechanism and the spent cartridge case flew out.
The feeding mechanism snicked and the fresh shell clicked as it slid
into the breech.

He lay for a moment, watching. And on the knoll where the thing
had fallen, the grass was twitching as if the wind were blowing, only
there was no wind. But despite the twitching of the grass, there was
no sign of the Cytha. It did not struggle up again. It stayed where it
had fallen.

Duncan got to his feet, dug out the bandanna and mopped at his
face. He heard the soft thud of the step behind him and turned his
head. It was the tracker.

"It's all right, Sipar," he said. "You can quit worrying. I got it. We
can go home now."

It had been a long, hard chase, longer than he had thought it might
be. But it had been successful and that was the thing that counted.
For the moment, the *vua* crop was safe.

He tucked the bandanna back into his pocket, went down the
slope and started up the knoll. He reached the place where the Cytha
had fallen. There were three small gouts of torn, mangled fur and
flesh lying on the ground and there was nothing else.

He spun around and jerked his rifle up. Every nerve was scream-
ingly alert. He swung his head, searching for the slightest movement,
for some shape or color that was not the shape or color of the bush

or grass or ground. But there was nothing. The heat droned in the hush of afternoon. There was not a breath of moving air. But there was danger—a saw-toothed sense of danger close behind his neck.

"Sipar!" he called in a tense whisper, "Watch out!"

The native stood motionless, unheeding, its eyeballs rolling up until there was only white, while the muscles stood out along its throat like straining ropes of steel.

Duncan slowly swiveled, rifle held almost at arm's length, elbows crooked a little, ready to bring the weapon into play in a fraction of a second.

Nothing stirred. There was no more than emptiness—the emptiness of sun and molten sky, of grass and scraggy bush, of a brown-and-yellow land stretching into foreverness.

Step by step, Duncan covered the hillside and finally came back to the place where the native squatted on its heels and moaned, rocking back and forth, arms locked tightly across its chest, as if it tried to cradle itself in a sort of illusory comfort.

The Earthman walked to the place where the Cytha had fallen and picked up, one by one, the bits of bleeding flesh. They had been mangled by his bullet. They were limp and had no shape. And it was queer, he thought. In all his years of hunting, over many planets, he had never known a bullet to rip out hunks of flesh.

He dropped the bloody pieces back into the grass and wiped his hand upon his thighs. He got up a little stiffly.

He'd found no trail of blood leading through the grass, and surely an animal with a hole of that size would leave a trail.

And as he stood there upon the hillside, with the bloody finger-prints still wet and glistening upon the fabric of his trousers, he felt the first cold touch of fear, as if the fingertips of fear might momentarily, almost casually, have trailed across his heart.

He turned around and walked back to the native, reached down and shook it.

"Snap out of it," he ordered.

He expected pleading, cowering, terror, but there was none.

Sipar got swiftly to its feet and stood looking at him and there was, he thought, an odd glitter in its eyes.

"Get going," Duncan said. "We still have a little time. Start circling and pick up the trail. I will cover you."

He glanced at the sun. An hour and a half still left—maybe as much as two. There might still be time to get this buttoned up before the fall of night.

A half mile beyond the knoll, Sipar picked up the trail again and they went ahead, but now they traveled more cautiously, for any bush, any rock, any clump of grass might conceal the wounded beast.

Duncan found himself on edge and cursed himself savagely for it. He'd been in tight spots before. This was nothing new to him. There was no reason to get himself tensed up. It was a deadly business, sure, but he had faced others calmly and walked away from them. It was those frontier tales he'd heard about the Cytha—the kind of superstitious chatter that one always heard on the edge of unknown land.

He gripped the rifle tighter and went on.

No animal, he told himself, was unkillable.

Half an hour before sunset, he called a halt when they reached a brackish waterhole. The light soon would be getting bad for shooting. In the morning, they'd take up the trail again, and by that time the Cytha would be at an even greater disadvantage. It would be stiff and slow and weak. It might be even dead.

Duncan gathered wood and built a fire in the lee of a thorn-bush thicket. Sipar waded out with the canteens and thrust them at arm's length beneath the surface to fill them. The water still was warm and evil-tasting, but it was fairly free of scum and a thirsty man could drink it.

The sun went down and darkness fell quickly. They dragged more wood out of the thicket and piled it carefully close at hand.

Duncan reached into his pocket and brought out the little bag of rockahominy.

"Here," he said to Sipar. "Supper."

The native held one hand cupped and Duncan poured a little mound into its palm.

"Thank you, mister," Sipar said. "Food-giver."

"Huh?" asked Duncan, then caught what the native meant. "Dive into it," he said, almost kindly. "It isn't much, but it gives you strength. We'll need strength tomorrow."

Food-giver, eh? Trying to butter him up, perhaps. In a little while, Sipar would start whining for him to knock off the hunt and head back for the farm.

Although, come to think of it, he really was the food-giver to this bunch of sexless wonders. Corn, thank God, grew well on the red and stubborn soil of Layard—good old corn from North America. Fed to hogs, made into corn-pone for breakfast back on Earth, and here, on Layard, the staple food crop for a gang of shiftless varmints who still regarded, with some good solid skepticism and round-eyed wonder, this unorthodox idea that one should take the trouble to grow plants to eat rather than go out and scrounge for them.

Corn from North America, he thought, growing side by side with the *vua* of Layard. And that was the way it went. Something from one planet and something from another and still something further from a third and so was built up through the wide social confederacy of space a truly cosmic culture which in the end, in another ten thousand years or so, might spell out some way of life with more sanity and understanding than was evident today.

He poured a mound of rockahominy into his own hand and put the bag back into his pocket.

"Sipar."

"Yes, mister?"

"You were not scared today when the donovan threatened to attack us."

"No, mister. The donovan would not hurt me."

"I see. You said the donovan was taboo to you. Could it be that you, likewise, are taboo to the donovan?"

"Yes, mister. The donovan and I grew up together."

"Oh, so that's it," said Duncan.

He put a pinch of the parched and powdered corn into his mouth and took a sip of brackish water. He chewed reflectively on the resultant mash.

He might go ahead, he knew, and ask why and how and where Sipar and the donovan had grown up together, but there was no point to it. This was exactly the kind of tangle that Shotwell was forever getting into.

Half the time, he told himself, I'm convinced the little stinkers are doing no more than pulling our legs.

What a fantastic bunch of jerks! Not men, not women, just things. And while there were never babies, there were children, although never less than eight or nine years old. And if there were no babies, where did the eight- and nine-year-olds come from?

"I suppose," he said, "that these other things that are your taboos, the stiltbirds and the screamers and the like, also grew up with you."

"That is right, mister."

"Some playground that must have been," said Duncan.

He went on chewing, staring out into the darkness beyond the ring of firelight.

"There's something in the thorn bush, mister."

"I didn't hear a thing."

"Little pattering. Something is running there."

Duncan listened closely. What Sipar said was true. A lot of little things were running in the thicket.

"More than likely mice," he said.

He finished his rockahominy and took an extra swig of water, gagging on it slightly.

"Get your rest," he told Sipar. "I'll wake you later so I can catch a wink or two."

"Mister," Sipar said, "I will stay with you to the end."

"Well," said Duncan, somewhat startled, "that is decent of you."

"I will stay to the death," Sipar promised earnestly.

"Don't strain yourself," said Duncan.

He picked up the rifle and walked down to the waterhole.

The night was quiet and the land continued to have that empty feeling. Empty except for the fire and the waterhole and the little micelike animals running in the thicket.

And Sipar—Sipar lying by the fire, curled up and sound asleep already. Naked, with not a weapon to its hand—just the naked animal, the basic humanoid, and yet with underlying purpose that at times was baffling. Scared and shivering this morning at mere mention of the Cytha, yet never faltering on the trail; in pure funk back there on the knoll where they had lost the Cytha, but now ready to go on to the death.

Duncan went back to the fire and prodded Sipar with his toe. The native came straight up out of sleep.

"Whose death?" asked Duncan. "Whose death were you talking of?"

"Why, ours, of course," said Sipar, and went back to sleep.

III

Duncan did not see the arrow coming. He heard the swishing whistle and felt the wind of it on the right side of his throat and then it thunked into a tree behind him.

He leaped aside and dived for the cover of a tumbled mound of boulders and almost instinctively his thumb pushed the fire control of the rifle up to automatic.

He crouched behind the jumbled rocks and peered ahead. There was not a thing to see. The hula-trees shimmered in the blaze of sun and the thorn-bush was gray and lifeless and the only things astir were three stilt-birds walking gravely a quarter of a mile away.

"Sipar!" he whispered.

"Here, mister."

"Keep low. It's still out there."

Whatever it might be. Still out there and waiting for another shot. Duncan shivered, remembering the feel of the arrow flying past his throat. A hell of a way for a man to die—out at the tail-end of nowhere with an arrow in his throat and a scared-stiff native heading back for home as fast as it could go.

He flicked the control on the rifle back to single fire, crawled around the rock pile and sprinted for a grove of trees that stood on higher ground. He reached them and there he flanked the spot from which the arrow must have come.

He unlimbered the binoculars and glassed the area. He still saw no sign. Whatever had taken the pot shot at them had made its get-away.

He walked back to the tree where the arrow still stood out, its point driven deep into the bark. He grasped the shaft and wrenched the arrow free.

"You can come out now," he called to Sipar. "There's no one around."

The arrow was unbelievably crude. The unfeathered shaft looked as if it had been battered off to the proper length with a jagged stone. The arrowhead was unflaked flint picked up from some outcropping or dry creek bed, and it was awkwardly bound to the shaft with the tough but pliant inner bark of the hula-tree.

"You recognize this?" he asked Sipar.

The native took the arrow and examined it. "Not my tribe."

"Of course not your tribe. Yours wouldn't take a shot at us. Some other tribe, perhaps?"

"Very poor arrow."

"I know that. But it could kill you just as dead as if it were a good one. Do you recognize it?"

"No tribe made this arrow," Sipar declared.

"Child, maybe?"

"What would child do way out here?"

"That's what I thought, too," said Duncan.

He took the arrow back, held it between his thumbs and forefingers and twirled it slowly, with a terrifying thought nibbling at his brain. It couldn't be. It was too fantastic. He wondered if the sun was finally getting him that he had thought of it at all.

He squatted down and dug at the ground with the makeshift arrow point. "Sipar, what do you actually know about the Cytha?"

"Nothing, mister. Scared of it is all."

"We aren't turning back. If there's something that you know—something that would help us . . ."

It was as close as he could come to begging aid. It was further than he had meant to go. He should not have asked at all, he thought angrily.

"I do not know," the native said.

Duncan cast the arrow to one side and rose to his feet. He cradled the rifle in his arm. "Let's go."

He watched Sipar trot ahead. Crafty little stinker, he told himself. It knows more than it's telling.

They toiled into the afternoon. It was, if possible, hotter and drier than the day before. There was a sense of tension in the air—no, that was rot. And even if there were, a man must act as if it were not there. If he let himself fall prey to every mood out in this empty land, he only had himself to blame for whatever happened to him.

The tracking was harder now. The day before, the Cytha had only run away, straight-line fleeing to keep ahead of them, to stay out of their reach. Now it was becoming tricky. It backtracked often in an attempt to throw them off. Twice in the afternoon, the trail blanked out entirely and it was only after long searching that Sipar picked it up again—in one instance, a mile away from where it had vanished in thin air.

That vanishing bothered Duncan more than he would admit. Trails do not disappear entirely, not when the terrain remains the same, not when the weather is unchanged. Something was going on, something, perhaps, that Sipar knew far more about than it was willing to divulge.

He watched the native closely and there seemed nothing suspicious. It continued at its work. It was, for all to see, the good and faithful hound.

Late in the afternoon, the plain on which they had been traveling suddenly dropped away. They stood poised on the brink of a great escarpment and looked far out to great tangled forests and a flowing river.

It was like suddenly coming into another and beautiful room that one had not expected.

This was new land, never seen before by any Earthman. For no one had ever mentioned that somewhere to the west a forest lay beyond the bush. Men coming in from space had seen it, probably, but only as a different color-marking on the planet. To them, it made no difference.

But to the men who lived on Layard, to the planter and the trader, the prospector and the hunter, it was important. And I, thought Duncan with a sense of triumph, am the man who found it.

"Mister!"

"Now what?"

"Out there. *Skun!*"

"I don't—"

"Out there, mister. Across the river."

Duncan saw it then—a haze in the blueness of the rift—a puff of copper moving very fast, and as he watched, he heard the far-off keening of the storm, a shiver in the air rather than a sound.

He watched in fascination as it moved along the river and saw the boiling fury it made out of the forest. It struck and crossed the river, and the river for a moment seemed to stand on end, with a sheet of silvery water splashed toward the sky.

Then it was gone as quickly as it had happened, but there was a tumbled slash across the forest where the churning winds had traveled.

Back at the farm, Zikkara had warned him of the *skun*. This was the season for them, it had said, and a man caught in one wouldn't have a chance.

Duncan let his breath out slowly.

"Bad," said Sipar.

"Yes, very bad."

"Hit fast. No warning."

"What about the trail?" asked Duncan. "Did the Cytha—"

Sipar nodded downward.

"Can we make it before nightfall?"

"I think so," Sipar answered.

It was rougher than they had thought. Twice they went down blind trails that pinched off, with sheer rock faces opening out into drops of hundreds of feet, and were forced to climb again and find another way.

They reached the bottom of the escarpment as the brief twilight closed in and they hurried to gather firewood. There was no water, but a little was still left in their canteens and they made do with that.

After their scant meal of rockahominy, Sipar rolled himself into a ball and went to sleep immediately.

Duncan sat with his back against a boulder which one day, long ago, had fallen from the slope above them, but was now half buried in the soil that through the ages had kept sifting down.

Two days gone, he told himself.

Was there, after all, some truth in the whispered tales that made the rounds back at the settlements—that no one should waste his time in tracking down a Cytha, since a Cytha was unkillable?

Nonsense, he told himself. And yet the hunt had toughened, the trail become more difficult, the Cytha a much more cunning and elusive quarry. Where it had run from them the day before, now it fought to shake them off. And if it did that the second day, why had it not tried to throw them off the first? And what about the third day—tomorrow?

He shook his head. It seemed incredible that an animal would become more formidable as the hunt progressed. But that seemed to be exactly what had happened. More spooked, perhaps, more frightened—only the Cytha did not act like a frightened beast. It was acting like an animal that was gaining savvy and determination, and that was somehow frightening.

From far off to the west, toward the forest and the river, came the laughter and the howling of a pack of screamers. Duncan leaned his rifle against the boulder and got up to pile more wood on the fire. He stared out into the western darkness, listening to the racket. He made a wry face and pushed a hand absent-mindedly through his hair. He put out a silent hope that the screamers would decide to keep their distance. They were something a man could do without.

Behind him, a pebble came bumping down the slope. It thudded to a rest just short of the fire.

Duncan spun around. Foolish thing to do, he thought, to camp so near the slope. If something big should start to move, they'd be out of luck.

He stood and listened. The night was quiet. Even the screamers had shut up for the moment. Just one rolling rock and he had his hackles up. He'd have to get himself in hand.

He went back to the boulder, and as he stooped to pick up the rifle, he heard the faint beginning of a rumble. He straightened swiftly to face the scarp that blotted out the star-strewn sky—and the rumble grew!

In one leap, he was at Sipar's side. He reached down and grasped the native by an arm, jerked it erect, held it on its feet. Sipar's eyes snapped open, blinking in the firelight

The rumble had grown to a roar and there were thumping noises, as of heavy boulders bouncing, and beneath the roar the silky, ominous rustle of sliding soil and rock.

Sipar jerked its arm free of Duncan's grip and plunged into the darkness. Duncan whirled and followed.

They ran, stumbling in the dark, and behind them the roar of the sliding, bouncing rock became a throaty roll of thunder that filled the night from brim to brim. As he ran, Duncan could feel, in dread anticipation, the gusty breath of hurtling debris blowing on his neck, the crushing impact of a boulder smashing into him, the engulfing flood of tumbling talus snatching at his legs.

A puff of billowing dust came out and caught them and they ran choking as well as stumbling. Off to the left of them, a mighty chunk of rock chugged along the ground in jerky, almost reluctant fashion.

Then the thunder stopped and all one could hear was the small slitherings of the lesser debris as it trickled down the slope.

Duncan stopped running and slowly turned around. The campfire was gone, buried, no doubt, beneath tons of overlay, and the stars had paled because of the great cloud of dust which still billowed up into the sky.

He heard Sipar moving near him and reached out a hand, searching for the tracker, not knowing exactly where it was. He found the native, grasped it by the shoulder and pulled it up beside him.

Sipar was shivering.

"It's all right," said Duncan.

And it *was* all right, he reassured himself. He still had the rifle. The extra drum of ammunition and the knife were on his belt, the bag of rockahominy in his pocket. The canteens were all they had lost—the canteens and the fire.

"We'll have to hole up somewhere for the night," Duncan said. "There are screamers on the loose."

He didn't like what he was thinking, nor the sharp edge of fear that was beginning to crowd in upon him. He tried to shrug it off, but it still stayed with him, just out of reach.

Sipar plucked at his elbow.

"Thorn thicket, mister. Over there. We could crawl inside. We would be safe from screamers."

It was torture, but they made it.

"Screamers and you are taboo," said Duncan, suddenly remembering. "How come you are afraid of them?"

"Afraid for you, mister, mostly. Afraid for myself just a little. Screamers could forget. They might not recognize me until too late. Safer here."

"I agree with you," said Duncan.

The screamers came and padded all about the thicket. The beasts sniffed and clawed at the thorns to reach them, but finally went away.

When morning came, Duncan and Sipar climbed the scarp, clambering over the boulders and the tons of soil and rock that covered their camping place. Following the gash cut by the slide, they clambered up the slope and finally reached the point of the slide's beginning.

There they found the depression in which the poised slab of rock had rested and where the supporting soil had been dug away so that it could be started, with a push, down the slope above the campfire.

And all about were the deeply sunken pug marks of the Cytha!

IV

Now it was more than just a hunt. It was knife against the throat, kill or be killed. Now there was no stopping, when before there might have been. It was no longer sport and there was no mercy.

"And that's the way I like it," Duncan told himself.

He rubbed his hand along the rifle barrel and saw the metallic glints shine in the noonday sun. One more shot, he prayed. Just give me one more shot at it. This time there will be no slip-up. This time there will be more than three sodden hunks of flesh and fur lying in the grass to mock me.

He squinted his eyes against the heat shimmer rising from the river, watching Sipar hunkered beside the water's edge.

The native rose to its feet and trotted back to him.

"It crossed," said Sipar. "It walked out as far as it could go and it must have swum."

"Are you sure? It might have waded out to make us think it crossed, then doubled back again."

He stared at the purple-green of the trees across the river. Inside that forest, it would be hellish going.

"We can look," said Sipar.

"Good. You go downstream. I'll go up."

An hour later, they were back. They had found no tracks. There seemed little doubt the Cytha had really crossed the river.

They stood side by side, looking at the forest.

"Mister, we have come far. You are brave to hunt the Cytha. You have no fear of death."

"The fear of death," Duncan said, "is entirely infantile. And it's beside the point as well. I do not intend to die."

They waded out into the stream. The bottom shelved gradually and they had to swim no more than a hundred yards or so.

They reached the forest bank and threw themselves flat to rest.

Duncan looked back the way that they had come. To the east, the escarpment was a dark-blue smudge against the pale-blue burnished sky. And two days back of that lay the farm and the *vua* field, but they seemed much farther off than that. They were lost in time and distance; they belonged to another existence and another world.

All his life, it seemed to him, had faded and become inconsequential and forgotten, as if this moment in his life were the only one that counted; as if all the minutes and the hours, all the breaths and heartbeats, wake and sleep, had pointed toward this certain hour upon this certain stream, with the rifle molded to his hand and the cool, calculated bloodlust of a killer riding in his brain.

Sipar finally got up and began to range along the stream. Duncan sat up and watched.

Scared to death, he thought, and yet it stayed with me. At the campfire that first night, it had said it would stick to the death and apparently it had meant exactly what it said. It's hard, he thought, to figure out these jokers, hard to know what kind of mental operation, what seethings of emotion, what brand of ethics and what variety of belief and faith go to make them and their way of life.

It would have been so easy for Sipar to have missed the trail and swear it could not find it. Even from the start, it could have refused to go. Yet, fearing, it had gone. Reluctant, it had trailed. Without any need for faithfulness and loyalty, it had been loyal and faithful. But loyal to what, Duncan wondered, to him, the out-lander and intruder? Loyal to itself? Or perhaps, although that seemed impossible, faithful to the Cytha?

What does Sipar think of me, he asked himself, and maybe more to the point, what do I think of Sipar? Is there a common meeting ground? Or are we, despite our humanoid forms, condemned forever to be alien and apart?

He held the rifle across his knees and stroked it, polishing it, petting it, making it even more closely a part of him, an instrument of his deadliness, an expression of his determination to track and kill the Cytha.

Just another chance, he begged. Just one second, or even less, to draw a steady bead. That is all I want, all I need, all I'll ask.

Then he could go back across the days that he had left behind him, back to the farm and field, back into that misty other life from which he had been so mysteriously divorced, but which in time undoubtedly would become real and meaningful again.

Sipar came back. "I found the trail."

Duncan heaved himself to his feet. "Good."

They left the river and plunged into the forest and there the heat closed in more mercilessly than ever—humid, stifling heat that felt like a soggy blanket wrapped tightly round the body.

The trail lay plain and clear. The Cytha now, it seemed, was intent upon piling up a lead without recourse to evasive tactics. Perhaps it had reasoned that its pursuers would lose some time at the river and it may have been trying to stretch out that margin even further. Perhaps it needed that extra time, he speculated, to set up the necessary machinery for another dirty trick.

Sipar stopped and waited for Duncan to catch up. "Your knife, mister?"

Duncan hesitated. "What for?"

"I have a thorn in my foot," the native said. "I have to get it out."

Duncan pulled the knife from his belt and tossed it. Sipar caught it deftly.

Looking straight at Duncan, with the flicker of a smile upon its lips, the native cut its throat.

V

He should go back, he knew. Without the tracker, he didn't have a chance. The odds were now with the Cytha—if, indeed, they had not been with it from the very start.

Unkillable? Unkillable because it grew in intelligence to meet emergencies? Unkillable because, pressed, it could fashion a bow and arrow, however crude? Unkillable because it had a sense of tactics, like rolling rocks at night upon its enemy? Unkillable because a native tracker would cheerfully kill itself to protect the Cytha?

A sort of crisis-beast, perhaps? One able to develop intelligence and abilities to meet each new situation and then lapsing back to the level of non-intelligent contentment? That, thought Duncan, would be a sensible way for anything to live. It would do away with the inconvenience and the irritability and the discontentment of intelligence when intelligence was unneeded. But the intelligence, and the abilities which went with it, would be there, safely tucked away where one could reach in and get them, like a necklace or a gun—something to be used or to be put away as the case might be.

Duncan hunched forward and with a stick of wood pushed the fire together. The flames blazed up anew and sent sparks flying up into the whispering darkness of the trees. The night had cooled off a little, but the humidity still hung on and a man felt uncomfortable—a little frightened, too.

Duncan lifted his head and stared up into the fire-flecked darkness. There were no stars because the heavy foliage shut them out. He missed the stars. He'd feel better if he could look up and see them.

When morning came, he should go back. He should quit this hunt which now had become impossible and even slightly foolish.

But he knew he wouldn't. Somewhere along the three-day trail, he had become committed to a purpose and a challenge, and he knew that when morning came, he would go on again. It was not hatred that drove him, nor vengeance, nor even the trophy-urge—the hunter-lust that prodded men to kill something strange or harder to kill or bigger than any man had ever killed before. It was something more than that, some weird entangling of the Cytha's meaning with his own.

He reached out and picked up the rifle and laid it in his lap. Its barrel gleamed dully in the flickering campfire light and he rubbed his hand along the stock as another man might stroke a woman's throat.

"Mister," said a voice.

It did not startle him, for the word was softly spoken and for a moment he had forgotten that Sipar was dead—dead with a half-smile fixed upon its face and with its throat laid wide open.

"Mister?"

Duncan stiffened.

Sipar was dead and there was no one else—and yet someone had spoken to him, and there could be only one thing in all this wilderness that might speak to him.

"Yes," he said.

He did not move. He simply sat there, with the rifle in his lap.

"You know who I am?"

"I suppose you are the Cytha."

"You have done well," the Cytha said. "You've made a splendid hunt. There is no dishonor if you should decide to quit. Why don't you go back? I promise you no harm."

It was over there, somewhere in front of him, somewhere in the brush beyond the fire, almost straight across the fire from him, Duncan told himself. If he could keep it talking, perhaps even lure it out—

"Why should I?" he asked. "The hunt is never done until one gets the thing one is after."

"I can kill you," the Cytha told him. "But I do not want to kill. It hurts to kill."

"That's right," said Duncan. "You are most perceptive."

For he had it pegged now. He knew exactly where it was. He could afford a little mockery.

His thumb slid up the metal and nudged the fire control to automatic and he flexed his legs beneath him so that he could rise and fire in one single motion.

"Why did you hunt me?" the Cytha asked. "You are a stranger on my world and you had no right to hunt me. Not that I mind, of course. In fact, I found it stimulating. We must do it again. When I am ready to be hunted, I shall come and tell you and we can spend a day or two at it."

"Sure we can," said Duncan, rising. And as he rose into his crouch, he held the trigger down and the gun danced in insane fury, the muzzle flare a flicking tongue of hatred and the hail of death hissing spitefully in the underbrush.

"Anytime you want to," yelled Duncan gleefully, "I'll come and hunt you! You just say the word and I'll be on your tail. I might even kill you. How do you like it, chump!"

And he held the trigger tight and kept his crouch so the slugs would not fly high, but would cut their swath just above the ground, and he moved the muzzle back and forth a lot so that he covered extra ground to compensate for any miscalcuations he might have made.

The magazine ran out and the gun clicked empty and the vicious chatter stopped. Powder smoke drifted softly in the campfire light and the smell of it was perfume in the nostrils and in the underbrush many little feet were running, as if a thousand frightened mice were scurrying from catastrophe.

Duncan unhooked the extra magazine from where it hung upon his belt and replaced the empty one. Then he snatched a burning length of wood from the fire and waved it frantically until it burst into a blaze and became a torch. Rifle grasped in one hand and the torch in the other, he plunged into the underbrush. Little chittering things fled to escape him.

He did not find the Cytha. He found chewed-up bushes and soil churned by flying metal, and he found five lumps of flesh and fur, and these he brought back to the fire.

Now the fear that had been stalking him, keeping just beyond his reach, walked out from the shadows and hunkered by the campfire with him.

He placed the rifle within easy reach and arranged the five bloody chunks on the ground close to the fire and he tried with trembling fingers to restore them to the shape they'd been before the bullets struck them. And that was a good one, he thought with grim irony, because they had no shape. They had been part of the Cytha and you killed a Cytha inch by inch, not with a single shot You knocked a pound of meat off it the first time, and the next time you shot off another pound or two, and if you got enough shots at it, you finally carved it down to size and maybe you could kill it then, although he wasn't sure.

He was afraid. He admitted that he was and he squatted there and watched his fingers shake and he kept his jaws clamped tight to stop the chatter of his teeth.

The fear had been getting closer all the time; he knew it had moved in by a step or two when Sipar cut its throat, and why in the name of God had the damn fool done it? It made no sense at all. He had wondered about Sipar's loyalties, and the very loyalties that he had dismissed as a sheer impossibility had been the answer, after all. In the end, for some obscure reason—obscure to humans, that is— Sipar's loyalty had been to the Cytha.

But then what was the use of searching for any reason in it? Nothing that had happened made any sense. It made no sense that a beast one was pursuing should up and talk to one—although it did fit in with the theory of the crisis-beast he had fashioned in his mind.

Progressive adaptation, he told himself. Carry adaptation far enough and you'd reach communication. But might not the Cytha's power of adaptation be running down? Had the Cytha gone about as far as it could force itself to go? Maybe so, he thought. It might be worth a gamble. Sipar's suicide, for all its casualness, bore the overtones of last-notch desperation. And the Cytha's speaking to Duncan, its attempt to parley with him, contained a note of weakness.

The arrow had failed and the rockslide had failed and so had Sipar's death. What next would the Cytha try? Had it anything to try?

Tomorrow he'd find out. Tomorrow he'd go on. He couldn't turn back now.

He was too deeply involved. He'd always wonder, if he turned back now, whether another hour or two might not have seen the end of it. There were too many questions, too much mystery—there was now far more at stake than ten rows of *vua*.

Another day might make some sense of it, might banish the dread walker that trod upon his heels, might bring some peace of mind.

As it stood right at the moment, none of it made sense.

But even as he thought it, suddenly one of the bits of bloody flesh and mangled fur made sense.

Beneath the punching and prodding of his fingers, it had assumed a shape.

Breathlessly, Duncan bent above it, not believing, not even wanting to believe, hoping frantically that it should prove completely wrong.

But there was nothing wrong with it. The shape was there and could not be denied. It had somehow fitted back into its natural shape and it was a baby screamer—well, maybe not a baby, but at least a tiny screamer.

Duncan sat back on his heels and sweated. He wiped his bloody hands upon the ground. He wondered what other shapes he'd find if he put back into proper place the other hunks of limpness that lay beside the fire.

He tried and failed. They were too smashed and torn.

He picked them up and tossed them in the fire. He took up his rifle and walked around the fire, sat down with his back against a tree, cradling the gun across his knees.

Those little scurrying feet, he wondered—like the scampering of a thousand busy mice. He had heard them twice, that first night in the thicket by the waterhole and again tonight.

And what could the Cytha be? Certainly not the simple, uncomplicated, marauding animal he had thought to start with.

A hive-beast? A host animal? A thing masquerading in many different forms?

Shotwell, trained in such deductions, might make a fairly accurate guess, but Shotwell was not here. He was at the farm, fretting, more than likely, over Duncan's failure to return.

Finally the first light of morning began to filter through the forest and it was not the glaring, clean white light of the open plain and bush, but a softened, diluted, fuzzy green light to match the smothering vegetation.

The night noises died away and the noises of the day took up— the sawings of unseen insects, the screechings of hidden birds and something far away began to make a noise that sounded like an empty barrel falling slowly down a stairway.

What little coolness the night had brought dissipated swiftly and the heat clamped down, a breathless, relentless heat that quivered in the air.

Circling, Duncan picked up the Cytha trail not more than a hundred yards from camp.

The beast had been traveling fast. The pug marks were deeply sunk and widely spaced. Duncan followed as rapidly as he dared. It was a temptation to follow at a run, to match the Cytha's speed, for the trail was plain and fresh and it fairly beckoned.

And that was wrong, Duncan told himself. It was too fresh, too plain—almost as if the animal had gone to endless trouble so that the human could not miss the trail.

He stopped his trailing and crouched beside a tree and studied the tracks ahead. His hands were too tense upon the gun, his body keyed too high and fine. He forced himself to take slow, deep breaths. He had to calm himself. He had to loosen up.

He studied the tracks ahead—four bunched pug marks, then a long leap interval, then four more bunched tracks, and between the sets of marks the forest floor was innocent and smooth.

Too smooth, perhaps. Especially the third one from him. Too smooth and somehow artificial, as if someone had patted it with gentle hands to make it unsuspicious.

Duncan sucked his breath in slowly.

Trap?

Or was his imagination playing tricks on him?

And if it were a trap, he would have fallen into it if he had kept on following as he had started out.

Now there was something else, a strange uneasiness, and he stirred uncomfortably, casting frantically for some clue to what it was.

He rose and stepped out from the tree, with the gun at ready. What a perfect place to set a trap, he thought. One would be looking at the pug marks, never at the space between them, for the space between would be neutral ground, safe to stride out upon.

Oh, clever Cytha, he said to himself. Oh, clever, clever Cytha!

And now he knew what the other trouble was—the great uneasiness. It was the sense of being watched.

Somewhere up ahead, the Cytha was crouched, watching and waiting—anxious or exultant, maybe even with laughter rumbling in its throat.

He walked slowly forward until he reached the third set of tracks and he saw that he had been right. The little area ahead was smoother than it should be.

"Cytha!" he called.

His voice was far louder than he had meant it to be and he stood astonished and a bit abashed.

Then he realized why it was so loud.

It was the only sound there was!

The forest suddenly had fallen silent. The insects and birds were quiet and the thing in the distance had quit falling down the stairs. Even the leaves were silent. There was no rustle in them and they hung limp upon their stems.

There was a feeling of doom and the green light had changed to a copper light and everything was still.

And the light was *copper!*

Duncan spun around in panic. There was no place for him to hide.

Before he could take another step, the *skun* came and the winds rushed out of nowhere. The air was clogged with flying leaves and debris. Trees snapped and popped and tumbled in the air.

The wind hurled Duncan to his knees, and as he fought to regain his feet, he remembered, in a blinding flash of total recall, how it had looked from atop the escarpment—the boiling fury of the winds and the mad swirling of the coppery mist and how the trees had whipped in whirlpool fashion.

He came half erect and stumbled, clawing at the ground in an attempt to get up again, while inside his brain an insistent, clicking voice cried out for him to run, and somewhere another voice said to lie flat upon the ground, to dig in as best he could.

Something struck him from behind and he went down, pinned flat, with his rifle wedged beneath him. He cracked his head upon the ground and the world whirled sickeningly and plastered his face with a handful of mud and tattered leaves.

He tried to crawl and couldn't, for something had grabbed him by the ankle and was hanging on.

With a frantic hand, he clawed the mess out of his eyes, spat it from his mouth.

Across the spinning ground, something black and angular tumbled rapidly. It was coming straight toward him and he saw it was the Cytha and that in another second it would be on top of him.

He threw up an arm across his face, with the elbow crooked, to take the impact of the wind-blown Cytha and to ward it off.

But it never reached him. Less than a yard away, the ground opened up to take the Cytha and it was no longer there.

Suddenly the wind cut off and the leaves once more hung motionless and the heat clamped down again and that was the end of it. The *skun* had come and struck and gone.

Minutes, Duncan wondered, or perhaps no more than seconds. But in those seconds, the forest had been flattened and the trees lay in shattered heaps.

He raised himself on an elbow and looked to see what was the matter with his foot and he saw that a fallen tree had trapped his foot beneath it.

He tugged a few times experimentally. It was no use. Two close-set limbs, branching almost at right angles from the bole, had been driven deep into the ground and his foot, he saw, had been caught at the ankle in the fork of the buried branches.

The foot didn't hurt—not yet. It didn't seem to be there at all. He tried wiggling his toes and felt none.

He wiped the sweat off his face with a shirt sleeve and fought to force down the panic that was rising in him. Getting panicky was the worst thing a man could do in a spot like this. The thing to do was to take stock of the situation, figure out the best approach, then go ahead and try it.

The tree looked heavy, but perhaps he could handle it if he had to, although there was the danger that if he shifted it, the bole might settle more solidly and crush his foot beneath it. At the moment, the two heavy branches, thrust into the ground on either side of his ankle, were holding most of the tree's weight off his foot.

The best thing to do, he decided, was to dig the ground away beneath his foot until he could pull it out.

He twisted around and started digging with the fingers of one hand. Beneath the thin covering of humus, he struck a solid surface and his fingers slid along it.

With mounting alarm, he explored the ground, scratching at the humus. There was nothing but rock—some long-buried boulder, the top of which lay just beneath the ground.

His foot was trapped beneath a heavy tree and a massive boulder, held securely in place by forked branches that had forced their splintering way down along the boulder's sides.

He lay back, propped on an elbow. It was evident that he could do nothing about the buried boulder. If he was going to do anything, his problem was the tree.

To move the tree, he would need a lever and he had a good, stout lever in his rifle. It would be a shame, he thought a little wryly, to use a gun for such a purpose, but he had no choice.

He worked for an hour and it was no good. Even with the rifle as a pry, he could not budge the tree.

He lay back, defeated, breathing hard, wringing wet with perspiration.

He grimaced at the sky.

All right, Cytha, he thought, you won out in the end. But it took a *skun* to do it. With all your tricks, you couldn't do the job until . . .

Then he remembered.

He sat up hurriedly.

"Cytha!" he called.

The Cytha had fallen into a hole that had opened in the ground. The hole was less than an arm's length away from him, with a little debris around its edges still trickling into it.

Duncan stretched out his body, lying flat upon the ground, and looked into the hole. There, at the bottom of it, was the Cytha.

It was the first time he'd gotten a good look at the Cytha and it was a crazily put-together thing. It seemed to have nothing functional about it and it looked more like a heap of something, just thrown on the ground, than it did an animal.

The hole, he saw, was more than an ordinary hole. It was a pit and very cleverly constructed. The mouth was about four feet in diameter and it widened to roughly twice that at the bottom. It was, in general, bottle-shaped, with an incurving shoulder at the top so that anything that fell in could not climb out. Anything falling into that pit was in to stay.

This, Duncan knew, was what had lain beneath that too-smooth interval between the two sets of Cytha tracks. The Cytha had worked all night to dig it, then had carried away the dirt dug out of the pit and had built a flimsy camouflage cover over it. Then it had gone back and made the trail that was so loud and clear, so easy to make out and follow. And having done all that, having labored hard and stealthily, the Cytha had settled down to watch, to make sure the following human had fallen in the pit.

"Hi, pal," said Duncan. "How are you making out?"

The Cytha did not answer.

"Classy pit," said Duncan. "Do you always den up in luxury like this?"

But the Cytha didn't answer.

Something queer was happening to the Cytha. It was coming all apart.

Duncan watched with fascinated horror as the Cytha broke down into a thousand lumps of motion that scurried in the pit and tried to scramble up its sides, only to fall back in tiny showers of sand.

Amid the scurrying lumps, one thing remained intact, a fragile object that resembled nothing quite so much as the stripped skeleton of a Thanksgiving turkey. But it was a most extraordinary Thanksgiving skeleton, for it throbbed with pulsing life and glowed with a steady violet light.

Chitterings and squeakings came out of the pit and the soft patter of tiny running feet, and as Duncan's eyes became accustomed to the darkness of the pit, he began to make out the forms of some of the scurrying shapes. There were tiny screamers and some donovans and sawmill birds and a bevy of kill-devils and something else as well.

Duncan raised a hand and pressed it against his eyes, then took it quickly away. The little faces still were there, looking up as if beseeching him, with the white shine of their teeth and the white rolling of their eyes.

He felt horror wrenching at his stomach and the sour, bitter taste of revulsion welled into his throat, but he fought it down, harking back to that day at the farm before they had started on the hunt.

"I can track down anything but screamers, stilt-birds, longhorns and donovans," Sipar had told him solemnly. "These are my taboos."

And Sipar was also their taboo, for he had not feared the donovan. Sipar had been, however, somewhat fearful of the screamers in the dead of night because, the native had told him reasonably, screamers were forgetful.

Forgetful of what!

Forgetful of the Cytha-mother? Forgetful of the motley brood in which they had spent their childhood?

For that was the only answer to what was running in the pit and the whole, unsuspected answer to the enigma against which men like Shotwell had frustratedly banged their heads for years.

Strange, he told himself. All right, it might be strange, but if it worked, what difference did it make? So the planet's denizens were sexless because there was no need of sex—what was wrong with that? It might, in fact, Duncan admitted to himself, head off a lot of trouble. No family spats, no triangle trouble, no fighting over mates. While it might be unexciting, it did seem downright peaceful.

And since there was no sex, the Cytha species was the planetary mother—but more than just a mother. The Cytha, more than likely, was mother-father, incubator, nursery, teacher and perhaps many other things besides, all rolled into one.

In many ways, he thought, it might make a lot of sense. Here natural selection would be ruled out and ecology could be controlled in considerable degree and mutation might even be a matter of deliberate choice rather than random happenstance.

And it would make for a potential planetary unity such as no other world had ever known. Everything here was kin to everything else. Here was a planet where Man, or any other alien, must learn to tread most softly. For it was not inconceivable that, in a crisis or a clash of interests, one might find himself faced suddenly with a unified and cooperating planet, with every form of life making common cause against the interloper.

The little scurrying things had given up; they'd gone back to their places, clustered around the pulsing violet of the Thanksgiving skeleton, each one fitting into place until the Cytha had taken shape again. As if, Duncan told himself, blood and nerve and muscle had come back from a brief vacation to form the beast anew.

"Mister," asked the Cytha, "what do we do now?"

"You should know," Duncan told it. "You were the one who dug the pit."

"I split myself," the Cytha said. "A part of me dug the pit and the other part that stayed on the surface got me out when the job was done."

"Convenient," grunted Duncan.

And it *was* convenient. That was what had happened to the Cytha when he had shot at it—it had split into all its component parts and had got away. And that night beside the waterhole, it had spied on him, again in the form of all its separate parts, from the safety of the thicket.

"You are caught and so am I," the Cytha said. "Both of us will die here. It seems a fitting end to our association. Do you not agree with me?"

"I'll get you out," said Duncan wearily. "I have no quarrel with children."

He dragged the rifle toward him and unhooked the sling from the stock. Carefully he lowered the gun by the sling, still attached to the barrel, down into the pit.

The Cytha reared up and grasped it with its forepaws.

"Easy now," Duncan cautioned. "You're heavy. I don't know if I can hold you."

But he needn't have worried. The little ones were detaching themselves and scrambling up the rifle and the sling. They reached his extended arms and ran up them with scrabbling claws. Little sneering screamers and the comic stilt-birds and the mouse-size kill-devils that snarled at him as they climbed. And the little grinning natives—not babies, scarcely children, but small editions of full-grown humanoids. And the weird donovans scampering happily.

They came climbing up his arms and across his shoulders and milled about on the ground beside him, waiting for the others.

And finally the Cytha, not skinned down to the bare bones of its Thanksgiving-turkey-size, but far smaller than it had been, climbed awkwardly up the rifle and the sling to safety.

Duncan hauled the rifle up and twisted himself into a sitting position.

The Cytha, he saw, was reassembling.

He watched in fascination as the restless miniatures of the planet's life swarmed and seethed like a hive of bees, each one clicking into place to form the entire beast.

And now the Cytha was complete. Yet small—still small—no more than lion-size.

"But it is such a little one," Zikkara had argued with him that morning at the farm. "It is such a young one."

Just a young brood, no more than suckling infants—if suckling was the word, or even some kind of wild approximation. And through the months and years, the Cytha would grow, with the growing of its diverse children, until it became a monstrous thing.

It stood there looking at Duncan and the tree.

"Now," said Duncan, "if you'll push on the tree, I think that between the two of us—"

"It is too bad," the Cytha said, and wheeled itself about.

He watched it go loping off.

"Hey!" he yelled.

But it didn't stop.

He grabbed up the rifle and had it halfway to his shoulder before he remembered how absolutely futile it was to shoot at the Cytha.

He let the rifle down.

"The dirty, ungrateful, double-crossing—"

He stopped himself. There was no profit in rage. When you were in a jam, you did the best you could. You figured out the problem and you picked the course that seemed best and you didn't panic at the odds.

He laid the rifle in his lap and started to hook up the sling and it was not till then that he saw the barrel was packed with sand and dirt.

He sat numbly for a moment, thinking back to how close he had been to firing at the Cytha, and if that barrel was packed hard enough or deep enough, he might have had an exploding weapon in his hands.

He had used the rifle as a crowbar, which was no way to use a gun. That was one way, he told himself, that was guaranteed to ruin it.

Duncan hunted around and found a twig and dug at the clogged muzzle, but the dirt was jammed too firmly in it and he made little progress.

He dropped the twig and was hunting for another stronger one when he caught the motion in a nearby clump of brush.

He watched closely for a moment and there was nothing, so he resumed the hunt for a stronger twig. He found one and started poking at the muzzle and there was another flash of motion.

He twisted around. Not more than twenty feet away, a screamer sat easily on its haunches. Its tongue was lolling out and it had what looked like a grin upon its face.

And there was another, just at the edge of the clump of brush where he had caught the motion first.

There were others as well, he knew. He could hear them sliding through the tangle of fallen trees, could sense the soft padding of their feet.

The executioners, he thought.

The Cytha certainly had not wasted any time.

He raised the rifle and rapped the barrel smartly on the fallen tree, trying to dislodge the obstruction in the bore. But it didn't budge; the barrel still was packed with sand.

But no matter—he'd have to fire anyhow and take whatever chance there was.

He shoved the control to automatic and tilted up the muzzle.

There were six of them now, sitting in a ragged row, grinning at him, not in any hurry. They were sure of him and there was no hurry. He'd still be there when they decided to move in.

And there were others—on all sides of him.

Once it started, he wouldn't have a chance.

"It'll be expensive, gents," he told them.

And he was astonished at how calm, how coldly objective he could be, now that the chips were down. But that was the way it was, he realized.

He'd thought, a while ago, how a man might suddenly find himself face to face with an aroused and cooperating planet. Maybe this was it in miniature.

The Cytha had obviously passed the word along: *Man back there needs killing. Go and get him.*

Just like that, for a Cytha would be the power here. A life force, the giver of life, the decider of life, the repository of all animal life on the entire planet.

There was more than one of them, of course. Probably they had home districts, spheres of influence and responsibility mapped out. And each one would be a power supreme in its own district.

Momism, he thought with a sour grin. Momism at its absolute peak.

Nevertheless, he told himself, it wasn't too bad a system if you wanted to consider it objectively.

But he was in a poor position to be objective about that or anything else.

The screamers were inching closer, hitching themselves forward slowly on their bottoms.

"I'm going to set up a deadline for you critters," Duncan called out. "Just two feet farther, up to that rock, and I let you have it."

He'd get all six of them, of course, but the shots would be the signal for the general rush by all those other animals slinking in the brush.

If he were free, if he were on his feet, possibly he could beat them off. But pinned as he was, he didn't have a chance. It would be all over less than a minute after he opened fire. He might, he figured, last as long as that.

The six inched closer and he raised the rifle.

But they stopped and moved no farther. Their ears lifted just a little, as if they might be listening, and the grins dropped from their faces. They squirmed uneasily and assumed a look of guilt and, like shadows, they were gone, melting away so swiftly that he scarcely saw them go.

Duncan sat quietly, listening, but he could hear no sound.

Reprieve, he thought. But for how long? Something had scared them off, but in a while they might be back. He had to get out of here and he had to make it fast.

If he could find a longer lever, he could move the tree. There was a branch slanting up from the topside of the fallen tree. It was almost four inches at the butt and it carried its diameter well.

He slid the knife from his belt and looked at it. Too small, too thin, he thought, to chisel through a four-inch branch, but it was all he had. When a man was desperate enough, though, when his very life depended on it, he would do anything.

He hitched himself along, sliding toward the point where the branch protruded from the tree. His pinned leg protested with stabs of pain as his body wrenched it around. He gritted his teeth and pushed himself closer. Pain slashed through his leg again and he was still long inches from the branch.

He tried once more, then gave up. He lay panting on the ground.

There was just one thing left.

He'd have to try to hack out a notch in the trunk just above his leg. No, that would be next to impossible, for he'd be cutting into the whorled and twisted grain at the base of the supporting fork.

Either that or cut off his foot, and that was even more impossible. A man would faint before he got the job done.

It was useless, he knew. He could do neither one. There was nothing he could do.

For the first time, he admitted to himself: He would stay here and die. Shotwell, back at the farm, in a day or two might set out hunting for him. But Shotwell would never find him. And anyhow, by nightfall, if not sooner, the screamers would be back.

He laughed gruffly in his throat—laughing at himself.

The Cytha had won the hunt hands down. It had used a human weakness to win and then had used that same human weakness to achieve a viciously poetic vengeance.

After all, what could one expect? One could not equate human ethics with the ethics of the Cytha. Might not human ethics, in certain cases, seem as weird and illogical, as infamous and ungrateful, to an alien?

He hunted for a twig and began working again to clean the rifle bore.

A crashing behind him twisted him around and he saw the Cytha. Behind the Cytha stalked a donovan.

He tossed away the twig and raised the gun.

"No," said the Cytha sharply.

The donovan tramped purposefully forward and Duncan felt the prickling of the skin along his back. It was a frightful thing. Nothing could stand before a donovan. The screamers had turned tail and run when they had heard it a couple of miles or more away.

The donovan was named for the first known human to be killed by one. That first was only one of many. The roll of donovan-victims ran long, and no wonder, Duncan thought. It was the closest he had ever been to one of the beasts and he felt a coldness creeping over him. It was like an elephant and a tiger and a grizzly bear wrapped in the selfsame hide. It was the most vicious fighting machine that ever had been spawned.

He lowered the rifle. There would be no point in shooting. In two quick strides, the beast could be upon him.

The donovan almost stepped on him and he flinched away. Then the great head lowered and gave the fallen tree a butt and the tree bounced for a yard or two. The donovan kept on walking. Its power-fully muscled stern moved into the brush and out of sight.

"Now we are even," said the Cytha. "I had to get some help."

Duncan grunted. He flexed the leg that had been trapped and he could not feel the foot. Using his rifle as a cane, he pulled himself erect. He tried putting weight on the injured foot and it screamed with pain.

He braced himself with the rifle and rotated so that he faced the Cytha.

"Thanks, pal," he said. "I didn't think you'd do it."

"You will not hunt me now?"

Duncan shook his head. "I'm in no shape for hunting. I am head-ing home."

"It was the *vua*, wasn't it? That was why you hunted me?"

"The *vua* is my livelihood," said Duncan. "I cannot let you eat it."

The Cytha stood silently and Duncan watched it for a moment. Then he wheeled. Using the rifle for a crutch, he started hobbling away.

The Cytha hurried to catch up with him.

"Let us make a bargain, mister. I will not eat the *vua* and you will not hunt me. Is that fair enough?"

"That is fine with me," said Duncan. "Let us shake on it."

He put down a hand and the Cytha lifted up a paw. They shook, somewhat awkwardly, but very solemnly.

"Now," the Cytha said, "I will see you home. The screamers would have you before you got out of the woods."

VI

They halted on a knoll. Below them lay the farm, with the *vua* rows straight and green in the red soil of the fields.

"You can make it from here," the Cytha said. "I am wearing thin. It is an awful effort to keep on being smart. I want to go back to ignorance and comfort."

"It was nice knowing you," Duncan told it politely. "And thanks for sticking with me."

He started down the hill, leaning heavily on the rifle-crutch. Then he frowned troubledly and turned back.

"Look," he said, "you'll go back to animal again. Then you will forget. One of these days, you'll see all that nice, tender *vua* and—"

"Very simple," said the Cytha. "If you find me in the *vua*, just begin hunting me. With you after me, I will quickly get smart and remember once again and it will be all right."

"Sure," agreed Duncan. "I guess that will work."

The Cytha watched him go stumping down the hill.

Admirable, it thought. Next time I have a brood, I think I'll raise a dozen like him.

It turned around and headed for the deeper brush.

It felt intelligence slipping from it, felt the old, uncaring comfort coming back again. But it glowed with anticipation, seethed with happiness at the big surprise it had in store for its new-found friend.

Won't he be happy and surprised when I drop them at his door, it thought.

Will he be ever pleased!

ALIEN OFFER

AL SEVCIK

"You are General James Rothwell?"

Rothwell sighed. "Yes, Commander Aku. We have met several times."

"Ah, yes. I recognize your insignia. Humans are so alike." The alien strode importantly across the office, the resilient pads of his broad feet making little plopping sounds on the rug, and seated himself abruptly in the visitor's chair beside Rothwell's desk. He gave a sharp cry, and another alien, shorter, but sporting similar, golden fur, stepped into the office and closed the door. Both wore simple, brown uniforms, without ornamentation.

"I am here," Aku said, "to tell you something." He stared impassively at Rothwell for a minute, his fur-covered, almost human face completely expressionless, then his gaze shifted to the window, to the hot runways of New York International Airport and to the immense gray spaceship that, even from the center of the field, loomed above the hangars and passenger buildings. For an instant, a quick, unguessable emotion clouded the wide black eyes and tightened the thin lips, then it was gone.

Rothwell waited.

"General, Earth's children must all be aboard my ships within one week. We will start to load on the sixth day, next Thursday." He stood.

Rothwell locked eyes with the alien, and leaned forward, grinding his knuckles into the desk top. "You know that's impossible. We can't select 100,000 children from every country and assemble them in only six days."

182

"You will do it." The alien turned to leave.

"Commander Aku! Let me remind you . . ."

Aku spun around, eyes flashing. "General Rothwell! Let *me* remind you that two weeks ago I didn't even know Earth existed, and since accidentally happening across your sun system and learning of your trouble I have had my entire trading fleet of a hundred ships in orbit about this planet while all your multitudinous political subdivisions have filled the air with talk and wrangle.

"I am sorry for Earth, but my allegiance is to my fleet and I cannot remain longer than seven more days and risk being caught up in your destruction. Now, either you accept my offer to evacuate as many humans as my ships will carry, or you don't." He paused. "You are the planet's evacuation coordinator; you will give me an answer."

Rothwell's arms sagged, he sunk back down into his chair, all pretense gone. Slowly he swung around to face the window and the gray ship, standing like a Gargantuan sundial counting the last days of Earth. He almost whispered. "We are choosing the children. They will be ready in six days."

He heard the door open and close. He was alone.

Five years ago, he thought, we cracked the secret of faster-than-light travel, and since then we've built about three dozen exploration ships and sent them out among the stars to see what they could see.

He stared blankly at the palms of his hands. I wonder what it was we expected to find?

We found that the galaxy was big, that there were a lot of stars, not so many planets, and practically no other life—at least no intelligence to compare with ours. Then . . . He jabbed a button on his intercom.

"Ed Philips here. What is it Jim?"

"Doc, are you sure your boys have hypo'd, couched, and hypno'd the Leo crew with everything you've got?"

The voice on the intercom sighed. "Jim, those guys haven't got a memory of their own. We know everything about each one of them, from the hurts he got falling off tricycles to the feel of the first girl he kissed. Those men aren't lying, Jim."

"I never thought they were lying, Doc." Rothwell paused for a minute and studied the long yellow hairs that grew sparsely across the back of his hand, thickened to a dense grove at his wrist, and vanished under the sleeve of his uniform. He looked back at the intercom. "Doc, all I know is that three perfectly normal guys got on board that ship, and when it came back we found a lot of jammed instruments and three men terrified almost to the point of insanity."

"Jim, if you'd seen . . ."

Rothwell interrupted. "I know. Five radio-active planets with the fresh scars of cobalt bombs and the remains of civilizations. Then radar screens erupting crazily with signals from a multi-thousand ship space fleet; vector computers hurriedly plotting and re-plotting the fast-moving trajectory, submitting each time an unvarying answer for the fleet's destination—our own solar system." He slapped his hand flat against the desk. "The point is, Doc, it's not much to go on, and we don't dare send another ship to check for fear of attracting attention to ourselves. If we could only be *sure.*"

"Jim," over the intercom, Philip's voice seemed to waver slightly, "those men honestly saw what they say. I'd stake my life on it."

"All of us are, Doc." He flipped the off button. Just thirty days now, since the scout ship Leo's discovery and the panicked dash for home with the warning. Not that the warning was worth much, he reflected. Earth had no space battle fleet. There had never been any reason to build one.

Then, two weeks ago, Aku's trading fleet had descended from nowhere, having blundered, he said, across Earth's orbit while on a new route between two distant star clusters. When told of the impending attack, Aku immediately offered to cancel his trip and evacuate as many humans as his ships could hold, so that humanity would at least survive, somewhere in the galaxy. Earth chose to accept his offer.

"Hobson's choice," Rothwell growled to himself. "No choice at all." After years of handling hot and cold local wars and crises of every description, his military mind had become conditioned to a complete disbelief in fortuitous coincidence, and he gagged at the thought of Aku "just happening by." Still frowning, he punched a yellow button on his desk, and reviewed in his mind the things he wanted to say.

"Jim! Isn't everything all right?"

Chagrined, Rothwell scrambled to his feet. The President had never answered so quickly before. He faced the screen on the wall to his right and saluted, amazed once again at how old the man looked. Sparse white hair criss-crossed haphazardly over the President's head, his face was lined with deep trenches that not even the most charitable could call wrinkles, and the faded eyes that stared from deep caverns no longer radiated the flaming vitality that had inspired victorious armies in the African war.

"Commander Aku was just here, sir. He demands that the children be ready for evacuation next Thursday. I told him that it would be damned difficult."

The face on the screen paled perceptibly. "I hope you didn't anger the commander!"

Rothwell ground his teeth. "I told him we'd deliver the goods on Thursday."

Presidential lips tightened. "I don't care for the way you said that, General."

Rothwell straightened. "I apologize, sir. It's just that this whole lousy setup has me worried silly. I don't like Aku making like a guardian angel and us having no choice but to dance to his harp." His fingers clenched. "God knows we need his help, and I guess its wrong to ask too many questions, but how come he's only landed one of his ships, and why is it that he and his lieutenant are the only aliens to leave that ship—the only aliens we've ever even seen? It just doesn't figure out!" There, he thought, I've said it.

The President looked at him quietly for a minute, then answered softly, "I know, Jim, but what else can we do?" Rothwell winced at the shake in the old man's voice.

"I don't know," he said. "But Aku's got us in a hell of a spot."

"Uh, Jim. You haven't said this in public, have you?"

Rothwell snorted. "No, *sir*, I don't care for a panic."

"There, there, Jim." The President smiled weakly. "We can't expect the aliens to act like we do, can we?" He began to adopt the preacher tone he used so effectively in his campaign speeches. "We must be thankful for the chance breeze that wafted Commander Aku to these shores, and for his help. Maybe the war fleet won't arrive after all and everything will turn out all right. You're doing a fine job, Jim." The screen went blank.

Rothwell felt sick. He felt sorry for the President, but sorrier for the Western Democratic Union, to be captained by such a feeble thing. Leaning back in his chair, he glared at the empty screen. "You can't solve problems by wishing them away. You knew that once."

His mind wandered, and for a minute he thought he could actually feel the growing pressure of three billion people waiting for the computers of Moscow Central to make their impartial choice from the world's children. Trained mathematicians, the best that could be mustered from every major country, monitored each phase of the project to insure its absolute honesty. One hundred thousand children were to be picked completely at random; brown, yellow, black, white, red; sick or well; genius or moron; every child had an equal chance. This fact, this fact alone gave every parent hope, and possibly prevented worldwide rioting.

But with the destruction of the planet an almost certainty, the collective nervous system was just one micron away from explosion. There was nothing else to think about or talk about, and no one tried to pretend any different.

Rothwell's eyes moved involuntarily to the little spherical tri-photo on his desk, just an informal shot he'd snapped a few months back of Martha and her proudest possessions, their rambunctious, priceless off-spring. Jim, Jr., in his space scouts uniform, and Mary Ellen with that crazy hair-do. She was so proud of them, but had already forgotten.

"Damn!" he said aloud. "Dammit to hell!" In one quick movement, he spun his chair around and jabbed at the intercom. "Get the heli!" His voice crackled.

Grabbing his hat, he yanked open the door and strode into the sudden quiet of the small office. He turned right and went out through a side entrance to a small landing ramp, arriving just as his personal heli touched down. He climbed in. "To the ship."

As he settled back in the hard seat, Rothwell offered a silent thanks that, instead of asking which ship, Sergeant Johnson promptly lifted and headed for the gray space vessel that dominated the field.

A few hundred yards from the craft he said, "You'd better set her down here, Sarge, and let me walk in. Our friends might get nervous about something flying in at them."

He jumped out, squinting against the hot glare off the concrete, and then, with a slight uneasiness, stepped into the dark shadow that pointed a thousand feet along the runway, away from the setting sun. He walked towards the ship.

A few seconds later, his eye caught a small, unexplained flash and he threw himself flat just as a section of pavement exploded, a dozen feet ahead.

Cursing, Rothwell picked himself off the ground, brushed the dust off his uniform, and stood quietly. He didn't have long to wait.

A small cubicle jutted out from the ship and lowered itself along a monorail running down to the ground. The side nearest him opened revealing, as Rothwell expected, Commander Aku and his lieutenant who both hurried over to where he was standing, as if to keep him from coming forward to meet them—and in so doing coming nearer the ship. As the commander trotted rapidly towards him, Rothwell noted that he was still buttoning his jacket and that the shirt underneath looked suspiciously as if it hadn't been buttoned at all. Funny, he thought, that my presence should cause such a panic.

"General, what a pleasure." The commander's disconcerted look belied his words, but even as he spoke he began to regain his composure and assume the poker face that Rothwell had come to expect.

"I do hope," said Rothwell, "that my visit hasn't inconvenienced you."

Aku and his lieutenant traded swift glances, neither said anything.

"Well," Rothwell began again, "I am here to convey to you the good wishes of the President of our country and to submit a request from him and from the other governments of the Earth."

Aku straightened. "Though merely the commander of a poor trading fleet, I feel sure I speak for my empire when I wish your President good health. The request?"

Rothwell spoke evenly, trying to keep the bitterness out of his voice. "Commander, when the attack comes we expect that Earth with all its life will be annihilated. But your offer to transport a hundred thousand children to your own home worlds has prevented despair, and has at least given us hope that if we will not see the future our children will."

Aku nodded slightly, avoiding his eyes. "You take it well."

"But it takes more than hope, Commander. We need some assurance, also, that our children will be all right." He took an involuntary step nearer the alien, whose facial muscles never moved, and who turned away slightly, refusing to meet Rothwell's eyes.

"Commander, you and your lieutenant are the only members of your race that we have ever seen, and then only on official business. We would like very much to meet the others. Why don't you land your ships and give the crews liberty, so that we can meet them informally and they can get to know us, also? That way it won't seem as if we are giving our kids over to complete strangers."

Without turning his head, Aku said flatly, "That is impossible. Do you want reasons?"

"No," Rothwell said quietly. "If you don't want to do something, it's easy enough to think up reasons." He ached to reach out and grab the alien neck, to shake some expression into that frozen face. "Look, Commander, surely the friendship of a doomed race can't bring any harm to your crew!"

Aku faced him now. "What you ask is impossible."

Ashamed of the desperate note that crept inadvertently into his voice, Rothwell said, "Commander, will you let me, alone, briefly enter your ship, so that I can tell my people what it is like?"

Aku and the lieutenant traded a long, silent look, then the lieutenant almost imperceptibly shrugged his shoulders. Without moving, turned partly away from Rothwell, Aku said, simply, "No." The two started to walk back to the ship.

"Commander!"

They stopped, but didn't turn.

"Commander Aku, if you have any sort of God in your empire, or any sort of honor that your race swears by, please tell me one thing— tell me that our children will be safe. I won't ask you anything else."

The two aliens stood still, facing away from him, towards their ship. Minutes passed. Rothwell stood quietly, looking at their backs, human appearing, but hiding unguessable thoughts. Neither of them moved, or said a word. Finally, he turned and walked away, back towards his heli.

He leaned back in the little heli's bucket seat and ran a large hand through unruly yellow hair that was already flecked with white. The first evening lights of Brooklyn and Queens and, off to the left, Manhattan, moved unseen beneath him as the craft headed towards his home. Dammit, he thought, is it that Aku just doesn't care what we think, or that he cares very much what we would think if we knew whatever it is he's hiding?

He banged his fists together in frustration. How the hell can anyone guess what goes on in an alien mind? His whole damn brain is probably completely different! Maybe to him a poker face is friendly. Maybe he's honestly not hiding anything at all. He looked out as the heli slowly started its descent. No evidence, he thought. Not a shred, except a suspicious mind and, he glanced at the dirt on his trousers, and a shell exploding in my face.

He slapped his hat back on and whirled to the surprised pilot. "Dammit, I don't make the decisions. I'm just in charge of loading, and if the President says it's okay, then it's okay with me!" He stepped out onto the grass of his yard, and quashed a little shriek of conscience somewhere in the back of his mind.

Blinding lights pinned him in mid-stride. A familiar voice sprang out of the glare, "Here he is now viewers, General James Rothwell, commander of the western armies, and head of the Earth evacuation project. General, International-TV cameras have been waiting secretly in your yard for hours for your return."

As his eyes adjusted, Rothwell distinguished a camera crew, their small portable instrument, and a young, smooth talking announcer that he had seen several times on television. He forced the annoyance out of his eyes. This, he thought, is all I need.

"What the general doesn't know," the announcer went on, "is that earlier this evening it was announced by Moscow Central that the computers had picked his son as one of the evacuees!"

The shock was visible on 150,000,000 TV sets. Completely unexpected, the surprise of the announcement hit Rothwell like a physical blow; his eyes widened, his chin dropped, and for an instant the world's viewers read in his face the frank emotions of a father, unshielded by military veneer. Then years of training took command, and he faced the camera, apparently calm, though churning internally. The odds, he thought confusedly, the odds must be at least ten thousand to one! Then he realized that someone was talking to him, waving a microphone.

"Er, I'm sorry, I didn't quite catch . . ." he mumbled at the camera.

The announcer laughed amiably. "Certainly can't blame you, this must be a really big night! How does it feel, General, for your son to be one of the evacuees?"

Something in the back of his mind twisted the question. How does it feel, General, to turn your only son over to a poker-faced alien who shoots when you walk near his ship? "I'm not sure," he said, "how I feel."

Talking excitedly, the announcer drew closer. "To think that your name will live forever in the vast star clusters of the galaxy!" He lowered his voice. "General, speaking now unofficially, as a parent, to the thousands of other parents whose children may also be selected, and to the rest of us who . . ." he seemed to stumble for a word, and for an instant Rothwell saw him, too, as a man worried and afraid, instead of as part of a television machine. "Well, General, *you've* had contact with the aliens, are you glad your son is going?"

Rothwell looked at the strained face of the announcer, at the camera crew quietly eyeing him, and at the small huddled group of neighbors hovering in the background, and he knew that his next words might be the most critical he would ever use in his life. In a world strained emotionally almost beyond endurance, the wrong words, a hint of a suspicion, could spark the riots that would kill millions and bring total destruction.

He faced the camera and said calmly, "I am glad my son is going. I wish it could happen for everyone. Commander Aku has assured me that everything will turn out all right." Mentally he begged for forgiveness, there was nothing else he could say. Sweat glistened on his forehead as he tried to fight down the memory of Aku turning his back on the plea that echoed in his brain—"tell me that our children will be safe."

The front door of the house banged open and all at once Martha was in his arms, crying, laughing. "Oh, Jim, I'm so glad, so very glad!" Rothwell blinked his eyes as he put his arm around her and waved the camera away. Tears sparkled on his cheeks; but neither Martha nor the viewers knew why.

The next morning Aku and his ever-present lieutenant were waiting when Rothwell's heli set him down in front of the administration building, a few minutes later than usual. They followed him into his office.

"Coffee?" Rothwell held out a paper cup.

"No thank you," said Aku, as expressionless as ever. "We are here to make final arrangements for the evacuation."

"I see. Well," said Rothwell, "Thursday will be a very painful day for us and we will want to expedite things as much as possible."

Aku nodded.

Rothwell went on. "I have made arrangements to have a hundred air fields cleared at various population centers around the world. That way your ships can land simultaneously, one at each field, and the loading can be finished in very little time. Now," he opened a desk drawer, "here is a list of . . ."

Aku held up a fur-covered hand. "That will not be possible."

Rothwell looked down at his desk and closed his eyes briefly. I knew it, he thought, I knew this would happen, sure as hell. He raised his head. "Impossible?"

"We will first land twenty ships. These twenty must be fully loaded and back in orbit before the next will land. We will use the first twenty air fields on your list."

Rothwell took a deep breath. "But I thought you wanted to get away as soon as possible! It will take at least an extra day to load according to your scheme."

"Will it?" Aku moved to go, his lieutenant reached to open the door.

On an impulse, Rothwell stepped forward. "Commander, if you had a son would you send him away like this?"

Aku stopped, and looked directly at him with even, black eyes; then the gaze moved through and past him, to the window and the ship beyond. For a minute his expression altered, changing almost to one of pain. When he spoke, it was almost to himself. "My father loved his children more than . . ." He started as his lieutenant suddenly clapped a hand on his shoulder. The expression vanished.

They left together, without looking at Rothwell or saying another word.

For several minutes Rothwell stared frowning at the closed door. He walked thoughtfully back to his desk, and lowered himself slowly into the chair.

He sat for a long time, trying to puzzle through the picture. Finally he stood and paced the room. "Suppose," he said to himself, "just suppose that not all of those hundred ships up there are really cargo ships. Suppose that, say, only twenty are. Then, after those twenty were loaded . . ." He swung around to look again at the long, slim silhouette poised high against the main runway. "With ocean vessels, it's the fighting ships that are lean and slender."

Bending over his desk, he nudged an intercom button with his finger. "Doc, how would one go about trying to understand an alien's reactions?"

Philip's voice shot right back. "Well, Jim, the very first thing, you'd have to be sure they weren't exactly the same as a human's reactions."

Rothwell paused, startled. "It can't be, Doc. Why, if Aku was a human I'd say . . ." He stiffened, feeling the hair rise at the back of his neck. The short, curt answers, the refusal to meet his eyes, the frozen expression clicked into pattern. "Doc . . . I'd say he was being forced to do something he hated like hell to do."

Tensely, he straightened and contemplated the lean, gray spaceship. Then he whirled around and slapped every button on the intercom.

Thursday. The sun pecked fitfully at the low overcast while a sullen crowd watched a squat alien ship descend vertically, to finally settle with a flaming belch not far from the first. Similar crowds watched similar landings at nineteen other airports around the world, but the loading was to start first in New York.

An elevator-like box swung out from the fat belly of the ship and was lowered rapidly to the ground. Two golden-hued aliens, in uniforms resembling Aku's, stepped out and walked about a thousand

feet towards the crowd. Only children actually being loaded were to
go beyond this point; parents had to stay at the airport gates.

"When do I go, Dad?"

"Shortly, son." Rothwell laid his hand on the lean shoulder. "You're
in the second hundred." There was a brief, awkward silence. "Martha,
you'd better take him over to the line." He held out his hand. "So
long, son."

Jim, Jr., shook his hand gravely, then, without a word, suddenly
threw his hands tight around his younger sister. He took his mother's
hand, and they walked slowly over to the sad line that was forming
beyond the gate.

Rothwell turned to his daughter. "You going over there too, kitten?" The words were gruff in his tight throat.

She wiped a hand quickly across her cheek. "No, Dad, I guess I'll
stay here with you." She stood close beside him.

Aku, forgotten until now, cleared his throat. "I think the loading
should start, General."

Raising his hand in a half-salute, Rothwell signaled to a captain
standing near the gate who turned and motioned to a small cordon
of military police. Shortly, a group of fifty of the first youngsters in
the line separated from the others and moved slowly out onto the
concrete ribbon towards the waiting ship. The rest of the line hesitated, then edged reluctantly up to the gate, to take the place of the
fifty who had left. They waited there, the children of a thousand fam-
ilies, suddenly dead quiet, staring after the fifty that slowly moved
away.

They walked quietly, in a tight group, without any antics or
horseplay which, in itself, gave the event an air of unreality.
Approaching the ship, they seemed to huddle even closer together,
forming a pathetically tiny cluster in the shadow of the towering
space cruiser. The title of a book that he had read once, many years
before, flashed unexpectedly in Rothwell's memory, *The Story of
Mankind*. He looked sadly after the fifty, then back at the silent
line. Were these frightened kids now writing the final period in the

last chapter? He shook himself, work to be done, no time now for daydreams.

As the fifty reached the ship and started to enter the elevator, Rothwell turned and beckoned to some technicians standing out of sight just inside the entrance to the control tower. Three of them ran out and set up what looked like a television set, only with three screens. One ran back, unreeling a power cable, while a fourth flicked on a bank of switches, making feverish, minute adjustments. Rothwell felt the sweat in his hands. "Is it okay, Sergeant?"

The back of the sergeant's shirt was wet though the air was cool. "It's got to be, sir!" His fingers played across the knobs. "All that metal, the whole thing is critical as . . . Ah!" He jumped back. The screens flashed into life.

Aku stiffened. His lieutenant gasped audibly, made a jerky movement towards the screens, then suddenly became aware of three MP's standing beside him, hands nonchalantly cradling bluntnosed weapons.

All three receivers showed similar scenes, the milling youngsters and the ship, but from up close, the pictures jerking and swaying erratically as if the cameras were somehow fastened to moving human beings. Then the scenes condensed into a cramped, jostling blackness as the fifty crowded into the elevator and were lifted up the side of the ship.

Next, were three views of a large room, bare except for what appeared to be overhead cranes and other mechanical paraphernalia of a military shop or warehouse. For a while the fifty moved about restlessly, then the cameras swung about simultaneously to face a wall that slowly slid apart.

Rothwell froze. "Good Lord!"

Six murky *things* moved from the open wall towards the cameras, which fell back to the opposite side of the room. Each was large, many times the size of a man, but somehow indistinct, for the cameras didn't convey any sense of shape or form. For an instant, one of the screens flashed a picture of a terrified human face, and arms raised protectively as the shadowy things moved in upon the group.

A projection snapped out from one, grabbed two of the humans, and hurled them into a corner. Then it motioned a dozen or so others over to the same spot. With similar harsh, sweeping movements, the group of humans was quickly broken up into three roughly equal segments. One of the groups seemed to be protecting someone who appeared seriously hurt. A black tentacle lashed out and one of the screens went blank. Then another.

The third showed a small group pushed stumbling through a narrow door, down a short passageway, and abruptly into blackness. Something that looked like bars flashed across the screen, then a dark liquid trickled across the camera lens, blotting out the view.

Eyes blazing, Rothwell whirled on Aku. "Throughout our history, Commander, humans have had one thing in common, our blasted pride! We will not turn over our young to slavery, and by hell if we die, we'll die fighting!" He jerked up his coat sleeve, barked an order into a small transmitter on his wrist, and, grabbing his daughter, threw himself flat on the concrete.

Hesitating only an instant, Aku, his lieutenant, and the MP's hit the ground as both spaceships vanished in a cataclysmic eruption of flame and steel.

Raising his head, Rothwell grinned crazily into the exploding debris, imagining nineteen other ships suddenly disintegrating under the rocket guns of nineteen different nations. He saw Earth, like a giant porcupine, flicking thousands of atom tipped missiles into space from hundreds of submarines and secret bases—the war power of the great nations, designed for the ruin of each other, united to destroy the alien fleet.

He turned to Aku, "Midgets, volunteers with miniature TV cameras . . ." he stopped.

The commander and his lieutenant had flung their arms about each other and were crying like babies. Tentatively, Aku reached towards him. "Those things, the *Eleele*, from another galaxy." He struggled for words. "They captured your scout crew and implanted memories of thousands of ships to create fear and make it easier to take slaves before blasting you." He glanced up at the flashes in the sky. "This was their only fleet."

Rothwell glared. "You helped them."

Aku nodded miserably. "We had to. They thought you'd trust us because we look almost human. It was a trick that worked before." Tears streamed across his face, matting the golden fur. "You see, the radioactive planets your men reported, one of them was—home."

EARTHMEN BEARING GIFTS

FREDRIC BROWN

Dhar Ry sat alone in his room, meditating. From outside the door he caught a thought wave equivalent to a knock, and, glancing at the door, he willed it to slide open.

It opened. "Enter, my friend," he said. He could have projected the idea telepathically; but with only two persons present, speech was more polite.

Ejon Khee entered. "You are up late tonight, my leader," he said.

"Yes, Khee. Within an hour the Earth rocket is due to land, and I wish to see it. Yes, I know, it will land a thousand miles away, if their calculations are correct. Beyond the horizon. But if it lands even twice that far the flash of the atomic explosion should be visible. And I have waited long for first contact. For even though no Earthman will be on that rocket, it will still be first contact—for them. Of course our telepath teams have been reading their thoughts for many centuries, but—this will be the first *physical* contact between Mars and Earth."

Khee made himself comfortable on one of the low chairs. "True," he said. "I have not followed recent reports too closely, though. Why are they using an atomic warhead? I know they suppose our planet is uninhabited, but still—"

"They will watch the flash through their lunar telescopes and get a—what do they call it?—a spectroscopic analysis. That will tell them more than they know now (or think they know; much of it is erroneous) about the atmosphere of our planet and the composition

198

of its surface. It is—call it a sighting shot, Khee. They'll be here in person within a few oppositions. And then—"

Mars was holding out, waiting for Earth to come. What was left of Mars, that is; this one small city of about nine hundred beings. The civilization of Mars was older than that of Earth, but it was a dying one. This was what remained of it: one city, nine hundred people. They were waiting for Earth to make contact, for a selfish reason and for an unselfish one.

Martian civilization had developed in a quite different direction from that of Earth. It had developed no important knowledge of the physical sciences, no technology. But it had developed social sciences to the point where there had not been a single crime, let alone a war, on Mars for fifty thousand years. And it had developed fully the parapsychological sciences of the mind, which Earth was just beginning to discover.

Mars could teach Earth much. How to avoid crime and war to begin with. Beyond those simple things lay telepathy, telekinesis, empathy . . .

And Earth would, Mars hoped, teach them something even more valuable to Mars: how, by science and technology—which it was too late for Mars to develop now, even if they had the type of minds which would enable them to develop these things—to restore and rehabilitate a dying planet, so that an otherwise dying race might live and multiply again.

Each planet would gain greatly, and neither would lose.

And tonight was the night when Earth would make its first sighting shot. Its next shot, a rocket containing Earthmen, or at least an Earthman, would be at the next opposition, two Earth years, or roughly four Martian years, hence. The Martians knew this, because their teams of telepaths were able to catch at least some of the thoughts of Earthmen, enough to know their plans. Unfortunately, at that distance, the connection was one-way. Mars could not ask Earth to hurry its program. Or tell Earth scientists the facts about

Mars' composition and atmosphere which would have made this preliminary shot unnecessary.

Tonight Ry, the leader (as nearly as the Martian word can be translated), and Khee, his administrative assistant and closest friend, sat and meditated together until the time was near. Then they drank a toast to the future—in a beverage based on menthol, which had the same effect on Martians as alcohol on Earthmen—and climbed to the roof of the building in which they had been sitting. They watched toward the north, where the rocket should land. The stars shone brilliantly and unwinkingly through the atmosphere.

In Observatory No. 1 on Earth's moon, Rog Everett, his eye at the eyepiece of the spotter scope, said triumphantly, "Thar she blew, Willie. And now, as soon as the films are developed, we'll know the score on that old planet Mars." He straightened up—there'd be no more to see now—and he and Willie Sanger shook hands solemnly. It was an historical occasion.

"Hope it didn't kill anybody. Any Martians, that is. Rog, did it hit dead center in Syrtis Major?"

"Near as matters. I'd say it was maybe a thousand miles off, to the south. And that's damn close on a fifty-million-mile shot. Willie, do you really think there are any Martians?"

Willie thought a second and then said, "No."

He was right.